Daedalus

and

The Deep

DAEDALUS AND THE DEEP

BY

MATT WILLIS

Cortero Publishing
An Imprint of Fireship Press

Daedalus and The Deep by Matt Willis

Copyright © Matt Willis, copyright 2012

All rights reserved. No part of this book may be used or reproduced by any means without the written permission of the publisher except in the case of brief quotation embodied in critical articles and reviews.

ISBN-13: 978-1-61179-267-6 (Paperback)
ISBN -978-1-61179-268-3   (e-book)

BISAC Subject Headings:
FIC023000 FICTION-Mythology
FIC028100 FICTION- Science Fiction-Adventure
FIC047000 FICTION / Sea Stories

Cover Illustration by Christine Horner

Address all correspondence to:
Fireship Press, LLC
P.O. Box 68412
Tucson, AZ 85737
Or visit our website at:
www.FireshipPress.com

Acknowledgements

I'd like to thank the following people, who were extremely generous with their time and knowledge, and who undoubtedly made this a better book that it would otherwise have been.

First of all, Lars Opland, who patiently helped me get the mechanics of square-rig sailing right. Lars has the kind of experience of sailing square riggers that most of us can only dream of. He also has a fine sense of the dramatic and his comments on the story were as helpful as his comments on the nautical detail.

Equally, Ken Pastore, David Hayes and Bob Barrows from the Historic Naval Fiction forum were unstinting with their time and freely gave of their vast knowledge of historical naval matters. They were directly responsible, not just for improving the accuracy of the narrative, but making it a better story too.

Thanks also to my father, Brian Willis, and uncle, Tony Willis, who both read early drafts of the manuscript and offered encouragement when it was needed most. The author Richard Woodman very kindly read the manuscript and offered both encouragement and suggestions. I am also indebted to Captain Woodman for the inspiration provided by his many wonderful works of historic sea fiction.

I'd also like to acknowledge the main texts that I referred to for historical context during the writing of the novel. These were *Trincomalee: the Last of Nelson's Frigates* by Andrew Lambert,

Fisher's Face by Jan Morris, *HMS Warrior: Britain's First and Last Iron-Hulled Warship* by John McIlwain, *The Immortal Warrior* by Captain John Wells, RN. In addition, *Quarterdeck*, the newsletter of the Friends of HMS *Trincomalee* provided wonderful contemporary anecdotes and colour.

The team at the Office of Letters and Light deserve my profound thanks for making National Novel Writing Week such a success year after year—2011 was certainly successful for me, as a last minute decision to take part ended with the novel you hold in your hands.

Finally, but of vital importance, my wife Ros, without whose patience, encouragement, support and love the novel would not have been started, let alone finished—my eternal thanks.

PART I

THE CORVETTE

Prologue

SHE lanced up through the fluid atmosphere, out of the home depth, towards the unknown sky. Her body was utterly straight, the pace of her upward motion imparted by rippling fins on her flanks.

At first it was easy. The pressure below forced her upward, and the thinning atmosphere above was softer to penetrate. For hours she continued, never deviating or slowing. Her long snout parted the surrounding ether, which spun past her slender form. The undulations of her fins corkscrewed the diffusing fluid, which was quickly pressed back into an inanimate mass after her passing.

After many more hours relentless upward flight, the atmosphere started to become unbearably thin. Instead of helping her upwards, the rarified substance now made progress harder. Her breathing became ragged, and the lightening pressure gave her fins little to grip on. It became difficult to stay on a straight course, and she started to feel as though she was about to topple over.

She grasped her resolve harder, and started to flex the rear of her body to help push against the unsettling thinness. Was this the sky? Had she plunged out of the atmosphere already and into space? No, it would be much longer yet. How could anyone stand it? Well, they could and they had, said the legends and stories, even within her own lifetime. She would not be beaten so easily, so soon.

Daedalus and The Deep

Ahead of her, the atmosphere started to take on a colour she had only ever seen in tiny spots, or flickers of luminescence. The entire vista before her was becoming unnaturally bright and blue, slowly at first then overwhelmingly. The blue was everywhere above, and before long she was inside *it. She bridled at its unfamiliarity, quivering with muted panic—but still pressed onward.*

The glow of the upper atmosphere did nothing to prepare her for the edge of space. The light had grown until it burned around her...but through the intensity she saw a solid, glittering sheet encompassing the whole sky—a boundary. She slowed finally and adjusted her trajectory, curving out of her vertical trajectory until she was cruising level, parallel to the great shining sweep. A knot of fear heavy in her gut, she inspected the barrier. It seemed to undulate, slickly, but no breaks appeared in it. Her people's lore said nothing of this. Was this why no one had made the long journey upwards in generations? Or was it simply that no one had needed to?

She needed to now, or lose everything.

She slowed once again, maintaining altitude with her lateral fins, and worked gradually closer to the luminous boundary, her course narrowly intersecting with its plane. As the two angles began to merge, she resisted the urge to close her eyes. And then...

Nothing. No resistance. The top edge of her long head softly broke into blazing and sensationless light. Her nictitating membranes slammed shut, and through the translucent tissue her eyes began to adjust. It was more light in one moment than she had experienced in her whole life, but somehow her eyes remembered and started to make sense of the alien world. This was it—she had flown all the way out of the atmosphere, and found the edge of space.

After the long flight from the depths of her home, the quest was now truly beginning.

CHAPTER 1

PAIN bloomed inside Midshipman Colyer's head like the roiling of smoke from a powder explosion. For a moment nothing existed but that pure rush, shooting up from the spine, then seeming to roll around the lining of the skull.

Darkness.

Bright flashing. And a face lurched suddenly in view, eyes wide, lips working furiously, lit as though by flame. The only sound was a constant, rushing roar like the *Daedalus'* wake when the ship ran along before a strong quarter breeze.... *The raid!* How had it ended? Colyer tried to remember what had happened.

Gradually, and in an instant, the midshipman realised the raid was not over—it was presumably still underway.... They had been third in the line of ship's boats pulling steadily towards the boom stretched by the pirates across the river. Lieutenant Garrard had just given the order to ready the carronade when—

Colyer's world had fractured at that moment. Bright lights in the dark and a noise like nothing on Earth...

Orders! Where was Lieutenant Garrard? It was then that the man who had been gesticulating before again thrust his face into the midshipman's own, and started yelling again. It was the bosun, Granby. The all-consuming roar had faded to a whine but the words still struggled to make themselves understood.

"...tenan'...bit o'...nister....st....nder....teenpou...aught us...."
Colyer could hear the desperation in the man's voice even if the words were themselves like fragments of shrapnel.

Something about guns?

Of course. Some long guns on a raft raking the boats as they attempted to tackle the boom. Each moment of clarity was like one more step up the ratlines on a bright day, and a tiny spark of something buried deep in the youth seized on them and started forming a plan. But what of...? Ah, there was Garrard lying between the thwarts with one ear a ragged mess, his blood mixing with the bilgewater in flowing black scrolls.

Which meant—

I'm in charge

The thought was almost as devastating as the roar of the heavy calibre ordnance right in one ear had been. Colyer scratched one temple, trying to think—and the hand came away bloody. No time for that now. The raft guns would cut them to pieces. Someone should take a party to attack them.

The raft had to be tackled. Why was no one doing it? If only they could...

Then why not...?

The midshipman grabbed Granby by the elbow and stabbed a finger at where the muzzle flashes betrayed the cannonade originated. Three big guns, 18 or 24 pounders. "We can't hit them from here with our boat carronade, but if we can get it to the tip of the headland we can rake them like they're raking us."

"Aye, Sir," answered Granby and set the men rowing toward the shore. Colyer felt a moment's euphoric disbelief that the man had neither sought to argue nor simply laughed at the order. The launch scraped on the sand and the men began to leap into the shallows, dragging the heavy carvel-planked boat as far up the strand as they could.

With Granby's help, Colyer directed men to carry the carronade and others to drag its carriage. The pirates appeared not to have seen them, thank God.... But they had. A couple of ill-aimed musket shots whined overhead from out of the black jungle, off to the left. Colyer's heart thundered, but fear was momentarily replaced by shame as the youth felt the trickle of urine down one leg.

That was the second time, damn it all!

Unbidden, a lascar called Panna, one of the midshipman's own sub-division, shook the arms of a couple of the other men and the three of them darted for the trees. They moved at a crouching run, drawing sabres as they went. Colyer glanced at Granby—who nodded his assent—and ordered the rest of the boat's crew to push ahead with the carronade.

In a brief lull in the roaring of the cannon, a scream, of fear, agony or possibly aggression, drifted out of the night, some way away.

The dawn was clearly coming on now. The boats from *Vixen*, *Wolverine* and *Vestal* could dimly be seen floating on the river, dark shapes on a mud brown mass. Those at the far side of the river were trying to cut the boom, those on the near side desperately trying to maintain fire on the forts with whatever cannon had been loaded onto the small craft—though it was likely that nothing they had could fire far enough to get anywhere near the enemy.

Panna and his companions returned, their cutlasses dark with blood. Colyer saw a wide-eyed madness in two of the men as they panted with the rush of slaughter, but not Panna. He was serenely, eerily calm, but he kept his gaze turned down.

Colyer pointed to the place identified earlier. Here the river turned sharply to the left and almost bent back on itself. The boom was stretched almost from the tip of the corner to a point somewhere downstream on the far bank. Colyer had earlier idly wondered why the cable had been placed diagonally across the river—now it was obvious. A raft with some long guns stationed just beyond the spit could pour devastating enfilading fire onto a boat anywhere along the line of the boom, while the boats could not fire back for fear of hitting each other.

"We was bloody lucky, Sir," muttered Granby as the men struggled to set the carronade in place. "The shot from that langridge missed us completely. You and Mister Garr'd must have caught a couple o' bits o' the tin case." Colyer nodded. Just one of the iron balls in a langridge case would be enough to take a man's head off, or put a ragged hole through it at any rate.

A cartridge and canister shot was loaded, wadding rammed and the gun primed. Seconds ticked by. Surely the raft had seen them and in seconds they would be cut to ribbons by a storm of shot. Colyer forced down a desperate compulsion to run, or huddle down, or urinate again. The men working at the carronade, and the marines busy loading their muskets just kept working away as if it was a drill on the *Daedalus*, miles out to sea and no enemy anywhere to be seen. Colyer—'Mister Midshipman Colyer of Her

DAEDALUS AND THE DEEP

Britannic Majesty's Navy'—could not but do the same, however strange the title still sounded.

All the while the big guns out on the river kept up their deafening fire. Surely no one on any of the other boats was alive! Finally, it was reported that the gun was ready—Granby stood at the breech holding the lanyard and wearing an expectant expression. Colyer gulped audibly, and gave the order to fire. It had seemed like hours. In fact it was still only twenty or thirty minutes since they had come ashore.

The carronade roared and its load of pistol shot scythed across the water. The Daedaluses heard screams and snatches of broken Malay floating out of the morning gloom, but by then the gun was ready to fire again. The gunners relished the destruction and spurred each other on to reload and fire the small artillery piece ever faster. Soon, only one of the three raft guns was firing, and that only sporadically. There was a distinct paleness to the scene now, and before long the sun would be up. They were not a moment too soon in dealing with the cannon. In the gloom of the predawn, the pirates had had to use case shot in the hope of hitting anything at all—enough to do fierce damage to human flesh but only likely to sink a boat with a very lucky shot. And it seemed they had been firing high in any case. With light to see by, they could switch to ball shot and clear the boats away at their leisure.

Colyer saw the boom part with a white streak momentarily forming on the river as the cable whipped away. The boats surged on towards the fort over the far side just round the bend. "We have to go back to the boat!" Colyer yelled, "Mr. Granby, do you see to the carronade and bring everyone back as fast as possible." A headlong rush back to the launch ensued. The gun was hastily re-embarked and the boat forged into the stream once more. Colyer, although quite entitled to jump into the sternsheets and give orders, helped push and only jumped back in when the water was waist-deep. Panna grabbed an arm and hauled the cadet officer bodily into the craft. Colyer couldn't help notice an exchange of looks between the men, and that twist in the guts returned with a snap.

Granby, unbidden, called stroke and the launch pushed on towards the fort, rounding the bend just as *Agincourt's* whaler touched the sand below the first palisade. The young midshipman finally gave some thought to the wound sustained earlier.

Fortunately the cut was shallow and had already turned to a dried, crusted mat.

Colyer gave silent thanks that she had not been wounded anywhere on her body. Even their dull surgeon would be likely to notice certain of her more distinctive features under treatment. She had no idea what would happen to her if she was discovered posing as a boy, and had no desire whatsoever to find out.

Chapter 2

CAPTAIN MacQuarrie was annoyed. No, he was livid. He had hoped and believed men from his crew would be the first to storm the fortress walls. Instead, his third lieutenant, Garrard, had got himself wounded in the opening exchanges and the *Daedalus'* boat had been last into the action. True, the midshipman, Colyer, had done tolerably well tidying up the matter of the gun raft, but he had left his station to do so, which had of course meant that the launch was late getting to the attack on the fortresses themselves. There was little he could do about that—Paynter of the *Agincourt* had gone out of his way to mention Colyer most favourably in his report and Vice-Admiral Cochrane was said to be satisfied.

Still, he did not believe it was conducive to discipline for one so young and inexperienced to be displaying initiative. *Initiative*, he fumed, *is for post-rank. Until that time a man would do well to confine himself to obeying orders, efficiently and without question.* He would have a word with the first lieutenant about it.

He paced the *Agincourt's* quarterdeck intemperately.

The admiral's flag lieutenant stepped out of the main cabin and ushered MacQuarrie through the door. The Captain thundered silently as he was kept waiting for a second time, while Cochrane finished dictating to his clerk.

"...had attacked, at Malloodoo Bay, the pirate chief of all Borneo, Seriff Housman," declaimed the admiral. "The boats of the squadron succeeded in taking his forts, being three in number, and mounting altogether fifteen guns; they destroyed his town, and all the goods they came across. The boats were under the fire of the batteries, and some portable guns, while forcing the boom, for a period upwards of fifty minutes, at little more than two

Daedalus and the Deep

hundred yards distance. Our loss was six killed and fifteen wounded—two of the latter since dead. Do you have that? Very well. You are dismissed, Buckley. Please prepare the papers for Captain MacQuarrie. Ah, MacQuarrie, do come over, sit, sit, there's a good fellow." He gestured impatiently at the chair only just vacated by the clerk. MacQuarrie sat.

"I am most pleased with the operation," Cochrane uttered greasily. "We certainly told these ugly bastards that we will not tolerate any of their bestial habits here! Taylor tells me your young gentleman—what was his name?"

"Midshipman Colyer," said MacQuarrie through gritted teeth. Sometimes he felt the first lieutenant thought himself the real Captain, with MacQuarrie just a superannuated figurehead. "He is acting lieutenant currently due to Lieutenant Garrard's injuries." That had been at Malory's insistence.

Cochrane spoke again. "Indeed, it was useful of him to keep the raft-mounted cannon occupied while my men dealt with the boom." MacQuarrie heard the emphasis on *my men* and the muscles in his jaw tautened like weather braces.

"Now Captain, yours is a fine old ship is it not?" MacQuarrie muttered his assent. "But not so handy in these restricted waters, to be sure." MacQuarrie opened his mouth to protest, but Cochrane raised his hand. "No, a corvette of the nature of *Daedalus* is less useful to me than a steam sloop which is not dependent on the wind to work in these shallow bays. I am therefore detaching you and your ship to cruise independently in the Indian Ocean and apprehend whatever pirates or slavers you chance to meet. Ah, here is Buckley with your orders." The clerk handed over a sealed canvas package weighted with shot for quick disposal should the ship be captured. MacQuarrie snorted inwardly—was some corsair or slavemaster likely to be interested in the laughably vague instructions that were no doubt bound into the packet?

"You will cruise until the end of the year whereupon you shall put into the Cape for further orders. That will be all."

MacQuarrie stood and saluted, half turned in his impatience to get out of the cabin which suddenly seemed claustrophobic despite its generous size and wide windows.

"There is one more thing, actually," uttered Cochrane in a tone MacQuarrie did not like in the least. He turned back towards the admiral. "That lieutenant of yours who was wounded, Garrard isn't it? I'm having him transferred onto the *Agincourt*. You'll need a full complement of officers for your cruise and he can recover better here. I'll transfer one of our luffs to you. Talbot has recommended his fifth, a chap called Spencer. It's a shame for your fellow Colyer, it's true, but he's young and will get another chance. Mention it to my flag lieutenant would you, and he can see to the transfer."

Once again MacQuarrie opened his mouth to speak, but stopped himself. Garrard may have been a fool to get himself injured like that but he was a good officer, the right sort. No doubt Taylor of the *Agincourt* was taking full use of the opportunity to divest himself of some wastrel or incompetent. The Captain stormed out of the cabin with as much dignity as he could muster and vented his frustration with a curt order to the flag lieutenant.

As his gig was rowed back to the *Daedalus*, MacQuarrie picked over the exchange, finding more fuel to throw on the fire of his resentment. An independent cruise might have meant something forty years ago when ships like *Daedalus* had harried French, Spanish, Dutch and American trade on the busy sea lanes. Now all he could hope for was to pick up a small schooner or two and hope the slavers didn't throw too much of their human cargo overboard before it could be liberated—in addition to the prize money for any ships seized, he would be paid a bounty on the head of every slave that could be freed. He didn't hold with the abolition himself, but policing the seas did at least keep the Navy busy during the long peace.

To add insult to injury, a third of the powder from each ship had been requisitioned to blow up the forts. If he found any slavers he would have to husband every shot.

Moreover, he had been ordered to part with 15 of his marines to make up losses on the other ships, who would need them for further shore raids. That only left him with 20 to police the ship and help the officers maintain discipline. Less than one marine for every ten sailors! There had better be no ill-discipline on the cruise...

More of the Admiral's words jumped back into the officer's turbulent mind. He had called *Daedalus* a corvette. Well, technically that was what she was, now the Admiralty in its wisdom had equipped all ships of the *Leda*-class with a smaller number of more powerful guns. True, she threw a weight of broadside far greater than before, and with a longer range, but the

DAEDALUS AND THE DEEP

Navy in its arcane way classed vessels purely on the number of guns they carried. So what would have been a fine, 46-gun frigate became a paltry 20-gun corvette. In addition to being pushed out of the Borneo squadron he was robbed of the chance of emulating his heroes Pellew and Broke, who were after all *frigate* captains. Even Cochrane, the Admiral who had just given him his worthless orders, had been a frigate captain of some note; but now, it seemed, he was determined to ruin things for any possible successors.

His previous command had been a sloop—a small ten-gun brig—but now there were paddle sloops bigger than *Daedalus*. His career was going backwards thanks to the quill-pushers and amateurs at the Admiralty. MacQuarrie had made lieutenant two years after Trafalgar but had spent the rest of the war on the quarterdeck of a 74, wearing a groove in the sea on blockade duty outside Brest. The war had ended before he got the chance to distinguish himself. Now, in the closest thing the Royal Navy had got to another war in decades, he was being sent away! It was too much to bear.

He resolved to make a success of this cruise come what may. The men might not have a war to motivate them, so it would have to be wartime discipline that would do it. No transgression must be allowed to escape without the severest sanction possible, he reflected. His officers and men had let him down once—he was determined not to let them do so again.

Nevertheless, as the gig rounded the spit and *Daedalus* came into view, he could not suppress a swell of pride and satisfaction. It was a gloriously bright day, and the sea breeze had whipped up a short chop on the startlingly green waters. Sitting amongst the waves as if set in malachite was his ship. Long and lean, the black hull glistened with new paint and the white strake running from stem to stern emphasized her thoroughbred lines. Since most of the upper deck broadside guns had been removed, the bulwarks had been rebuilt as a low, flush sheer curve running the length of the ship, which made the vessel even more elegant.

Her masts raked elegantly, and he noted with satisfaction the perfectly squared yards. At least Malory and Gilpin, that awful antique of a sailing master, were able to keep the ship tidy-looking.

Even the modern round stern he hated so passionately could not detract from the inspiring sight today. And there was not so much as a paddlewheel or funnel to ruin the purity of his ship

The coxswain put the helm over as the boat passed into the shadow of the hull and the oarsmen tossed their oars. He stood, then jumped for the entry port, not waiting for the bowman to snag a lifeline with his boathook.

...And when his foot slipped on the wet step, Captain Robert MacQuarrie RN, commander of Her Majesty's Ship *Daedalus*, plunged into the two foot wide strip of brilliant green sea between the gig and the corvette. When he finally boarded his command to be greeted by the shrill whistle of bosuns' calls and the salute of the officer of the watch he was dripping wet, hatless, and his temper was fouler than the air in the orlop deck.

He sentenced his coxswain to four lashes for dereliction of duty, but even the punishment failed to lift his mood. Fuming, he had no choice but to break into another bottle in his dwindling supply of spirits.

Chapter 3

COLYER'S last 24 hours had been deeply unsettling. First, she had been called before the captain and curtly informed that she had been given an acting commission as fourth lieutenant until Garrard was fit to return to duty. "I wish you joy of it," he said, sounding as though he wished her head wound had been fatal.

Then, barely had she moved her few possessions into the wardroom before she was informed that Garrard was to be replaced and her acting commission was revoked. In fact, the emotion that had chiefly pushed itself to the fore was relief. She could continue to hide, drawing as little attention to herself as possible. To keep doing just enough to avoid accusations of slackness, but not to put her head above the parapet by excelling. To get to the end of this voyage unnoticed, undiscovered...

Beneath this was a bitter tang of disbelief. She had not quite been able to believe that someone thought her worthy of promotion and had not been surprised when it was snatched away. Life became simpler again. She had been proved right about herself.

Before that morning on the river she had been afraid to do so much as bid the first lieutenant good morning. She had spent her time keeping her head down as if avoiding attention was a vocation in itself. And yet without realising how, she had led a group of sailors and marines—hardened men, some of them former criminals—in an attack on a gun emplacement. It was as if in the heat of battle, someone else had taken over her body— perhaps that was the real Tom Colyer, her brother's spirit guiding her from...wherever it might be now. Or perhaps she had acted simply as the character she was masquerading as would. Was she now bound to act according to the dictum of her assumed personality?

Surely it was just a bang on the head followed by the confusion of battle. But she had acted without thinking too much and somehow she had acted like a naval officer. The thought was frightening but exciting at the same time—that perhaps she did not have to hide all the time. She had spent the majority of the commission acting a part, trying not to get noticed, just getting by until the ship returned home. She reflected ruefully that until the action against the forts, the greatest initiative she had shown was in identifying that a quarter of an hour before the end of the first watch was the safest time for her to use the heads. Maybe it didn't always have to be like that...

There was of course one more ordeal to undergo before she could return to the anonymity of the midshipmen's berth. The captain had invited all the officers not on watch to dinner that evening, before Garrard's replacement had been sprung on the ship. Since it would have been a slight to withdraw the invitation, Colyer was still required to attend. She had never socialised formally with the ship's officers before and was apprehensive to say the least.

It was true that the atmosphere had been distinctly more adult in the wardroom and, even after only a day, returning to the midshipmen's berth felt like entering a nursery overseen by the elderly.

Billeting the midshipmen with the junior warrant officers was supposed, she understood, to mean that the older, experienced professional seamen could keep an eye on the young trainee officers and impart some of their wisdom and steadiness. On the *Daedalus*, however, it seemed that the warrant officers were only exasperated at the presence of the midshipmen, who in their turn sought to outdo each other in annoying their elders. Even a string of mastheadings and liaisons with the 'gunner's daughter' had not cooled the boys' ardour. The two groups had little to do with each other.

The fact that her brief promotion had been over the heads of more senior midshipmen had not gone unnoticed, either—and it had not made life any easier. While to the youngest boys, Gower and MacLeod, she had briefly become a minor hero, the older pair Johnson and Holford had already stopped addressing her in anything other than monosyllables. She suspected it was them who had twice smeared her hammock with the foetid scum that grew on the iron water tanks.

There had been a more senior mid, a steady if unimaginative lad of 17 called Herbert, who had at least seen a fair amount of time at sea. He had been left behind along with a sprinkling of men when the squadron left Penang in a hurry after news of Seriff Housman's piracy had reached the Navy. His loss 'promoted' Johnson to that level, and the pudgy 14 year old had not forgotten it.

It had not helped Colyer's mood therefore when she discovered that Johnson and Holford's 'seniority' was entirely illusory. Both boys had supposedly been to sea before, Johnson on the *Boyne* and Holford on the *Queen Charlotte*. That indeed was what the books of those two ships said. In fact, Gower had whispered to her, they had done no such thing. The only thing connecting those two boys with those ships was their names, entered onto the ship's papers as a favour by the captains to their influential fathers to buy more time 'at sea' on the records of the midshipmen.

The sound of bosun's pipes indicated all hands were to be mustered for weighing anchor. While Colyer made her way to her post, the hands were already placing the long wooden bars in the capstans and readying themselves to hoist the huge anchors from the silt below.

As they began to push at the spokes, some of the men started to sing. It was something of a custom on *Daedalus* that, although unusual elsewhere in the Navy, was indulged in with some enthusiasm here. It was usually some simple sea song or shanty with a refrain every few lines that the whole company could join in with. Colyer secretly enjoyed this idiosyncrasy though most of the officers were disdainful. At times she even longed to take part. This time it was "The Wild Goose," with its rousing chorus of 'Ranzo, my boys, ranzo weigh-hey' getting the crew shouting. Although when they reached the line, 'I met with a pretty girl, her topsails all-aquiver,' Colyer blushed brightly, while the other midshipmen sniggered.

The new Lieutenant, Spencer, stood nearby. It was the first time she had seen the 'cuckoo in the nest' properly—he was a gangling fellow with a surprisingly scruffy appearance. His left shirt front was untucked, his round jacket rumpled and a dusting of stubble covered his jaws. His expression could best be described as simpering. He noticed her gaze and addressed her cheerily.

DAEDALUS AND THE DEEP

"You are partial to music, Midshipman? *Agincourt* had a brass band—I fear the caterwauling of the hands cannot compare."

"Sir?" she responded, but he merely laughed—at least, he uttered what she assumed was a laugh but came out as a bizarre wheeze of inhaled air dragged across the back of his throat. Her eyes widened with amusement and she glimpsed nearby Midshipman Holford who was doubled up in hysterical laughter. Spencer appeared not to notice.

The stern anchor was raised and stowed and the slack taken in on the bow anchor, while sails set fore-and-aft started to move the ship, imperceptibly at first. As the *Daedalus* gradually passed over the anchor, a final heave on the capstan plucked the iron shanks from the bottom, and the ship was free of the land. Topmen scrambled up the ratlines to set more sail, and the ship gathered more and more way. Soon she was standing out into the bay, gathering distance rapidly from the anchored ships of the squadron.

"Mr. Colyer!" It was Lieutenant Malory, shouting from the windward side of the quarterdeck over the noisy creak of the cable being hauled through the hawse. She scuttled over and tapped the peak of her cap with a deferential knuckle.

"Sir?"

"Please give the captain my compliments, and inform him I intend to tack ship to ensure we clear the headland. I shall be doing so in...eight minutes." He glanced at his fob watch as if to confirm his intentions. Colyer saluted again and dashed to the companionway. It was only then she realised that the captain was not on deck. Unusual, for getting under-way before a long cruise...

She had to knock three times at the door of the Captain's cabin before being given permission to enter. Instead of putting her head meekly round the door, she stepped boldly into the cabin. "Mr. Malory's compliments, Sir," she proclaimed, "and he intends to tack ship in ei..um, about seven minutes, Sir."

"When was that did you say?"

She stammered, all her momentum blown away in a moment. "Begging your pardon sir, but the lieutenant said eight minutes when he told me, but that was over a minute ago."

MacQuarrie looked bemused. Colyer noticed for the first time the half empty bottle of a dark liquid sitting on the chart table beside the captain, next to a single glass. The thick, white whiskers around his mouth were stained pink.

"Um, very well. Give the precise Mister Malory my compliments and tell him I assent to his evolution."

When she reached the quarterdeck and repeated the Captain's reply, Malory laughed. "I wasn't asking his permission, if we do not tack ship we cannot weather the point and we will run aground in..." he checked his watch again, "...sixteen minutes." Malory was the only person she knew with a watch and he was evidently rather proud of it. He was always checking it against the ship's chronometer.

Colyer mumbled something indistinct, highly uncomfortable to be caught dangling between the two most senior men on the ship. She had little enough navigation and found it astounding that other people were able to tell with such precision where the ship would be at this or that time in the future based on quadrants and vectors and Heaven only knew what else. She knew with total conviction that she would never be able to do that. For a moment, everything seemed to topple as if the ship was capsizing but she put a hand out to the compass binnacle which steadied her.

At the very nadir of her confidence, Malory spoke again. "It's time—will you give the order, Mr. Colyer?"

Give the order? She turned toward the forecastle and felt her face glowing bright pink, desperately trying to remember the right words.

"Stand by to tack ship!" she bellowed, "Hands to braces, sheets and clew-lines," before adding "Lively there!" almost as an afterthought.

Some of the nearer hands looked over at her, quizzically. One or two put their hands up to their ears as if to catch the sound better. Forward of the midships hatch coaming no one even reacted. Malory chuckled. "You need to work on your command voice, young snotty. Like this."

He uttered the same words Colyer had spoken, at what seemed a moderate volume, but within seconds, the mates were marshalling their teams and the deck had become abuzz with a kind of masculine ballet as men found their places.

"Mr. Gilpin, if you please," said Malory to the sailing master, who took up the order.

Daedalus and The Deep

"Rise tacks and sheets! Helm a-lee!" yelled Gilpin, and the square sails were loosened and temporarily hauled up out of the wind. Beneath Colyer's feet, the sense of the ship swinging could be felt. Columns of men on either gangway hauled the foreyards round.

"Let go and haul!" The ship's head continued yawing to port, and the foresails momentarily flapped with a heavy *whoof-smack! whoof-smack!* as the clewlines were released and the sheets hauled home. The big sails filled with a clap, aback, and added their weight to the helm driving the ship onto its new course. The great mechanical dance overhead continued, with the main and mizzen yards cranked round, safely blanketed by the foresails.

The jib boom had now swung past the eye of the wind. The men on what had been the windward side let go the sheets and braces, and the men on the new windward side hauled for all they were worth. With a deafening clatter and creak of ropes, blocks and flogging canvas, the sails filled and set and soon the wind was driving the vessel again, now from the other beam. The mates shouted back to confirm that all the sheets, tacks and braces were fully home.

"Steady close-hauled on the starboard tack," Malory ordered, before passing a new course to Gilpin. The sailing master made a couple of adjustments to the trim to keep the sails filled efficiently, and reported the helmsman's confirmation that *Daedalus* was steady on course.

HMS *Daedalus* stood out of the bay. Colyer's shoulders slumped, any thoughts of ever becoming a dashing and able naval officer like Malory now well and truly crushed. The sheer complexity of what she had just witnessed baffled her young mind, adding to her embarrassment.

It was not yet over. Malory beckoned. "Walk with me a while, young man," he invited, beginning to pace the windward length of the quarterdeck as the activity on the ship returned to normal. "You know," he confided, "I used to go up onto the hills behind the Portsmouth Dockyard and practise."

"Sir?"

"Commanding. I used to address an imaginary company. Did my declamation the world of good. You should try it."

"Yes—I mean, aye, Sir."

"I'm serious, man," Malory asserted. "An officer's voice is very important. Say you need to give orders quickly and clearly in a rising gale. Or in battle. You remember what gunfire is like?"

"Aye, Sir..." She recalled that first salvo from the raft. The confusion and disorientation. "I thought I'd been permanently deafened after the first cannon shot at us. I couldn't hear a thing for minutes and minutes."

The lieutenant laughed at that. "Indeed, it is the same for most men, I imagine. Still. You are how old now?"

"Sixteen last month, Sir." That was Tom's age, or would have been—she was a year younger, in fact.

"And remarkably you are neither the youngest nor the most stupid of your father's sons," Malory quipped. She smiled tiredly. It was not the first time she had heard the old saw.

"...Your voice not yet broken," Malory continued. "Yet you are already taller than most of your contemporaries—albeit fearfully skinny. We each of us grow up in different ways I suppose. I was a tiny squab at your age. The midshipman's diet you see. Completely inadequate. How is your navigation?"

"Er, I have not yet fully mastered some of the complexities, Sir."

"Well, you will need to. After today Spencer will be taking a watch so I will no longer be required to. I'll help you with some of the rudiments, but you must continue to learn seamanship from Gilpin with the other snotties, is that clear? Well, there it is," he concluded without waiting for a response. The lieutenant grasped the rail and peered out over the steadily receding rows of whitecaps that marched back to the horizon. He spoke after a spell without turning back, as if addressing the sea.

"I'm sorry about your acting commission young man. We are sometimes at the mercy of other powers. In all truth you are much too young for it to have been made permanent, but a little additional seniority never goes amiss. Nevertheless you will have plenty of chances. You should do all right Colyer, if you put your mind to it."

He seemed to draw himself up. "I'll wager that at this moment you don't believe you can fit half of what you need to be an officer in your head, nor carry out the other half nearly well enough. Well, I can tell you that you are wrong. You will learn it, you will carry it out and you will be an officer, and a good one. If you don't progress to my satisfaction you won't serve on my ship for long. At the moment, I believe you are worth working on. Needless to say," at this point he turned to face her—"I am more likely to be right in this than you."

"Thank you, Sir," she stammered, caught in a maelstrom of conflicting emotions. She seized onto a tiny kernel from the nebula —the thought that perhaps she could do more than just hide in this world, sending what money she could to her family until she was inevitably found out. She felt steadier, and sought for the right words. "I will labour night and day to be worthy of your indulgence, Lieutenant Malory."

He grinned at that uncharacteristic theatricality. Colyer reflected that he was not in the least bit handsome but his smile was intriguing—diabolical one moment, angelic the next. "I regret that I had until the late action considered you something of a dullard," he added. "However, it seems you can think. That's worth something to me. Now off with you."

She saluted and with permission, withdrew to the waist to keep an eye on her sub-division, over which she had nominal command. Panna caught her eye and smiled briefly, touching his forelock. She returned the salute, and the smile, and began to enjoy life a little more.

Chapter 4

"...AND to be supplanted for *steam*. Steam power is a dirty, impractical fad. Less handy indeed! A well-drilled brig like my old sloop *Fly* can turn in her own length and certainly avoid running onto sandbanks more easily than one of these glorified floating... pit pumps!"

Dinner with the captain was not going well. The occasion had begun in morose silence while the officers waited, as was the custom, for the Captain to instigate conversation. Instead of engaging with his guests, however, a saturnine Captain MacQuarrie had set out their new orders, and followed this immediately with a diatribe questioning the judgement of Admiral Cochrane, bemoaning the idiocy of the Admiralty, quibbling over ship ratings and, finally, attacking steam as a most un-British innovation.

The officers and Colyer sat crowded around the table running the width of the great cabin. Crammed as they were into their blue round jackets—which in her case had been starting to get a little tight across the chest of late—and white trousers, they were creating no small volume of steam of their own in the tropical heat.

Colyer was already beyond discomfort and hoped desperately that her position near the far end of the table would protect her from attention. It was evident that the Captain had not been particularly enthusiastic about her acting commission and her presence was evidently something of an embarrassment. If she could get through the evening without drawing any further attention to herself she would be eternally thankful. She did at least have the opportunity to see at close quarters some of the officers she had barely had anything to do with before—Kane, the Lieutenant of Marines (those that were left), and the surgeon, Owers.

MacQuarrie had been rattling on, "...infernal things can't carry enough coal to carry out a proper cruise without sails in any case. And steering a course with paddle-wheels either side of you is impossible—why with each roll, the ship tries to veer one way and then the other. What say you Malory?" MacQuarrie added passing the baton, to the general relief of everyone else.

"Well, Sir, the new screw promises to negate the failings of the paddle-wheel, and it seems to me that such an innovation must represent the future of powered vessels..."

MacQuarrie glowered. Malory continued, diplomatically, "...insofar as they can be said to have a future, as coastal or dockyard craft. For a long range cruiser, it is not possible to beat a well-found sailing vessel. We have no heavy, unreliable machinery to drag around with us, and in the open sea we do not need the ability conferred by steam to manoeuvre in confined waters." MacQuarrie looked mollified but suspicious. Malory nodded to Lieutenant Douglas, who took up the baton.

"Mr. Gilpin tells me that with the stores stowed in the most favourable way, and with a steady quartering gale *Daedalus* could conceivably log fourteen and a half knots. I don't know of any steam vessel that could sail faster, not for any length of time."

Owers, the surgeon, added mournfully "It's a fearful business when a boiler bursts, indeed it is. During my last spell at Haslar we saw to a party of stokers who'd been right in the midst of it when a steam-tug blew its tubes out. Those who hadn't been half-flayed had been riddled with shrapnel."

Lambert, Third Lieutenant piped up "...and besides the practicalities, I consider this to be a most unseemly practice for the Royal Navy of Nelson, Blake and Hood. After all, a man signs aboard one of Her Majesty's Ships in the full expectation that he may suffer injury or death falling from the rigging, being torn to shreds by splinters, crushed by shot or hacked to pieces by cutlasses. He does not go to sea in the expectation of being boiled alive!"

The others murmured their assent and nodded, sagely, at this *tour de force*. Even Kane—who had little to add to the debate and who rarely departed from an appearance of upright impassivity, like a roadside stone cross, as if he were at permanent sentry-duty.

The Captain, too, began to sit a little straighter, the humiliations of the day perhaps seeming a little less acute. Colyer found she had been holding her breath. At that point, the new fourth luff, Spencer, cleared his throat.

"Surely, gentlemen," he entreated, "you cannot deny the possibilities steam has to offer? Indeed the science may be yet to become fully perfected but I have no doubt that in twenty or thirty years, there may be no purely sail-powered warships in first-line service. And even now, such steam vessels we have are far better suited to the shallow, restricted bays around Borneo we recently experienced than sail of the line. We know the British Empire to be *imperium sine fine*, but to remain so we must remain masters of innovation. I cannot believe that such men of science that form the officer corps of the Royal Navy would so easily throw over the greatest development of our time?"

Malory said nothing, but simply closed his eyes and sat rigid, brows like thunder. The other officers shuffled awkwardly, and Lambert flashed Spencer a look that was positively Medusan. Kane gazed on, his eyes staring out from beneath an unruly density of black hair, but his face reddened, noticeably.

"Science! Science has little to with that clanking ironmongery," the Captain hissed, his voice level but his face turning purple. "And tell me, Mister Spencer, which vessels it happened to be that went aground during the operation off the mouth of the Sarawak?"

Spencer, like a drunk pilot drifting unwittingly down onto a well-marked reef, continued, "Why, Sir, *Pluto,* steam gunvessel and *Agincourt*, sail third-rate."

"And would you care for me to recount what happened in each case?"

"Sir, well, I—"

"*Agincourt* was brought off without any difficulty and the only problems arose when the steamer *Nemesis* ran into her, is it not so?"

"It is true, Sir, but—"

"While the steam gunvessel *Pluto* sustained considerable damage to her bottom and paddles and had to be beached, *is it not so?*"

"Why yes, Sir, but—"

"Does this not prove beyond all doubt that the much-vaunted *practicality* of steam is nothing but a chimera?"

Spencer's mouth flapped, and the look in his eyes reminded Colyer of some unfortunate beast that had found a trap and blundered obligingly into it. Malory made to speak but MacQuarrie gestured him to desist and looked expectantly to Spencer.

The main course, a ragout of beef with potatoes, was brought out and Spencer was afforded a precious few moments to consider his response.

"I see that there are, ah, indeed, ah, many circumstances where sail may be recommended over steam, and there is...ahem, no reason to suggest why that should not remain so, Sir." And he once again uttered the strange croaking laugh that had already become the cause of hilarity in the midshipmen's berth. A muted snigger went round the room, but once again MacQuarrie appeared happy, having enjoyed the double satisfaction of winning the argument and crushing with aplomb the officer that had been forced on him.

At that moment, Colyer happened to inhale a mote of pepper as she lifted a forkful of beef, and sneezed explosively. All eyes turned to her—many had clearly forgotten she had been there until now. For several seconds, all that could be heard was the wash of the stern wave under the quarter. Malory gazed imperiously across from the top end of the table.

"What's your opinion on the sail-versus-steam debate, Colyer?" he asked. *A test*, she thought, pulse racing.

She had nothing left but honesty and instantly gave up any notion of trying to hide. There could be no fudging now. She took a breath. "I don't have any experience of a steam vessel, Sir, it's true, but there's no doubt in my mind that *Daedalus* is a proper thoroughbred. I don't know what the future holds but..." Malory inclined his head, urging her on. "*Daedalus*...she's fine of line, well-balanced, carries her sail well, and is good and weatherly. Alright, she doesn't handle a seaway as well as some, but still manages better than any paddle-steamer could hope to under sail. Ships like *Pluto* and *Nemesis* which don't sail *or* steam all that well *can't* be the way forward."

MacQuarrie harumphed "Well said, young shaver," and asked Douglas to pass the Madeira, while she fancied she saw Malory's mouth twist into a smile somehow both beatific and triumphant.

Chapter 5

TO Sailing Master Daniel Gilpin, the *Daedalus* under sail represented a perfect balance of forces. Standing by the leeward after-chains with one hand on a shroud it was as though he was part of the ship. He felt the energy from the sails as it travelled through the masts and yards, along the stays and braces into the hull, which took on just the right amount of heel. The pig-iron ballast in the hold resisted the tendency of the sails to push the ship over, while the lines of the underbody converted useless sidewards and rolling forces into good, forward motion. It was akin to the best possible outcome of an equation made physical.

He allowed himself a certain pride in this. He had tuned the rig like a musical instrument over the course of the commission, and arranged the stowage of stores and munitions for the ideal fore-and-aft balance. These *Leda*-class frigates were fine, fast ships and their design had been tweaked and massaged to bring constant improvements since the first ship of the type was launched—modelled after a ship captured from the French as long ago as 1782.

After his thirty years and more at sea, it still never ceased to astound Gilpin that a ship such as this could work at all. She displaced more than a thousand tons, and yet the lightest breath of air could set her in motion. And the engine by which that motion was achieved was a series of enormous, heavy sheets of canvas, their surfaces interrupted with reefing points and boltropes, and themselves attached to massive yards the shortest of which would overtop most houses, while the tracery of rope and chain needed to control it all further sapped the power from the air. It was a wonder that the wind could disturb such a structure at all, never mind use it to force the hull of a man o' war through the resisting waves. Yet a zephyr which could barely be felt on a man's face could move a ship with *Daedalus*' bulk as fast as a man might stroll.

It was a sense of disbelief that a sailing ship could *really* work that had led Gilpin to his great skill in coaxing the best out of any vessel he had ever served on. After all, he reflected, anything that should not work by rights needs all the help it could get to persuade nature to let the miracle happen. One day nature might realise the impossibility of the task and decide not to push ships around the world for man's convenience any more.

It was therefore his duty to maintain the subterfuge.

The sun high overhead indicated that it was nearing the local midday. Which meant that soon the officers and midshipmen would assemble on the quarterdeck for the daily ritual of 'shooting the sun'. Each would use their sextant to measure the altitude of the sun, indicating both the time and the precise latitude.

First in place was Colyer, the skinny midshipman recently distinguished in battle—not that it had done him any good, by the look of things. Still, it was nice to see the lad keen, here a good ten minutes before he needed to be. That was good—Malory had already buttonholed him about Colyer's schooling.

Gilpin had been a little surprised by that. Up until then, Colyer's school work had been adequate, but no more. The midshipmen as a group were, to their misfortune, younger and less experienced than the average. Normally on a ship like *Daedalus* there would be at least one or two boys of sixteen or seventeen, preparing to take their lieutenant's examination and perhaps already qualified as a mate. At best they kept the young boys honest and were taken seriously as a supplement to the officers. It was a shame for all of them that Herbert had got himself lost in Penang.

On this ship, the mids were tolerated or ignored, not integrated into the daily life of the ship. Colyer had only been sent with Garrard on the fortress raid for form's sake. No doubt Johnson or Holford would have gone if they had not incurred Malory's wrath earlier in the week—their fathers would not be happy to learn that their offspring had been denied the rare opportunity to see some real action.

He reflected that twenty years ago, this ship would have been a plum for a young gentleman of promise. These days, all the midshipmen with a bit of influence behind them were going to the 50-gun frigates, ships of the line...or steam gunvessels. No, there were no future Nelsons or Collingwoods in the midshipmen's berth today. Until Malory had decided to pluck Colyer from obscurity, that is.

A rather serious boy, Gilpin thought. *Diffident*.... The midshipman was a slightly odd looking fellow, taller than his shipmates but without even the light fluff on the cheeks that the older lads were now sprouting, a somewhat narrow chin and large grey eyes, freckles sprinkled around his nose. He did not look like the typical naval officer in the slightest. Especially now the fashion was for extravagantly bushy whiskers. Colyer looked up from fiddling with his sextant and nodded to Gilpin, who returned the gesture.

"Morning Mister Colyer."

"Morning Mister Gilpin. Fine day."

"Indeed. Clear skies and a fair quartering breeze. I must say it is good to see you here early."

"I'm midshipman of the watch next, so I wanted to be ready," the boy replied.

"Nevertheless, keenness is always welcome."

They stood in companionable silence for a moment, both enjoying the undulating rush of the waves under the stern, the incandescent sparkle of sunlight off the sea, the thrum of wind through the rigging.

"I hear you have been singing the praises of our fine ship at dinner with the Captain last evening," Gilpin said after a while, breaking into the quiet.

"Oh, yes." The midshipman flushed, something he seemed to do rather a lot. "The argu—the conversation fell to steam and sail and which is better."

"So I heard. Well, the question, of course, is not as simple as 'better'. Are you familiar with Monsieur Lamarck's hypothesis on transmutation, Mister Colyer?"

"I've heard of him," said the boy, after a brief pause, puzzlement in his eyes, "but I don't really know what his theories are about."

"In a nutshell," Gilpin set out, "he suggests that variations spring up in animals and plants to make them better suited to their environment. The skeletons of large animals dug up in

Dorset suggest that many beasts have changed beyond all recognition over the ages."

"And you think the same applies to ship design?"

So this lad's sharper than he looks, Gilpin thought. *Has he been hiding his light under a bushel?* "Exactly so. No two ships are the same of course, and we frequently make specific alterations to try out theories. The better ones become accepted and universal."

"And in extreme cases, the worse ships might be lost in battle or in poor weather while the better ones survive to influence the shipyards?"

"Quite so, quite so—I had not thought of it like that," he grinned broadly. "And I trust you *have* heard of Sir Robert Seppings' innovations?"

"Oh yes...that is, Aye, Sir," Colyer answered brightly, "the iron bits and bobs—knees and suchlike? Lieutenant Spencer keeps banging his head on them."

Gilpin laughed. That came as no surprise. "They make sailing vessels stronger, drier and longer-lasting.

"Sometimes," he continued after a pause, getting into his stride on a favourite subject, "a change in the environment spurs an innovation elsewhere. Seppings'...ah, 'bits and bobs' as you put it, rendered hulls strong enough to bear the weight and forces of steam power though steam was barely thought of at that time. Without the iron trusses a steam engine would shake any ship to pieces—perhaps no one would have ever thought to put a steam engine inside a ship."

The sea stretched away, brilliant green. Its rhythmic rush soft, deafening.

Colyer looked puzzled but thoughtful. "So..." the boy frowned, "a ship might be made better and better, but its star could wane anyway?"

"Even at its zenith. You have the way of it. Where are the great Mediterranean galleys or Atlantic galleases in these times? We must strive to improve in all things, of course, but who and what wins out is for the Lord to decide.

"You know," Gilpin added, conspiratorially, "some Christians take Monsieur Lamarck's theories to be against the word of God. I don't see why—after all, does it not show that the creator has given us the ability to improve ourselves?"

Colyer's response to that was an awkward smile—Gilpin's ideas were by no means common currency and many preferred not to listen.

"I'll think on it, Sir," the midshipman answered.

"'Tis a pleasure conversing with you Mister Colyer," he smiled, before his attention was distracted elsewhere. Midshipmen Johnson and Holford had arrived on the quarterdeck in the meantime—Holford had successfully wrestled Johnson's cap off his head and was dangling it over the taffrail while Johnson vainly lunged for it. Gilpin dashed over to stop the squabbling pair, leaving Colyer to attempt a tentative, experimental sighting with his sextant.

"Stop that skylarking on the quarterdeck you boys!" he snapped. They both immediately spun round and attempted to look sheepish (Johnson) and angelic (Holford). He gave them a piece of his mind and ordered them to pick up their sextants which they had carelessly left lying on the deck, then turned to the exercise, as everyone was now here.

Shooting the sun was, for Gilpin, another of those minor miracles of science and nature. For nature to provide the means for sailors to divine their exact locations was to the sailing master utterly remarkable, as was the fact that it could be done simply with a sextant and a chronometer. Taking a number of readings either side of midday could, when combined with readings from the chronometer, fix their position anywhere on the globe with remarkable precision.

He peered into the sighting scope of his own instrument, lining up the horizon, then releasing the index arm so the right-hand half of the image slid upwards, questing. He found the sun in that image, then tweaked the index until it lined up with the horizon, Clamping the index again, he read the angle. The sun was all but directly overhead, indicating it was a minute or two to midday. He looked around the midshipmen to check that they were working the instruments properly.

"What angle do you have Mister Colyer?" he inquired.

"89.8 degrees, Sir," the boy answered. Similar to his own reading.

All the readings were within a minute or two, apart from Johnson and Holford's, which were nearly a degree short of the average. He checked both boys' sextants. Both appeared to be fine.

DAEDALUS AND THE DEEP

He demanded their journals. Clearly reluctant, the boys gave the books up. A string of identical initial readings going back for weeks in both books. Johnson whined that he had always checked his result against Holford's *to be sure of being correct*. Holford, looked at him blackly. He questioned them both relentlessly until Colyer, at his shoulder coughed politely and indicated that it was midday.

He experienced a sudden epiphany—one boy had simply made his result up every day, knowing all the other officers would be bound to be close to the mark. The other boy had copied the first, thinking he had done the measurement properly.

Both failings could have led to serious danger if they had gone unnoticed. After he had informed the captain it was now midday, he returned to the miscreants. Gilpin, uncharacteristically, ranted for a while and told them in no uncertain terms he would bring charges recommending they both 'kiss the gunner's daughter'.

His good mood of earlier had departed. Blackly, he signalled the officer of the watch, and the *tangtang, tangtang, tangtang, tangtang* of the bell sounded the change of watch and the beginning of a new naval day. The fading tones drew a line directly through the emptiness, imposing the Royal Navy's law anew onto the open sea.

Daedalus sailed on, out of the past, into the future. Its wake inscribed the ocean, which allowed the disturbance for a short while before engulfing the mark. Even the wind eroded the ring of the bell to nothing.

Sullenly, Gilpin ran through navigational exercises with the febrile gaggle, calculating the great circle distance between two points and resolving some problems of spherical trigonometry. Finally, as they had their sextants to hand and the moon was clearly visible in the blue sky, he began to take them through the process of establishing time by measuring the distance between the moon and another body.

Chronometers were all very well, but nature had provided all the means to navigate with accuracy. Cook had been an expert in moon-sighting, and what was good enough for Cook would be good enough for these reprobates.

"With the sextant on its side, first align the image with the limb of the moon, then find the limb of the sun. Using your almanacs, now correct the distance to the centre of each body with the measurements given..."

Holford and Johnson glowered at the back of the group, but were ostentatiously working hard on the calculation. He might make navigators of them yet. At that point Gilpin heard a bizarre, creaking sound behind him. He turned to see Lieutenant Spencer —who had just taken over as officer of the watch—clearly amused and...was that bizarre noise in the back of his throat *laughter*?

"Lunar distance, Mister Gilpin?" he chuckled, "is our chronometer no longer working?"

"The chronometer is functioning admirably, Mister Spencer," Gilpin asserted, careful not to appear rude to a superior, but nonetheless annoyed at the interruption.

"Then why not teach the snotties how to use that?"

"I will do so in due course, Mister Spencer but I believe it important to give the young...*gentlemen*" (and with this he darted a look at Holford and Johnson) "...the importance of a method that relies more on their own aptitude than the vagaries of a sensitive piece of equipment. If, for example, they find themselves one day with a broken chronometer, or shipwrecked in a boat with none at all?"

"Of course, Mister Gilpin, of course. But most ships carry at least two chronometers these days. And with lunar distance, an error as little as half an arc-minute will give rise to an error of about a minute in Greenwich Time, which, if I am not mistaken equates to around fifteen nautical miles at the—ahem—equator."

Johnson, understanding none of the detail, nonetheless realised that the implication that method they had been slaving over might be fallible. And not only that, but there was a simple alternative involving nothing so complicated as reading a clock.

"So we could do *all* this and *still* be fifteen miles away from where we *think* we are? What's the good of that?" he sneered.

"No, no," interjected Spencer, "the sailing master is quite correct to teach you lunar distance. It's important to know the rudiments. *Aut viam inveniam aut faciam,* eh?" He sauntered away, leaving Gilpin with an unruly classroom once more. The usual time at which the lesson ended had passed, and the boys leapt up to leave. He managed to set some exercises before they scattered, requiring the more or less unwilling students to calculate time using some lunar distances he specified, but when Johnson and Holford's tasks were returned they were pitifully lacking and suspiciously similar.

DAEDALUS AND THE DEEP

At least Colyer's was done properly. He did not know what it was that had made the lad come out of himself but he gave thanks nonetheless.

Chapter 6

COLYER was attempting to read *The Boys' Book of Seamanship* in the midshipmen's berth, with little success, when the invitation from Malory was delivered. The other midshipmen were chattering loudly to each other, and the youngest boy, Gower, was systematically turning the space upside down searching for his journal.

She had finished her watch a while ago but sleep was elusive. She might have been awake even if someone had not left a dead rat in her hammock when it had been rolled up. The canvas with its unfortunate occupant had subsequently been left in the sun all day in the hammock netting on the rail. The stink clinging to the cloth had been unbearable and with a sigh of resignation she hung it out to air and attended to her studies.

As it was, the ship was rolling heavily, sailing directly downwind in a steep swell. Consequently, the anchor hawsers (which passed directly through large openings in the deck above and below), thumped abominably, and the water in the bilges sloshed in unison. Frequently men would pass through the 'berth' (which was in effect simply part of the forward platform between the cable tiers and the magazine) on their way to and from the powder room or the carpenter's workshop, further adding to the disturbance.

After reading the same sentence on kedging a ship out of an anchorage against unfavourable tides, she had just about despaired of learning anything in this manner. Then, above the general cacophony, she heard a polite throat-clearing. Upon looking up, to her surprise, the wardroom steward was standing before her. This was a man rarely seen forward of the mainmast.

Daedalus and The Deep

"Lieutenant Malory's compliments, young Sir," he said softly, "and he wishes you to attend him in the wardroom. You may bring your books."

Colyer thanked the steward, who melted away as swiftly as he had arrived and, clutching her books, stepped aft to see what Malory wanted.

When she arrived, several of the officers were sitting at the single, long table that ran the length of the wardroom, studiously ignoring each other. Spencer was reading a worn copy of Virgil's *Eclogues*. Gilpin was dozing quietly in his chair but opened his eyes as she entered and nodded, hospitably.

Douglas was dabbing a brush at a small watercolour. Malory appeared to be poring over a treatise on modern naval tactics. He noticed her arrival and gestured her to take a seat. Spencer's look of deep concentration seemed to swell somehow. He was staring so hard at the page that it appeared as though the detonation of a 32-pounder by his head would have elicited no reaction.

Colyer, still puzzled, thanked Malory.

"Not at all," he breezed, "it's quieter back here and you'll be able to study. Would you care for a drop of blackstrap?"

Her face felt hot. "Yes please, Sir—just a small glass if I may."

He poured a glass for each of them. "Gilpin tells me your navigation is coming on apace."

"I think so, Sir. It's making more sense to me these days"

"Good, good. Astronomy?"

She sighed inwardly. "I've tried to read up on it but I feel like there's so much to take in."

"Indeed there is. But reading's no good on its own, we have the night sky to teach us. You're on duty again for the first watch tonight, yes?"

"Y—Aye, Sir."

"Very well, bring your astral charts and we will go over some particulars."

"Thank you, Sir."

"Don't mention it. We need to make an officer of you and that college doesn't seem to have taught you anything worth knowing. No doubt it was all how to hoist 'England expects', or listing the figureheads of Nelson's ships in reverse order."

She smiled, and noticed Spencer looking daggers at Malory for the briefest of moments. "A little like that, Sir."

"Well, you may stay here until the end of the watch. If you require anything, simply call the steward and he will attend to your needs. If you wish to discuss anything that confuses or interests you further by all means raise it with me or one of these good fellows here."

"Thank you, Sir. I'm really very grateful." She tried to stop herself blushing again, and busied herself with her exercises.

"Not at all. I'll speak to Gilpin about getting you a rating as mate, then depending on how you do we can start to give some thought to your examination for lieutenant." Malory smiled indulgently, and returned to his tactics, busily scribbling in the margins and occasionally snorting sceptically at something he disagreed with.

Colyer got more done in those few hours than she had managed in weeks, and told Malory so. He tested her on a few points and seemed pleased with her responses. The invitation to the wardroom was repeated every few days over the succeeding weeks, and Colyer began to feel brave enough to question the lieutenants on a number of issues. On one memorable occasion the Battle of Cape St Vincent was recreated on the wardroom table, cutlery representing the opposing fleets, and by the climax of the action nearly all the off-watch officers had joined in.

Malory was implacable on the point that Nelson had all but disobeyed a direct order when he put *Captain* right across the enemy van alone, while the rest of the fleet chased the Spanish rear.

(At this point Lambert made a reference to 'the Spanish rear' that Colyer was quite sure was not entirely proper, but this time she laughed with the rest and turned only slightly pink.)

"Nelson interpreted his orders just closely enough to avoid censure—but only if his tactics worked," lectured Malory. "If he'd have failed, he'd have been court-martialled and on the beach before the smoke had cleared.

"That's why we must always be thinking. Using our brains. We may be in a position to spot an opportunity no one else has. Success is the best way of avoiding a Court Martial."

"'*Westminster Abbey or glorious victory*'," quoted Douglas wistfully, not appearing to have heard a word Malory said. "I bet

Daedalus and The Deep

I'd never be able to think of something inspiring to say at a time like that."

"If you ever got near boarding an enemy first rate, you'd probably shout 'Mother'" needled Lambert, and the session collapsed into good-natured ribbing.

Colyer had started to feel quite at home with the officers. They were all at least six years older than her, but that gulf seemed much narrower than the epoch that separated her from the squabbling, infantile midshipmen.

The shine was only slightly taken off the visits when, after the fourth or fifth, she heard Spencer's nasal tones drifting through the curtain as she approached.

"...the slightest notion why you encourage that snotty Colyer, Malory. Do you know who his people are? The captain's clerk tells me his father is a provincial sawbones at a charity hospital—penniless I should think because the mother works too, if you can believe that—at a school. Not even a proper school. One of those church affairs for the poor. Don't misunderstand me—he's a fine fellow, I rather like him. Don't doubt he'd make a decent warrant officer. That's the proper level for his sort, wouldn't you say?"

Malory muttered something which Colyer couldn't hear, but the edge to his tone was audible. The dig was all the more surprising given that she had stood watch with Spencer a couple of times recently and while they had hardly struck up a great friendship, the time had been passed pleasantly enough.

Crestfallen, she coughed theatrically and knocked on the partition. When she entered, Malory said, pointedly, "Wasn't your father a naval surgeon, Colyer?"

"Yes, Sir. He was ship's doctor on the *Albion* at Navarino in '27." She left out the fact that he had rather fallen into it, going to sea as a boy seaman and helping the surgeon when one of his loblolly boys was killed at the Battle of Lissa. Only after years of assisting had he won the chance to train as a surgeon's mate, then as a surgeon in his own right. To his credit, he had done well.

"Indeed, indeed," was all Malory said by way of reply, with something of an air of satisfaction. She attempted to go through some navigational exercises but her heart was not in her work today, and after half an hour she made her excuses and left. She stepped through the curtain, feeling like a fraud, and heard Malory snapping something at Spencer, who piped up again.

"Very well, very well, but ships' surgeons can't be considered *proper* officers, can they?"

Colyer heard him muttering some more about *sharing a mess with the likes of....* She realised she had to stand watch with him in a day or two, and clenched her fists silently as she picked her way forward.

CHAPTER 7

THE gale had struck them in the dark of the middle watch, three weeks into their passage across the Bengal Bay. It caught the ship unawares.

The glass had plunged, and before long, *Daedalus* was close-reaching into a steep swell and a rising wind. They did not have the sea-room to run downwind and so life was going to become uncomfortable.

Colyer was awake, attempting to resolve mathematical problems relating to the altitude interception of celestial bodies. She jumped out of her hammock at the first desperate calls for all hands to muster on deck and struggled into her oilskins, reaching the deck while the boys stumbled blearily round the midshipmen's berth looking for their kit.

The wind was by now shrieking around the shrouds and Malory was fuming that Spencer, as officer of the watch, had not acted more quickly. Captain MacQuarrie appeared in a state of undress, cursing the cut down armament that had reduced the size of the crew from that of Nelson's day—*another hundred men would have sail shortened in no time.*

Gilpin arrived, quickly and calmly advising how to alleviate the mounting problems. The topgallants needed to be taken in, and reefs put into the courses and topsails. If the wind built any more, the t'gallant yards would need bringing down, to boot. Every able-bodied man was needed aloft. That meant midshipmen too. Colyer quickly fell her sub-division in and made for the rigging.

The windward bulwark was high in the air while the lee rail was trailing through the surface —the ship was heeling more than Colyer had ever seen. As she scrambled around the deadeyes onto the fore-shrouds, she caught a glimpse of tall, steel-grey waves marching off to infinity. She pulled herself up to windward, while a wave caught the flank beneath her with a hollow boom, and a vertical sheet of water squirted into the air like foaming glass. It soaked Colyer to the skin in an instant, despite the oilskins.

With each gust, the young midshipman was flattened against the ratlines. She found she could only climb by dashing up a few steps during the lulls. When the wind blew hardest, even breathing was a challenge—turning her head into the gale was like being drowned in air, while turning her head away felt like trying to breathe in a vacuum. The ship lurched into each trough, slamming against the next wave and sending a shiver up the masts.

Colyer reached the fighting top, scrambling round the futtock shrouds and on up the topmast rigging. Malory hollered incomprehensibly through a speaking trumpet on the quarterdeck below. She ignored him and concentrated on making the next step, then the next.

Finally, she made the topgallant yard and began shimmying out onto the port limb. The sea roiled below. She ignored that, too.

She noted with a stab of satisfaction that the lascar topman Panna was on the same end of the yard.

It had not been until the first gale she experienced on the *Daedalus,* back off the coast of West Africa, that Midshipman Colyer had fully comprehended the reason for Panna's popularity among the crew.

The man was quiet and seemingly spoke little English. He did not take part in the usual rough-and-tumble of forecastle life and although he could take a joke or two—no one lasted long who could not—he was hardly the spirit of frivolity. He did not match the usual pattern of the men in her sub-division—they were professional sailors and well-disciplined, thank God, but as loud, boisterous and sociable as any Jack Tar picked up in the press during the last war. And just as ready to start a fight or threaten bloody death at the merest provocation. Not Panna.

Halfway up the mainmast, though, half-frozen, pelted with rain and wrenched this way and that by the wind, Panna was in his element. With the men of the starboard watch balanced on the yard, taking in canvas soaked and stiffened by seawater, the lascar seemed to radiate calm like the galley stove radiated heat.

The men had wrapped themselves around the yard as the ship rolled and jibbed, swearing and flailing. Panna worked steadily, not hurrying but still at great speed, a small half-smile on his face.

His fingers moved at the gaskets and fabric with precision and his body seemed not to move at all. Even when when Colyer was attending to her own work—Lord knew there was no room to concentrate on anything else—it was possible to sense that he was there, dulling the fear and slowing the heartbeat until the sail was reefed and the crew moved to the next, or returned to the deck.

Three months before that first storm, Colyer had been safely at home, and she had not reckoned on the bowel-twisting terror of hanging on a slippery spar, while the ship bucked below and hands and feet went numb from the wind.

During that trip aloft early in her *Daedalus* career she splashed the fore-royal with vomit and pissed her best pair of cotton duck trousers. The youth was grateful for the rain washing most of the urine away as the team worked, and more grateful when the call came from the deck that the watch could come down. But she was most grateful to the quiet rock Panna, working away at the next loop.

He was like a totem, encapsulating his mates within the glowing orbit of his influence.

(She later discovered that he never touched a drop of alcohol and always shared his tot of rum out among his messmates. It was possible his popularity was connected to this too, but still...)

Colyer later wondered if it she—if any of them—could ever have secured those sails and climbed back down the twanging ratlines had it not been for Panna's mere presence. And in fact many of the younger men aboard *Daedalus* would have told similar tales if they cared to admit it. Having the lascar assigned to her sub-division was a singular stroke of luck.

The waisters began to haul on the buntlines, and Colyer and the men started gathering the canvas as it bunched up toward them. The yard began to drop beneath them as it was lowered to its stop. At that moment, she caught sight of a huge wave slewing toward the port bow. "Hang on lads!" she screamed, just as the bow thrust itself into the mass of water.

The ship seemed to stop dead, and behind her a sound like a cannon shot tore the air, hard followed by a cacophony of banging, rattling and flapping. A profound terror seized her for a flashing moment, and in her mind the whole rig came down, scattering the men like sycamore seeds.

A sail must have blown out, she thought, *but we're all right. concentrate, concentrate!* The yard jerked like an untamed horse.

Below, the deck was momentarily a boiling lagoon, water frothing feet-deep on its surface before gurgling back out of the scuppers. The captain had grabbed the speaking trumpet from Malory and was yelling inaudible gibberish at the men above even while knee deep in green sea.

The buntlines had been fully hauled in and Colyer grasped the ends of her gasket, securing the resisting bundle to the yard. She tested the knots—they were tight and would hold fast—and checked that the others had finished before starting to shuffle back to the mast.

At that moment she heard a stifled cry behind her, and glanced back to see the next man along, Livock, slumped over the yard, one leg seeming to hang limp from the foot rope. Panna reached him a moment later and had fastened his hand beneath the man's shoulder. Colyer gulped and slid back out. Between them, she and Panna lugged Livock's inert form along the yard, a foot at a time, toward the crosstrees. They rested for a moment, and Colyer coiled an aching arm gratefully around the jeer tackle. Her stomach lurched as she caught a glimpse of the topman's strangely twisted face.

With one of Livock's arms round each of them, Panna and Colyer inched down the ratlines to the foretop where a man was waiting with a line. Panna tied a bowline round the man's chest and they lowered him as gently as possible, through the lubber's hole to the deck below.

Panna looked at her quizzically but she motioned him to go ahead, before slipping onto the backstay herself. She took a firm grip, and a couple of deep breaths, and slid down after him.

The backstay was wet and vibrating like a bowstring but she gripped hard, took each hand at a time and eventually made the safety of the deck. When she got there, the men of her sub-division were gathered round, anxious. She knelt beside the prone figure.

Livock was lying on the deck, his face contorted. His left arm and leg were twisting and thumping the deck, while his right arm and leg, bizarrely, were completely motionless.

She caught sight of the surgeon bustling through the crowd of waisters, but before he could arrive, the blue coat of an officer appeared before her. She stood—it was the captain.

"What is happening, Midshipman?" he growled. "What is the matter with this man?"

At that point, Livock writhed again and a gurgling noise issued from his mouth.

"Gfffffffrrrrrrrrrrrrggggggggggg," he spluttered, "Gggggggggggj-j-j-j-rrrrrrrrrrrr"

Before Colyer could respond, MacQuarrie had turned purple. She saw his jaw clench. She inhaled to speak, but the captain beat her to it.

"This man is drunk," he hissed. "Drunk and insolent. Two dozen lashes. Take him below!"

Colyer looked up in disbelief. He was serious!

"Sir," she protested, "Livock isn't drunk, he's sick. He needs help!"

MacQuarrie whipped round, open-mouthed.

"Captain," she entreated, "I do not believe this man is drunk. He showed no signs of drunkenness when we ascended the rigging, and he seemed fine until we had secured the sail."

Panna leapt to his feet, looking at her with horror. "Sir—" he interjected, eyes wide as a warning, hands forming a pacifying gesture. Macquarrie turned and faced the lascar—Colyer realised with horror that he thought Panna's words directed at him.

"And a dozen for this man for insubordination!" he snapped, before staring at her, as he might regard an insect that had just bitten him. Quietly, he added "and you, Sir, shall kiss the gunner's daughter. A dozen strokes. I will have no challenge on my own ship." He turned and stormed away. The surgeon was finally able to attend to Livock who was burbling quietly on the deck.

"What the devil d'you think you were doing Colyer!" Malory had just appeared beside her and grasped her arm. "Never challenge the captain, especially...Just never challenge him, talk to me if you think there's a problem."

"Aye, Sir, sorry, Sir" she answered, eyes wide. "Poor Livock, Sir, he..."

"You silly little fool." Malory's grip was bitter. "Livock knew what he was signing up for." The lieutenant stormed away, muttering angrily to himself.

"Stroke or apoplexy I'd say," she heard the surgeon mutter, as Livock was carried below decks.

Chapter 8

COLYER had experienced pain before but nothing like the dozen strokes of the bosun's cane, nor had she ever felt such humiliation.

The storm had largely blown itself out. For the whole of the day she had had to await her punishment, she had vowed to herself that she would not cry—and after the fifth stroke, the tears streamed down her face and splashed off the scrubbed teak of the deck. Even the pose the punished had to assume—bent over the breech of a 32 pounder, trousers pulled down—seemed calculated to insult and taunt. *Seven...eight...*

Her entire lower half was now burning. She no longer felt each stroke as it happened, but a few seconds afterward like a wave breaking over her. She tried to think of navigational problems, of elements of seamanship, of the ships of famous admirals, techniques to gain the weather-gage, the common sequences of signal flags...

It was coming to an end! Thank the Lord. The pause between the last two strokes was the longest of her life, then, finally, it was over. She knelt, partly in pain and partly to pull the waistband of her trousers over her backside without displaying herself—and gasped with pain again. The universe was fractured. Her life before the first stroke seemed a distant memory, or belonging to someone else. Her life now was nothing but a glowing ember of agony and disgrace.

As she was led to the sick bay she caught sight of Holford and Johnson, wearing triumphant expressions. *Oh heavens*, she thought, catching sight of Spencer—the last man she wanted to see at this moment.

"Bear up Colyer," the lieutenant said cheerily as she passed him, "after all, *legum servi sumus ut liberi esse possimus.*" She pretended not to hear, but saw Lambert glowering in sympathy which gave her a brief, consolatory, satisfaction.

Owers, the surgeon curtly ordered her to remove her trousers so he could apply a salve and bandages. At that moment, Colyer wanted nothing more than to oblige but even through the fog in her brain she knew that she could not.

Gently, she shook the two men off her arms and stood, swaying with the roll of the ship. "No," she said. "Give me the salve, I'll put it on myself."

"Come now lad, there's no need to be shy," entreated Owers.

Colyer could have laughed. She had been dressed down by the captain in front of the entire crew and then thrashed. What was there left to be shy about? What indeed.

"I can...go away and apply the salve myself...or I can just go away," she said as firmly as she could. The surgeon was not unused to men refusing his care. He shrugged and rooted round in the wooden case full of tiny drawers before pulling out a small glass jar. He handed this over with some bandages and a disapproving look, all which she silently took, and shuffled off to the forward cable tier. Peeling her bloodstained trousers away from her scarred backside, she thought she would faint, but managed to apply the balm before shuffling back to the midshipmen's berth. Someone, she didn't even register who, slung her hammock for her and she lay there, broken, until a kind of dull unconsciousness took over.

Fortunately, Livock was not to be thrashed until he had recovered. Apparently, MacQuarrie had been all for flogging the topman as soon as the storm had subsided, but Malory had persuaded MacQuarrie to wait until the man was fit and could answer for himself. It was small consolation in a way—it did not look as though the topman would ever recover his senses.

Malory had a way with the captain, Colyer was learning. MacQuarrie agreed to things almost without realising it. The lieutenant reminded her of her brother, who had been able to mollify the most difficult horse and bend it to his will as if it were actually the will of the horse itself. Until the awful day of his return from the Naval College, that is. The memory of his tragic accident and the path it had set her on added to her desolation.

There was no such delay for Panna's punishment, however. As soon as the wind moderated enough to free up the crew, hours after her own flogging, a grating was rigged and hands called to witness punishment. Colyer had to fight back more tears. If she had only kept her mouth shut she could have spared the blameless seaman, not to mention herself.

She forced herself to watch as the boatswain's mate took the cat out of the bag and began issuing the strokes. The flogging seemed to take an age.

BdrdrdrdrdrdrdrdrdrdrdrThwack

"Five!"

BdrdrdrdrdrdrdrdrdrdrdrThwack

"Six"

She felt every stroke, added to her own. The rattan cane seemed mild compared with the vicious 'cat'.

BdrdrdrdrdrdrdrdrdrdrdrThwack

"Nine!"

BdrdrdrdrdrdrdrdrdrdrdrThwack

"Ten!"

The boatswain's mate had not moderated his strokes—he could not, or he would quickly be substituted for someone who would, and probably some additional strokes 'for luck' would be added.

Finally, the ghastly spectacle was over. She prayed no more men of her division—on the entire ship—were flogged again. At the same time she knew there would be more floggings, and she did not know how she would cope.

The following morning, her own wounds were excruciating and the bandages had stuck to the scabs. She applied more of the salve where she could and left the bandages in place. Colyer fervently hoped for a day of relative inaction—movement sent stabs of pain rippling through her.

It was then that the sound of a drum roll struck up once more from the spar deck. It was not for punishment duty this time.

It was the signal to beat to quarters. The ship was about to go into action.

And her post was on the fore-top.

She grabbed her telescope and made for the companionway. By the time she reached the spar deck she was already bleeding from broken scabs, and was almost numb by the time she had attained the fore-top. Panna was unshipping the swivel gun from its stowage so it could be mounted on the rail. But the lascar was not the usual seaman who shared her post.

"Where's Carson?", she asked.

"Swapped post with Carson, Sir. All right though. Checked with Mister Malory, Sir. If it's all right with you I mean, Sir."

That came as a surprise to her—Panna was evidently not near-silent because of his nationality. She had assumed he spoke little English, and that little mostly technical sailor's language. Such a thing was by no means uncommon, but she reddened a little at her presumption.

"Thank you, Panna," she replied, trying to raise a smile for him, "of course it is." Finally, it occurred to her to wonder why they had beaten to quarters. "Why have we cleared for action?" she enquired.

"Sighted a slaver. 'Bout four points off lee bow, there."

She followed his pointing finger, and indeed, there it was. The tiny double-sail profile of a hull-down ship. She pulled her pocket telescope out and scanned for the vessel. It was a hermaphrodite brig, with two large quadrilateral sails abaft the masts and a square topsail and course on the foremast. Ships with that rig were invariably fleet of foot. She looked around, searching for the full picture. The schooner was down to leeward, which gave *Daedalus* the weather-gage. It was evidently trying to escape by beam-reaching with the wind square on its port side. It was probably the brig's fastest point of sailing, but it meant that the Daedalus could work down towards her. *Daedalus* was fastest with the wind on the quarter, so both ships were playing to their strengths.

All things being equal, *Daedalus* would not catch the brig before sundown if at all, but with luck all things would not be equal. Their slide-mounted chasers could fire accurately over nearly two miles and the vessel's rig made a tempting target. If hobbled, the other ship would surely surrender. A single broadside from ten 32-pounders would tear a lightly built brig into splinters.

There was nothing to do for the moment but wait. The wind was building, slowly but steadily. That should favour the corvette—it could carry full sail far longer than the delicate schooner. She sensed more activity beneath her, and shifted her position to see what was going on. Men swarmed over the lower yards breaking out the stunsail spars—gear for the extra sails that could be added on either side of the great square sails. The stunsails were hoisted in a tight package, then unfurled in a single hearty flap of canvas.

Through the mast and the rigging she felt she could sense the extra push from the stunsails, and the creamy moustache flowing away from the ship's bow became noticeably larger.

"She's got a bone in her teeth today, eh Panna?" she quipped with a lighthearted skip in her voice that she did not feel in the least.

"Aye, Sir," Panna answered, grinning broadly despite the pain he must be in. The wind was beginning to whip his hair, which was long and black, into his face so he tied it back with a strip of fabric and shoved it into the back of his jacket. Colyer instinctively moved to do the same, before remembering that she had had her hair cut short since the journey by packet out from Portsmouth. Panna was gazing at her, quizzically. She grinned, foolishly, and looked away.

The activity below died away as the crew settled into the routine of waiting for action. She had heard it was common to send the hands for dinner when a long chase was underway but there seemed to be no sign of that happening here. She shifted to the back of the platform, trying to catch a glimpse of the officers on the quarterdeck in the gaps between the sails. She spotted the captain and Malory as they paced together, walking forward to the gangway then turning and disappearing behind the mainsail, clearly deep in conversation.

She extended her telescope and searched for the brig again. There it was, still somewhat forward of the beam but now she could see the top of the hull above the horizon. So they were gaining some ground. It could be hours before they were in range of a shot though...

"How are you...today, Sir?" Panna asked, after a long spell of silence. The implication was clear.

"Fine, thank you, Panna," she responded, feeling anything but fine.

"First time was it?" He asked, clearly uncomfortable. It was more words than she'd ever heard him say. His voice was warm, and in the middle range. He spoke English like a native, and his voice had not so much an accent as a kind of tang.

"Yes, it was. I hope it'll be the last," she said with a little too much passion.

"Not so bad after," he concluded.

"How are you?" she asked, not sure if it was appropriate but not wanting to ignore his own punishment—which was after all, her fault.

"You get used to it," he said, flatly.

She managed a smile at that. She couldn't imagine a man as skilled and sober as Panna needing to be beaten enough to 'get used to it'. Nevertheless, she reflected ruefully, recent experience showed that punishment did not always limit itself to reprimanding the unjust and protecting the just.

It was clearly a struggle to Panna to speak—probably embarrassing to the man as much as anything else. She weighed up returning to silence to spare his blushes, but after the previous day's pain and humiliation suddenly, desperately needed a little companionship with another human being for a moment or two. "Where are you from?" she enquired.

"Ratmalana, Sir," he answered. She knew vaguely where that was, but little about it.

She nodded. "I'm from Essex. Do you know Harwich?"

"Not me, Sir, not really. Sailed past a few times but.... Some of the lads was in *Blazer* before, she were a Harwich ship."

"Yes, I know her." Colyer had spent many hours as a child—as a younger child—lain on the hill overlooking the distant anchorage watching the comings-and-goings of the warships, dashing frigates and stately line-of-battle ships, and lately, puffing steamers of which the *Blazer* was one. She'd even got to recognise some individually from some quirk of their rig or distinctive stern decoration pointed out by her father, who had sailed on not a few of them.

"Have you been in *Daedalus* a long time?"

"Two commissions, Sir. Good ship. Good lads. I like her."

"That's good. How is that you're on a naval ship though? I thought there were lots of lascars on Indiamen. I reckon the John Company must pay better too."

He looked deeply uncomfortable. "Navy's all right."

"Do you have family in Ceylon?" she cast around for anything to keep the conversation going.

A look of utter desolation flickered over his features before they returned to their usual placid composure. "Wife and daughter," he said without joy. "Not seen them for...I dunno. Hope we catch that ship quick," he added with a nod to the schooner, changing the subject. She went along with it.

"Why so impatient? We have hours of light left."

"If it look like we're catchin' them slow but they've no way of gettin' out, they'll start pushin' the slaves over the side," he answered.

Her stomach turned at that. She imagined being pitched over the side of a rushing ship, still bound, unable to move freely, the weight of the chain pulling you down...

Panna reached absently into a jacket pocket and pulled out a string of beads, which he started running one by one through his fingers. He appeared deep in thought but every so often, muttered a few words very quietly to himself. Colyer caught a couple —"...*lord is with thee, blessed among...now...hour of our death...*"

Colyer dare not try continue the conversation after that. He clearly knew more about the horrors of the slave trade than she wanted to find out, and she doubted she would get any more out of him about his own life. Still, there weren't many lascars in Queen's Ships, while the East India Company was built on lascar sailors. In some Indiamen there were three to every Englishman. She was distinctly curious as to what his story might be, even more after the monosyllabic responses and evasion, but reluctantly accepted he was entitled to his privacy

After all, there was plenty that could be asked about her that she would rather avoid owning up to...

Panna lapsed back into silence, staring out at the horizon. Below, Colyer heard the shrill of bosun's calls piping hands to dinner by division. The captain had evidently decided that contact with the slaver was not imminent. She experimented with her position and found that lying on her front propped on her elbows was most comfortable. She could use her telescope that way, and started making regular sightings, marking the angle on the platform with a piece of charcoal and trying to gauge whether the brig was getting closer or further away.

Some time after midday, the stunsails were taken in again. The ship roared on through the heaving waves, which divided and streamed alongside the flying corvette. Colyer watched the water rushing by below and felt a flutter of excitement at the sheer sensation of speed. After a time the motion of the vessel started to become more uneven, more lurching, and it seemed that the bow was having more difficulty shrugging off the waves than it usually did.

"Midshipman! Colyer!" A voice called up from the deck below. She scrambled to the edge and peered over. It was Malory, his stentorian tones fighting with the shrill of wind around the rigging. "Kindly! report! to the quarterdeck! upon the instant!"

She cast around for a second, wondering what the least painful route to the deck would be. She decided upon sliding down the backstay—it would not involve moving her legs. On deck, the sensation of speed through the water was even greater, the whoosh of waves thundering back from the bow louder than she had ever heard. She presented herself to Lieutenant Malory.

"Mister Colyer," he started, raising his voice to be heard above the sea. "I see you have been following our friend through your telescope. Would you make a report to the captain and myself?"

"Aye, Sir," she gulped. Was this another test?

They waited while Gilpin pleaded with MacQuarrie. "...I wish to represent that the motion will be eased considerably by striking the royals, Sir," he entreated, "and in all probability we will gain half a knot."

"I'm not striking a damn thing more 'til she starts carrying the yards away. Now let that be an end to it!"

"Aye aye, Sir," muttered the master, and shuffled away. "A word with you, Sir?" he addressed to Malory as he and Colyer hurried astern.

"In a moment, Mister Gilpin," Malory snapped. Colyer found herself standing before the captain.

"Make your report, Midshipman," huffed MacQuarrie.

"Well, Sir, We're gaining on her downwind, perhaps 150 yards in every hour. She's definitely hull-up now. She isn't fore reaching on us—in fact we had started to make ground on her to the South West until the last half-hour when the motion started to get very confused. After that the slaver took back most of what we'd gained in that regard."

"Hmm, very well. Thank you Midshipman, dismissed."

"Aye aye, Sir," she responded and was about to withdraw when Malory motioned her to stand by.

The Captain was muttering, "...weather should be to our advantage. Damned lot of lubbers will lose us the prize."

"Captain, if I may?" Malory gently broke into MacQuarrie's reverie.

"What is it Malory?" the Captain asked cautiously, as if afraid of being tricked.

"I just wished to report that the bow seems to be rather depressed in the gusts, and she's making heavy weather of the larger waves. I fear we may start shipping it green if the wind continues to build."

"Very well." MacQuarrie paused and narrowed his eyes for a while and looked from the rig to the bow and back again. Finally, he said "we shall take the royals off her. If you please Malory?"

Malory turned and raised his speaking trumpet. "Hands aloft to take in royals," he shouted. Topmen scrambled for the rigging, and the boatswain's mates assembled long lines of waisters at the halliards. Gilpin sidled over to Malory.

"You wished for a word, Sailing Master?"

"Aye, Sir," Gilpin answered, bright with gratitude, "'twas to see if you could persuade the captain to shorten sail. However did you do it?"

"I didn't," he said with a wink. "Captain MacQuarrie thought to do so all by himself."

"Remarkable!" muttered Gilpin, and took his leave.

"Well now, Mister Colyer, you have been most useful. Back to the rigging with you. That is…if your physical state is conducive?"

"Thank you, Sir, I'm all right." She felt dizzy from time to time, and was aching terribly, but compared to yesterday she felt almost good.

"It's just that…er…you're bleeding."

Colyer's heart sank. The seat of her trousers was pink through the bandages. "Thank you for your concern, Sir…I'm all right. As long as the captain doesn't order me beaten again I'll be capital."

He laughed, heartily. "Very well, I'm sure the captain will find a very good reason not to."

She smiled to herself through the pain as she shuffled back up the rigging. After an hour it was plain that the rate they were overtaking the slaver meant they would not be in action until much later in the day. The hands were stood down and sent to dinner.

Daedalus and The Deep

After managing a few bites, Colyer went to the purser and bought a bolt of white cotton duck, some thread and a needle, returning with it all to the midshipmen's berth. Sitting there quietly, relatively undisturbed, she made herself a new pair of trousers. It was good—these would fit her better in any case. The work required concentration, just enough to blot out any other thoughts or sensations.

After a while she looked up to find Johnson scrutinising her from across the berth. "Is there anything you're not good at?" he sniped.

She smiled cherubically and returned to her sewing. "Can't everyone in the Navy sew?"

"Everyone forrard of the mainmast, perhaps," he snapped, pointedly, and stormed away.

Chapter 9

BY the late afternoon, the corvette had clawed close enough to the slaver to start firing regular shots with the bow chaser, so the crew beat to quarters once more. MacQuarrie only hoped they did not do too much damage in bringing the ship to heel. He wanted a prize, not a waterlogged wreck full of corpses.

The Captain was incandescent with anger. These days, he always was. The anger lived constantly with him, and by now he had forgotten what life was like without it. He barely remembered to order Malory to conn the ship during the operation so he could stand over the gunner.

As a younger man, the anger had seemed as though it was something in him but not of him—a formless force that had stealthily appropriated his consciousness in order to find expression. At times, he found himself able to step outside his own state of being. At those times he could see that perhaps there might be other ways to motivate the men of a watch or induce snotties to learn their business than by the forceful application of his unending reservoir of rage.

But no longer. The ceaseless routine of naval life, its casual hardships and the impersonal cruelty of the elements had left his original self dazed, weakened and docile. The only thing within him that had strength was the anger. It had allied itself with the litany of everday difficulties a naval officer had to survive, and battered away at him.

His anger had eroded his personality, carved hollows that it had nestled down into, and after long years, he and his anger had worn into each other.

Daedalus and The Deep

The slaver, his ill-disciplined and unskilled crew, his feckless officers and the obstructive Admiralty had converged on this spot in the ocean to fan his fury into a brightly glowing star. The universe revolved around it alone. He wanted to hang or flog them all, even turn the carronades on the waist and fire until his whole crew was nothing but a mess of torn flesh.

If they could only catch the slaver, he might feel a moment's calm.

Gilpin had taken the wheel to ensure as steady a course as possible, and Peddle, the gunner, was personally laying the fore 56-pounder. The massive cannon was mounted on a series of curved brass rails on which its crew were swinging it so it could fire diagonally over the bow. Peddle seemed to be spending minutes just gazing along the length of the oily-black barrel. MacQuarrie tapped his foot, impatiently. What if the wind changed? What if the weather closed in? What if the light started to fail?

"Up two degrees, for'rd five," The gun crew shuffled the enormous artillery piece by minute increments. The gunner sighted along the barrel again and nodded slightly.

"What an earth is keeping you, Mister Peddle?" growled the Captain.

"Adjusting for deflection and the wind angle, Sir," he replied conversationally. Peddle took the lanyard lightly in his hand and waited for the ship to move through two complete rolls. The Captain's anger thundered silently. At the top of the third roll, the gunner smartly tugged the lanyard and an almighty *boom*! reverberated around the ship, as a jet of smoke issued from the barrel and wafted delicately aft.

Half a dozen telescopes peered eagerly in the direction of the cannonball's trajectory.

"Deck there!" came a call from the fore-top. The young gentleman Colyer again. MacQuarrie's anger briefly impelled him to will the midshipman to fall, screaming, to the deck.

"Report!" Bellowed the captain before Malory or the gunner had a chance to respond.

"Shot fell a length ahead and a little over," the youngster shouted.

A ripple of satisfaction ran through the officers and men gathered on the bow. Even the Captain allowed himself a moment of something like pleasure, before wondering when the blazes the gunner was going to get round to firing another shot, and the anger crowded out all other sensations again.

Peddle made no more adjustments after the cannon was sponged out and reloaded. The second shot fell slightly further forward, so the gunner had the angle tweaked a touch and tried again. Another tug of of the lanyard, another *boom*!

"A few yards aft!" came the call from aloft. The next shots fell around the brig, never far away but never inflicting any damage either.

"Brig has borne up a point!" Colyer shouted from the fore-top. "Two points now."

"It's not a brig, it's a topsail schooner," muttered Lieutenant Spencer, uselessly, "what an earth has that sailing master been teaching the midshipmen now?"

Damnation! The captain could have stamped his feet with the inefficiency of it all. The gun would have to be re-laid. He could have pitched someone over the side in his frustration. Preferably that idiot Spencer.

"Mister Malory's compliments, Sir, and she's closing the distance," said a midshipman, suddenly appearing at his elbow. "He represents that should make her easier to hit, Sir."

"Indeed," responded the captain, his voice like crushed glass. The next move had just occurred to him. "We should run down on her for a while then bear up to maintain the weather-gage."

"Capital plan, Sir," Spencer affirmed, somewhat obsequiously.

MacQuarrie grunted. "Cease firing for a spell, Mister Peddle. We shall run down on her for a while." He grabbed the midshipman to send aft to inform Malory of the plan of attack. "Repeat it back to me boy!" the lieutenant snapped.

"Erm, Captain MacQuarrie's compliments, Sir," snivelled the boy who was either Holford or Johnson, "...and that he should maintain course until further notice, but that he will be required to bear up a point or two in due course."

"Fine, now go!" Snapped MacQuarrie, and the red-faced boy scampered off.

After ten minutes of the two vessels courses converging slightly, the brig's captain had evidently decided he had thrown off their aim sufficiently and returned to his favoured beam-reach. A little of the distance had been closed though, and Peddle resumed firing when he had assured himself of the angles.

Another six shots rang out with little discernible effect. "Perhaps we should try bar or chain shot, Sir." offered the gunner who apparently did not think enough of his skills to throw a single iron ball onto a small, moving ship at over a mile's distance.

"No, no, no Mister Peddle, chain-shot would tear her sticks out from this range and I want her in good condition."

The gunner lapsed into a sullen silence and kept up his fire.

Suddenly from above, a jubilant shout from the boy. "Deck there! Her topsail yard's dangling! Yes, it's fallen, we must have taken a halyard away."

"Excellent," crowed the captain, "Fine shooting, Mister Peddle. Now we must surely capture her in the next hour. Please see to the gun deck."

"Deck there, she's tacking. Sir, she means to cross our bows!"

"Damnation!" growled MacQuarrie. All the work undone! They had left it too late! He had known as much. His anger had expected it—known they would all let him down.

"Gun-deck bow-chasers fire as you bear, load chain-shot," he yelled.

"We shall cross astern, give her a broadside, tack ship and cover her wind," called Malory from the quarterdeck. MacQuarrie experienced a moment's fury at Malory's presumption before remembering that he *had* ordered the lieutenant to conn the ship.

A bustle of activity broke out, accompanied by a cacophony of bosun's pipes and orders being repeated fore and aft. The schooner was pointing high upwind now and perpendicular to their course. There was no time to swivel the big 56-pounder, so it was up to the two 32-pounder long guns at the forward end of the gun deck. Each one roared out as the brig sailed into its view. The first missed, the second punched a neat, circular hole in the slaver's mainsail, which did not appear to slow it in the least.

"Port battery, fire as you bear!" shouted Malory. MacQuarrie retreated to the quarterdeck, feeling like a lost duckling trailing after its mother, and overwhelmed by a swell of hatred for his intolerable first lieutenant. Each of the ten big 32-pounder cannon on the gun deck barked in a steady, rolling broadside. But, when the thick bands of bitter smoke diffused, the brig reappeared, sailing serenely on as if oblivious to the attentions of the men and weapons, mere yards away, desperately flinging death and destruction at it.

MacQuarrie was apoplectic. He could do nothing but fume at the inefficiency of the dockside scrapings that called itself a crew, the overprivileged adventurers who called themselves officers, the idiots and bureaucrats who had stripped away half his main battery and downgraded his command.

"Stand by to tack ship!" Malory sounded calm even now, damn his middle-class hide. Men ran for the braces and sheets as the commands were given. "Helm a-lee!"

Gilpin put the helm up and the bow began to slew round. After a few minutes, the sails were drawing once more on the other tack, but the schooner was noticeably more distant than she had been moments previously. There was no getting away from it—a large square rigger like *Daedalus* could not tack as swiftly as a trim fore-and-aft rigged vessel like the slaver and she would lose ground sailing to windward as well.

It was too much!

Malory asked for more reports from Midshipman Colyer, who confirmed that the brig was weathering on them and fore-reaching too. More shots were tried from the bow-chaser but, pitching into a short sea as they were now, the aim was all but impossible. They tried bar shot, chain shot and even case shot in the hope of peppering the sails with holes or killing men on deck, but it was to no avail. The brig steadily drew away and before much longer, darkness was falling.

With assiduous lookouts and careful handling, they followed the tiny hovering glow-worm that was the light from the brig's compass binnacle, but a rain squall hit the *Daedalus* shortly after midnight and when the corvette emerged, the light was nowhere to be seen. They held the same course until morning, but first light revealed nothing but a vast, wide, empty ocean glittering in the early light and swishing languidly beneath their feet. A sweep of telescopes around did not uncover so much as a single tiny masthead poking above the horizon. The lookouts boxed the compass twice and each call of all the 32 points ended in nothing.

MacQuarrie felt as though his chest would burst. He had been awake for 36 hours, as had most of his officers. A Royal Navy warship had been outwitted and outsailed by a scruffy, lawless, unprofessional, merchant vessel.

Daedalus and The Deep

"Find that brig, or find me another slaver," he snarled to whoever was near enough to hear. "I don't care which. But do it soon." And he stormed below decks where he drank half a bottle of Oporto, just enough to subdue his anger into dull embers, and slept for a watch and a half.

The ship's luck appeared to have deserted it completely. The Indian Ocean cruise was utterly fruitless. From time to time a sail was sighted, but more often than not it disappeared over the horizon before the *Daedalus* could make contact, or else it turned out to be a perfectly legitimate East Indiaman or a Royal Navy dispatch vessel.

A bleak, joyless Christmas passed with no further sightings, and with every one of *Daedalus*' crew experiencing the same heavy heart, the ship put into port at Cape Town for further orders. The second time that year in which MacQuarrie conferred with a flag officer was no more auspicious than the first. The Captain returned from his interview with the admiral aboard HMS *President* with both his mood and his news blacker than after he had been sent away by Cochrane many months earlier.

The ship was to sail for home. True there would be further cruising in the Atlantic, and similarly general instructions to 'interdict and apprehend what slavers and pirates you may run down', but at the end of the ship's four month supply of stores she must be back at Gibraltar, and thence to Portsmouth for decommissioning. The frigate would be laid up in ordinary—stripped of its masts and weapons and roofed over—ostensibly to be recommissioned when circumstances allowed. Everyone knew that if the corvette ever served again, it would be as a powder hulk or accommodation ship. This was to be their last cruise.

On the 18th January, HMS *Daedalus* slipped her moorings to the sound of the shanty *Bold Riley* echoing round the anchorage, and stood out into the Atlantic Ocean for a dwindling, last chance at glory, then home and retirement.

Neither crew nor officers had any idea at that time that the ship was being watched.

PART 2

THE CHASE

INTERLUDE

SO *this was the monster her quest had led her to. It was a creature the like of which she had never even imagined—the lore did not do these space-beasts justice. It was vast.*

From the tip of the vast single tusk at its snout to its strange, truncated tail it was twice her length. More than that, its body was bulky—rounded and robust like that of a Sperm Whale. It must exceed her weight a hundred times over or more.

Most impressive of all was the enormous collection of spines on its back. The creature had three, mighty spikes growing out of its upper surface, which were adorned with great membranes—a means of gathering food from the upper air?—and a delicate network of fibres running all over it—external muscle tissue or nerves?

The beast was so completely alien. She shuddered. How could she consider what she intended in the face of something so...other? It was a strange beauty, a fearsome beauty, but beauty nonetheless. Her mind struggled to accommodate it.

But what of her quest? In the face of such strangeness how could she possibly succeed?

...But if she did, it could change everything. Not just for her but her whole species. She had come so far. It was too far to turn back now.

She drew closer, inspecting the creature. She could not imagine it did not know she was there by now. Yet it continued to swim on, not heeding her in the slightest. No wonder, *she thought.*

Daedalus and the Deep

If I were so big and fearsome, I would expect nothing in the whole of sea or sky to pose any threat to me.

But make a challenge she must. She rippled her fins rapidly, and drew her head up above the fluid atmosphere, skirting towards the creature's tail.

As she approached, she saw something else that made her shudder. The beast was absolutely swarming with parasites. They stood all over her back, and were even scuttling up and down the external filaments around the spines.

This turned her stomach but also gave her a burst of hope. What if this meant the beast was sickening?

She began to track the creature, following it at a distance and studying its ways. It swam on, impassively. She observed, noted and planned. She studied it from all angles. After several days she still did not feel she understood the creature in the slightest. What did it eat? Did it always swim alone or was there a herd or pack? What drove it? Was it intelligent and thinking, or did it roam the seas in a mindless hunt for food like the sharks of the upper deep?

All remained a mystery. Soon though she would have to be ready to begin the next stage of her great quest.

Chapter 10

HMS *Daedalus* was practicing gunnery for the second time in a week, on the day that the lives of every man and officer on the corvette changed irrevocably.

The ship was somewhere around mid way between the Cape and St Helena, and all knew that they were unlikely to sight many slavers so far South. But Captain MacQuarrie had been furious at the results of the gunnery against the slaver in the Indian Ocean and was determined that should such an opportunity arise, they would not miss the capture again through poor shooting. Before they had put into the Cape, a shortage of powder had prevented much practice. Now they were fully restocked and there was no excuse. Lieutenant Malory was hardly less insistent on this point than the Captain, and he worked the gun crews mercilessly.

Colyer was not disappointed to have been banished to her action-station at the foretop with Panna. Being halfway up the mast reduced the assault on the ears from the great guns slightly. She would not be idle—Malory had insisted that she report the fall of shot to give the gunner better information. Panna, who was cleaning the swivel gun for want of anything better to do, observed the activity with his usual serene detachment and hummed a tune to himself.

The first practice run had simply tested the speed and regularity with which the gun crews could fire broadsides. It was loud and competitive and good for morale, but essentially proved little. This time they would actually have to hit something.

The carpenter had constructed a large, wood and canvas target which was lowered onto the water, whereupon the corvette sailed away until it was barely visible among the waves. Time and again, the ship sailed back and forth while port and starboard gun crews in turn tried to hit the target. Of course, a moving target would be better practice than a stationary one but here there was nothing to be done. The Captain had mooted the idea of using the launch under sail to tow the target but Malory had dissuaded him from that on the basis that the slow speed the launch could manage would not make things appreciably more realistic. The fact that no boat crew would be required to risk life and limb from errant 32-pound cannonballs was simply a happy coincidence.

Despite the difficulties with the slaver, the ship's gunnery was not of a particularly poor standard. No Royal Navy ship's gunnery was in this era, but the extended inshore operations rooting out pirates and slaver warlords had prevented regular practice. The exercises off the Cape therefore had more of the character of cleaning away rust than forging the ship's weapons anew.

On the first pass, the broadside was undeniably a touch ragged and the starboard gun crews chaffed the port in a good natured and competitive manner. The ship tacked and returned along a reciprocal course. The port broadside was a little better, each 32-pounder thumping along the side of the ship in a pleasingly rhythmic manner. It took too long to accomplish though, and the captain bellowed at the crews to do better.

The target floated on, completely unscathed.

None of the shots had gone anywhere close and Colyer shouted down to the deck that the splashes had been well short and spread over a wide area. Spencer, who was handling the ship while the Captain and Malory saw to the gunnery, passed the order to heave-to while the gun captains tapped the quoins out slightly to angle the guns further upward.

A second time the ship tacked and passed the target to port. Colyer heard the guns bark out again, noticeably closer together this time. The broadside had been mistimed though and the order to fire had been given before the ship had reached the top of the roll. The shot ploughed uselessly into the side of a wave some hundred yards from the target. The light raft with its canvas sides now seemed to mock them, as it bobbed on the water completely unharmed.

The second attempt from the starboard battery did the same. Perhaps they were not quite aware of the problem down on the gundeck—the roll could certainly be easier felt in the rigging, magnified as it was. She decided to clamber down the backstay to tell Malory personally—she was more likely to be listened to that way than hollering down from the gods.

Hand-over-hand she swayed down and dropped catlike onto the deck, reflecting that she was beginning to feel as much at home in the sky as ever she had on land, down through the companionway and attracted the first officer's attention.

"Sir, the last two salvoes have fallen short but were quite tightly grouped." She searched for the right expression. "I, er, wish to represent that the broadsides have been fired a little before the top of the roll—it may be harder to feel down here than it is on the foretop."

He smiled viciously. "Indeed, Mister Colyer, you could be right. Remember what I said about opportunities? I shall confer with the gunner, perhaps we may arrange the gunnery to your satisfaction next time around." She tapped the brim of her cap, to which Malory doffed his hat expansively in response, and she climbed back up to the spar deck.

As she reached the fore-chains, the waisters were preparing for the ship to tack, and as she scrambled onto the rigging, the helmsman had started heaving the wheel around. As she clambered around the futtock shrouds, hanging at an angle, the jib-boom was sweeping across the horizon, and as she brought one foot up onto the lip of the platform, a shout came from the forecastle.

"Deck there! Something in the water off starboard bow! Looks like a mainyard or a bloody big timber!"

"Helm up!" screeched Lieutenant Spencer. "Back the maincourse!"

Men scattered trying to reach the right ropes. The boatswain's mates yelled uselessly. The ship abruptly stopped swinging around and for a moment, felt as though it would start to turn back, but instead soggily came to a halt. The foresail, its tacks and sheets released, backed with an almighty clap and the rig shuddered. Colyer, who was reaching for a stay to pull her up found that the rope was no longer where it had been—her hand closed over nothing and with a yelp of surprise, she toppled backwards. Her arms flailed and the deck sprawled, wide and white and hard beneath her. With a wrench, something clamped around her ankle. For a second she hung there, terror thrashing in her chest like a living thing.

It was Panna. The lascar had grabbed her by the foot as she had fallen. She flapped her arms again and found a grip on the futtock shrouds. Panna lowered her leg as far as he could, then she managed to drop onto the ratlines, hanging on fiercely. It felt as though all her breath had been robbed from her. After moments like ages, she slowly crept the final few feet up to the top. It was the first and only time she had crept up through the lubber's hole rather than monkeying around the futtock shrouds. Panna helped her up and without thinking, or perhaps just without caring, she threw her arms around him and clung on for as long as it took for her heart to beat normally again.

The midshipman let go and slumped to the floor of the top. Panna squatted down and put a comforting hand on her shoulder. Below, the disarray that had reigned only minutes before had already dissipated. Dully, she realised what had happened—with Spencer's confused orders, the ship had been caught 'in stays', stuck pointing into the wind's eye before it could complete its turn.

Malory had taken over the quarterdeck and with a sequence of barked orders, the ship's head fell off the wind once more and the sails began to fill. The first lieutenant allowed himself a moment to pour abuse at Spencer. They had fallen back onto the original course and the ship slowly gathered way while the sailing master made his way from the beak to the taffrail checking for any damage that the ill-used rig might have sustained, or tangled and loose lines.

Nearly falling from the fore-top was not the only shock Colyer suffered that day.

"Sir..." started Panna, uncertainly. "I won't say nothing. Really. But...you're a girl, aren't you?"

The world dropped away. It was as if she was still falling. A jumble of emotions raced through her head. She was about to deny it, to order him to shut up. Even as the possibilities presented themselves she dismissed them, and simply nodded.

"How many people know?" she asked, as the clouds swirled and the sea roared in her ears. He looked surprised.

"Just me, Sir, honest. I won't say nothing. You understand?"

She nodded again, dumbly. "Thank you," she said, her voice sounding very small in her ears. A part of her brain that seemed to be separate from the rest of it wondered what might be required of her to keep the secret. "What do you want?"

He looked horrified. "Nothing, Sir! Nothing! I...want to help."

Could it be true? She had known that this might happen, of course. But somehow she had imagined being unmasked by the Captain, put in a dress and made to wash the crew's slops. She hadn't considered being discovered by the foremast hands. With a shudder, she pictured being...handed round.

At that moment she felt reckless, stupid and utterly desolate.

"How did you know?" she asked.

"I thought...but not sure. Then just now..." He patted his chest, apologetically. She had to smile at that. "Why?" he asked, finally.

The ship pushed on through the sea. The wind blew around the rigging. It already felt as though her life before *Daedalus* belonged to someone else.

"My brother," she began. "He's the real Midshipman Colyer. Or he was. He went away to train at the Naval College at Portsmouth. He died. I took his place."

Panna said nothing, but maintained a level gaze at her. Not knowing what else to do, she kept talking.

"Father had been a naval surgeon so Tom's training was paid for. He was at the college two years but he used to come back home from time to time. I couldn't hear enough about the college —would have loved to go there myself. I read all his books, talked to him for hours whenever he came home..."

She wiped away the beginning of a tear from the corner of one eye. She realised how much she had wanted to tell this to someone.

"He qualified last year and was assigned his first ship—*Daedalus*. He was so proud! He had a frigate." She smiled at the memory of his joy. "He was on his way there the last time we saw him. Only he...he wanted to ride a horse one more time before he went to sea. He had a friend who had one. It was a bad tempered thing, always biting people. Tom had ridden it before but..."

The tears were flowing freely now but inwardly she felt calm.

"It threw him and he broke his neck. He was dead, just like that. My parents were completely broken. They...Then the carriage came to take Tom to Portsmouth. I don't know why. But I told the driver Tom had already gone and I was following on with his dunnage. I just took all his things and jumped on the carriage. I just knew that.... The truth is we needed the money. Father was committed to the charity hospital he worked at but it only paid a nominal salary. Mother taught at the church school but that didn't pay much either. We were relying on Tom's wages. There were five of us children...well, four. I just thought...I don't know what I thought."

She broke off, tears finished, staring at the horizon as it scored its way all the way around their world. Her eyes momentarily fastened on a glint off something floating in the water, some way away. Long and slim. Dark. The waterlogged timber they had almost run into perhaps. She paid it no mind. She had barely thought of Tom or her family since the day she had arrived at Portsmouth. There had barely been time. But what kind of sister did that make her? Stealing his life then forgetting about him?

"When I got to Portsmouth I just put his uniform on and presented myself as Midshipman Tom Colyer. Simple as that." She had arranged to have most of her pay sent to her parents. That *was* why she had done what she had done, wasn't it?

"*Daedulus* was at Gibraltar of course, so I took the packet out there. I pestered the captain and did as much work as I could. I stood lookout duty, worked the halliards, furled the sails...I expected to be caught out right away but I wasn't. I suppose all my paperwork was in order and they were expecting me to be green anyway..."

They sat in silence for a moment.

"You can trust me, Sir," Panna said after a while. "I tell you something too? But you can't tell anyone. Then we're..." he searched for a word.

"Quits?" she offered.

"Yes, quits. Well..." he paused, appearing to dig deep into himself. "I was on an Indiaman. The *Beaufort*, Trincomalee. I...ran away. Deserted."

It didn't seem real. Panna was the most solid man she knew on *Daedalus*. She expected to feel disgusted with him but she didn't. Was there something wrong with her? "What happened?" she asked.

"There was a boatswain's mate. Always cursing at the lascars, using a rope's end on us. We were all 'black bastards' or 'filthy wogs' he says. But he had something against me particular. I was only young—three or four year older than you, maybe. Drank a bit more'n I should. Was a hard ship 'cause of him, not like most Indiamen. I took it though. For a couple of years.

"Well one trip, load of tea out of Bombay, glass was falling faster than you ever seen it. Had to get the sails off her fast like. He was starting us something terrible. Wasn't like we needed to be told, wind like that! He said something to me. Don't even remember what. I answered back and he started hitting me round the face with his bit of rope.

"I was going to hit him, or refuse orders...or I dunno. But I didn't. I went up the rigging. Quiet as a mouse. Didn't even say anythin'. Got the sails in. I thought I was all right but...when we got into London I couldn't face the thought of going back in the *Beaufort*. I tried to tell myself I was going home and I didn't need to go back out. But when it came to it...I just couldn't go. Left my *serang*, my gang...left them to that.... Let them down."

He continued his lookout all the while he told his story, professionally quartering the horizon. She watched him in silent wonder.

"But I couldn't go back to the Company. I'd jumped ship, even if they 'ad've taken me back I'd've been clapped in the bilboes and tried or flogged. But the boarding house robbed all me earnings. I went and signed on the first ship'd have me—it was a stacky barge in ballast, the mate 'ad broke 'is leg. Went over to Maldon to pick up a cargo and I signed on a coaster. Did that for a few years, up and down the coast.

"I made a mistake then. I'd been paid off in Hull, and signed on a whaler going for a cruise by Greenland. Was going to be a lot o' money. I thought mebbe would be enough to get me back to Ceylon. They said it'd be cold, but I thought London was cold. Couldn't think o' nothing could be colder. But when we got out there West o' Greenland I thought I was going to die with the cold. There were lumps of ice bigger than First Rates just floating around.... That was another year. We got some whales too. There was a gale and we put into Sumburgh. Captain wanted to go back out again. I couldn't face the cold so I ran again. Stupid. Would'a made good money.

"I managed to get on a fishing boat and got as far as Dundee. But word got round that I'd run—not many lascars goin' from ship to ship in Scotland. Ended up begging."

His silence filled the space. The sails stretched away above and below. They seemed to be listening intently.

"Well I thought I was goin' to die then, too. Thought I was going to freeze or starve. So far away from my wife and my girl. But when I ran, I was running away from them. I should've stayed, took my punishment. I was starving and...low. Mebbe I deserved to starve.

"But some lads off a Queen's ship started talking to me one day. Like I wasn't scum—like I was one of them. One lad had been on an Indiaman so he knew lascars. Said they were short good topmen and I should see about signing on with them."

He smiled. "It was a bit like I was back in my gang for a bit. Like I had a *serang* and my lads again. So I did. Signed on HMS *Hydra*, stayed with her 'till she decommission. Then *Daedalus* twice, last cruise and this one...couple of the lads—Barwell and Rayne—they were there when I signed on Hydra. Good lads. I 'int g'na leave another ship. Long as the lads need me, I 'int lettin' 'em down."

He paused, and for a while she thought he had finished, and tried to find something to say. They had both done terrible things she reflected. Maybe they didn't deserve forgiveness. But she forgave him everything, so far as it was her right to. It seemed important.

"Is that why you haven't seen your family?"

He nodded, and looked hopelessly sad again. "My daughter was three year old when I left. She'd be nearly your age now." He smiled weakly. "By now if I went back to Trincomalee Company'd prob'ly throw me in the clink anyway."

Colyer wondered what to say while the swell of the sea and the whistle of the wind through the shrouds became unbearable.

"Prob'ly married again by now," said Panna to the wind and the waves.

There was nothing more to say. Malory was tacking ship again. It was time to resume the gunnery practice. On the next pass the port battery shattered the target and then the starboard battery pounded the pieces into matchwood.

Perhaps, Midshipman Colyer reflected, nobody dared risk Lieutenant Malory's wrath by missing the target.

CHAPTER II

GILPIN sighed inwardly. Lieutenant Spencer was interrogating the seaman who had called the warning during the earlier gunnery practice for the third time. It was only around seven bells so there wasn't even the prospect of a change in watch to break up the ridiculous spectacle. He looked for anything he could find to interject. Fortunately, he saw the luff of the mizzen course shiver slightly suggesting the wind was a little close.

"...I swear t' ye le'tenant, twuz right there, huge 'n black and near as long as the ship it were. It were big as the mainyard on the old *Victory*. I swears it!"

"That's all very well but when *I* looked just after you shouted, I couldn't see a thing! And nor could anyone else I asked."

"Oi can't 'elp that le'tenant," the man sniffed, "twuz right there I tell ye."

"I should have you flogged for an insolent cur!"

"Mister Spencer," Gilpin broke in. "We may require a course change presently, the wind has backed and the yards will not brace round any further.

"Very well," Spencer grumbled. "Helmsman, is she holding her course?"

"Aye, Sir," the helmsman responded, "but if she backs any more I'll have to bear off half a point."

They moved down to leeward, as the captain had come on deck.

"...In any case, Mister Spencer, whether there was a mainyard or timber there or not, is entirely immaterial." Malory intoned, stepping onto the quarterdeck with Lieutenant Douglas and

Daedalus and The Deep

Midshipman Colyer. It seemed most of the officers were floating around after the morning's excitement, even those off-watch unwilling to relax below decks. Evidently he had heard the entire exchange.

"But surely, Sir!" Spencer's voice had jumped up an octave. "Hitting something like a mainyard could drive right through the planking!"

"At full speed, perhaps, but in the middle of a tack? I'd be surprised if it so much as scraped the paintwork! What are you doing aft? Get for'ard where you belong," he shouted at a seaman, who had been smirking quietly to himself, and now scuttled away before he could be sentenced to whatever punishment these arbitrary and unpredictable officers could think up.

"Lieutenant Malory, I must protest..." spluttered Spencer, after his second humiliation in one day. Malory simply shot a look of such venom at him that he stopped dead and just stood there with a disbelieving gape on his face.

"Actually, I thought I saw something like that in the water." said Midshipman Colyer. "It was off the port beam, fifty yards off perhaps. It sounded like Carson reported it—a long, black spar of some sort."

"Strange, it was to starboard when it was reported. When did you see it?"

Colyer looked thoughtful for a second, and then puzzled. "Actually, it must have been a couple of minutes after the tack was aborted and we continued on the port tack."

"We would have been well past it by then!" snorted Spencer until he was silenced by another look from Malory.

"Interesting we should get two such sightings within a few minutes," Malory mused.

"There could have been a wreck around here," Gilpin suggested, "and the debris's still floating around."

"Hmmm," offered Malory, evidently unconvinced. Spencer lapsed into silence, and any bonhomie following the successful gunnery evaporated like dew. For the next twenty minutes little was said by anyone on the quarterdeck beyond the odd curt command or report necessary for sailing the ship. Mercifully, it was nearly midday and before the ill mood became unbearable, some of the midshipmen and junior lieutenants had begun to take sun sightings and comparing the readings with each other.

Gilpin marked midday and ordered the glasses turned.

It was then that the second unusual hail of the day was heard.

"Deck there!" came the call from the mizzentop. "Big....fish in the water off the port quarter."

"What do you mean 'big fish'?" growled the Captain from the windward rail.

"Like a bloody big eel, Sir—there!" The lookout stabbed a finger. They could see how wide his eyes were even from the deck. The officers crowded to the lee rail.

It was a most remarkable 'fish', crossing their stern in, Gilpin estimated, a South Westerly direction.

A long head, with a streaming mane, rose above the water on a slender neck. Its narrow upper jaw overhung the lower, showing small, curved teeth.

The mane, a broad, frilled fin, extended back from the head, perhaps twenty feet.

"Look, there's the tail!" said Douglas, pointing at a loop of thick, black body breaking the water around twenty feet further back.

"That's not the tail, muttered Colyer, *there's* the tail". She indicated a fluked spear that broke the surface fully one hundred feet behind its nose.

As the creature came closer, Gilpin saw that it was actually a dark brown, and the underside of its jaw was a sort of dirty white. It opened its mouth slightly to reveal a maw lined with jagged teeth.

"Great God," blasphemed Malory, "those jaws would admit a man standing upright!"

"Must be doing twelve, thirteen knots!" said an awestruck-sounding Colyer. "It's overtaking us handsomely."

"Yes, indeed it is," said Malory, sounding most impressed. "Do you suppose those fins on its shoulders give it motive force?"

Every so often, a wave rolled away and revealed about sixty feet of the front part of the animal, gently undulating up and down. It was indeed like nothing so much as a giant eel or snake, though its skin was completely smooth without any appearance of scales or other irregularity apart from a sort of broad, fin growing out of each flank and running from its shoulders back as far as Gilpin could see, and which rippled sinuously.

DAEDALUS AND THE DEEP

"Ugly blighter!" someone muttered.

"Moves rather gracefully though, doesn't it?" said Gilpin, giving voice to a thought as it arose.

Douglas muttered dreamily "I saw a mermaid once, you know. Off Madagascar. She was sitting there in the water, just as close as this, combing her hair and looking into a glass."

The others snorted. "Poppycock," muttered Lambert.

"Do you think you could draw that thing, Douglas?" asked Malory, airily. "We ought to record it, and you're the best with a pencil."

"Aye, Sir, I suppose so," the officer replied. "Could paint it if you like. Does anyone have anything I could make some notes on?" They fished around and from somewhere a small notebook was produced. Officers were supposed to be proficient at drawing, though it was not something on which careers tended to hinge and while some had the gift, others did not.

"It seems to be swimming away, though hardly bothered at all by us," said Gilpin. "I've honestly never seen or heard of anything quite like it. Have any of you gentlemen?"

There was a general mutter of agreement from the officers crowded around the rail that they had not.

"No," muttered the captain, behind them. Gilpin jumped, having momentarily forgotten that MacQuarrie was there. "I have not. And we can perhaps presume that if this creature is unknown to us it may well be unknown to science. I think we would be shirking our duty as men of learning and the advancement of mankind if we did not observe this beast further. Mister Gilpin, a South-Westerly course if you please, and clap all the sail on her she'll handle.

"Aye aye, Sir," Gilpin responded, and began shouting orders to man the braces, swing the yards. The men pulled reluctantly away from the port hammock netting, from where most of them had been staring at the beast.

The serpent turned its head towards the ship briefly as it passed. The sailing master saw its cold, dark, narrow eyes and something inside him lurched. A single crescentic nostril snorted a puff of vapour and he jumped again.

After a few minutes the ship was bearing downwind and piling on royals and stunsails. For the first time in months the spirit of the ship seemed to rise a little. They had purpose for the time being, reflected Gilpin, although there was something he felt deeply uneasy about.

This could be a great discovery for science, and that was not to be taken lightly. But when those eyes had looked into his, he knew he had wanted nothing more than to set a course that would take him as far away from this creature as possible.

Chapter 12

LIEUTENANT Spencer was complaining again. Colyer had heard his nasal tones long before she came on deck. He was now remonstrating with the bosun while the ship was making sail, after having taken in the topgallants overnight.

There was no sign of the creature. They had followed it until dark the previous day—it had been all the fleet corvette could do to keep the giant serpent in sight.

At first light, all the officers had gathered on deck to see if the creature was in sight, and there was palpable disappointment that it was not. The captain had huffed and directed that they continue on the Sou'Westerly track, then repaired to his cabin. Yesterday's optimism had melted away and the previous gloom had been quick to reassert itself.

A few men of the watch below had begun singing as they skylarked on the forecastle, as was their way. Today, the song had been a Scottish sea song called *Sir Patrick Spens*. It had never been especially popular with the men before—perhaps unsurprisingly, as it told the story of an incompetent captain whose ship sank with all hands on its maiden voyage.

Nevertheless, the song had been heard several times of late. And, increasingly, when the men reached a line where the title character was mentioned, one or two would shout 'Le'tenant Spencer' instead. This time Spencer had heard and objected.

"I require you to tell me the names of the men who sang my name there, Bosun. We cannot have such an affront to discipline on this ship."

"I dare say it wa'n't meant in malice, Sir, and besides, I honestly couldn't tell ye who it was," entreated Granby.

Spencer huffed in exasperation. "I don't think we should let the men responsible off, Bosun. They deserve to be punished, surely you see that?"

"I'm sorry Mister Spencer, I really don't know who it were. Let me 'ave a word with the men, Sir, and I'll see it don't happen again."

"No need for that, I will request that the whole party's grog be stopped for a week. I believe the men drink too much in any case. It may do them some good."

"Mister Spencer, I really don't think—"

"I am decided, thank you Bosun. Kindly report their names." He sauntered from the deck leaving a burdened bosun and a resentful division of men muttering darkly.

The day wore on and no further sightings were made. Colyer's watch came around at noon and after shooting the sun, Lambert sent her up the foretop as an additional lookout. She turned her telescope forward and began dividing up the sea according to the points of the compass, determined to be the one who saw the creature first. Hours passed with no sign.

The men were still sulking about Spencer, and every so often a little band would gather on the forecastle to relate once again the scandal of the officer who wanted to separate the men from their rum.

Colyer pulled her attention away from the scene and scanned the sea down to leeward, focussing on every whitecap to see if anything was breaking the surface. Nothing was. After another two hours, near the end of her watch, she scrambled down and reported to the officer of the watch, Lambert. He sighed, dismissed her and as Douglas took over he sent Holford up the foremast in her stead.

She was about to go below and tackle some of the more advanced books on celestial navigation when the captain strode up from the companionway.

"Bait!" he exclaimed, grandly.

"Sir?" said Douglas, looking distinctly at a loss for how to respond to this outburst.

"We will trail some bait to draw the creature to us. And further to that I have decided upon a definitive course of action. I no longer wish us to simply observe and record the creature—I am resolved to capture it and return its body complete to England. It will look well as the centrepiece of the British Museum's Natural History collection, I think."

"I fear we have not sighted the creature since nightfall, Captain," Douglas apologised, in the same manner a parent might explain to a child that it may not play out of doors because of the rain.

"That is precisely why we shall bring the creature to us!" boomed the captain. "With bait! I have ordered that we sacrifice one of the bullocks to our mission, like heathens of old, and trail it behind the ship."

The captain moved up to the windward side of the quarterdeck while Douglas simply looked bewildered. The cook and his assistant soon appeared, manhandling a large bovine carcass which had previously been butchered and hung in the forecastle. With the aid of the bosun, they attached it securely to a length of light line and dangled it carefully over the stern. There were not a few hungry and disappointed glances at that prime beef now being hauled through the sea for the fish to nibble.

That will take half a knot off our speed, considered Colyer as the carcass bounced and slapped in their wake.

"No, no, no," snapped MacQuarrie. "The beast will never get a sniff of it there! Give it another five fathoms, ten indeed, 'til it sinks out of sight. And tip a few buckets of blood into the water if you have any."

More line was paid out and eventually the carcass sank beneath the waves. Colyer made her way below. She was not supposed to be on watch after all, and she needed to study and rest.

"Ah, there you are Colyer." It was Malory, emerging from the Wardroom as she stepped off the companionway. "You are planning to take to your books?"

"Yes, Sir, there hasn't been much time lately."

"No, no, we've all been rather under the lash, haven't we? Well, you may read in the wardroom but I'd like you to do me a favour."

"Of course, Sir, what is it?"

"I'd like you to find whatever material you can that might be pertinent to our pursuit of this creature. We have some texts on natural history in the ship's library, I have some books which touch on the study of marine life and the captain has some of Cook's writings on ocean life. I have no doubt it's a pitiful collection and you may find nothing at all. Still, as you can see the captain has set his mind to locating and capturing the creature, so anything we know is better than nothing. I'd like you to summarise everything you find."

"All right, Sir. When would you like my report?"

"The captain is entertaining the officers again tonight. I imagine you'll receive an invitation this time. Give it to me before that."

It wasn't a great deal of time, especially if she wanted to fit in any rest, not to mention any studies on navigation or seamanship.

There were, as Malory had said, a number of books and periodicals that touched upon natural history, even specific works about the oceans. She was slightly surprised to find that the sailing master had several books and a stack of *Loudon's Journal of Natural History* in his small cabin. But where on earth was she to find anything useful about hunting a giant sea serpent?

Her initial readings threw up remarkably little. Generally, the writings covered descriptions of the oceans that seemed too general to be of use. Indeed, one scholarly piece by Edward Forbes postulated that it was impossible for life to exist below 300 fathoms—although that seemed quite deep enough to Colyer—and that the depths below this were a lifeless desert.

After an hour, her notes covered barely half a page of her journal and she was beginning to despair of ever finding anything worth giving to the first lieutenant. He had of course said that he expected she might find nothing. Even so, she could imagine his reaction if she did go back without finding anything useful. Outwardly understanding of course, but in his eyes, and the twist of his lips there would be that hint of disappointment, that faintest suggestion of *I knew I shouldn't have expected too much from you.*

Things began to look up slightly when she found a text by James Rennell which discussed theories of deep-dwelling sea creatures. Some recently discovered fish had been found in areas known to be extremely deep, and these had only breached the surface when wounded or damaged in some way. Rennell suggested a theory of deep-water currents like rivers on the land, carrying veins of life that did not extend beyond their span. This could account for the occasional sightings of creatures like an implausibly huge squid, certain whales, an odd, slender shark which coiled itself up to launch at prey much as land-borne snakes do. She began to wonder if their 'serpent' was some creature of the deepest zones, and which had come to the surface for some inscrutable purpose.

It was then that she struck just what she had been looking for. She was skimming through a warped and stained volume entitled *The Natural History of Greenland*, dating from over a century before, written by a Scandinavian called Hans Egede. It was another one of the sailing master's, though quite what interest it held for him she could not fathom.

Initially, the book had not seemed to hold much promise. After all, the seas around Greenland were hardly like the South Atlantic. Quickly though, she realised she had struck gold. The task might not be as time consuming as she had feared.

She took a fresh sheet of paper and started scribbling feverishly. After a while longer she had just what she needed to present to give to Malory, folded the sheets and sought out the lieutenant.

He scanned over the pages, nodding, and *ha-h'm*-ing. Eventually, he uttered an offhand "Well done, Colyer, good work," folded the sheets and slipped them into an inside pocket, before cursorily acknowledging her salute and walking away. She felt utterly ill-used and wandered back to her berth, slung her hammock and lay there trying unsuccessfully to get back into the mindset for study before giving up and simply lying there.

There was a clatter of feet, and the top half of Midshipman MacLeod's face appeared above the side of her hammock. "Colyer," he puffed, "Captain requests the honour of your presence at dinner at eight o'clock this evening. Undress uniform." He scampered away. Well then, that would be four bells, second dog watch and it was now nearing eight bells in the afternoon watch. She had a four blessed hours to rest and study before dinner then.

No sooner did seem her eyes had closed than she heard the irregular thump of feet on the deck above, and MacLeod reappeared. "Colyer, it's the serpent! It's back!" She jumped out of her hammock and sprinted up to the quarterdeck.

Once again there was a crowd of waisters lining the rail at the gangway, and a similar, if better-dressed crowd at the rail on the quarterdeck. She peered between the heads of Spencer and

Lambert, into the sun which was setting into the sea in an amber blaze. The serpent was further away this time, its head clearly silhouetted raised above the water. It swam round their stern, at a distance, and once or twice dipped below the surface.

"It's going for the bait!" Lambert exclaimed.

At that point though, the serpent's head broke above the water, and it continued around the stern, at a distance of some hundred yards, sweeping alongside them, gradually overhauling the ship on the port beam.

"Haul that bait in closer there!" the captain ordered, and two members of the afterguard rushed to bring the carcass closer in. By the struggle they were having pulling the line against the speed of the ship, it was clear that the carcass was still there.

The serpent made another complete circuit of the ship, and dipped below the surface just as the sun did. At that moment, a yell came from one of the men hauling in the bullock. Another shout came and Colyer heard the line twanging against the taffrail and vibrating like a violin string.

Douglas was shouting now. "You men, Finnegan, Woodman! Here and lend a hand with this line."

Colyer rushed to the stern to see what was happening. Astern, where the line entered the water, there was a furious splashing, and occasionally, a dark shape visible through the turbulence.

"What on Earth..." she muttered, more to herself than anyone in particular.

"Sharks," said Lambert, at her elbow, grinning ghoulishly. "Vicious little bastards aren't they?"

She could not but agree. As the carcass was pulled closer, the sharks' frenzy seemed to increase. The furious rampage was only visible in a welter of spray for the most part, but occasionally, a long pectoral fin or a sharp, shovel nose would briefly dart out of the melee and disappear again just as swiftly. By the time the carcass was heaved out of the water, there was less than half of it left, and as it dangled from the taffrail, one of the sharks took a flying leap at the beef and seized another chunk from beneath the men's noses. Douglas thanked the men for their efforts as the mangled hunk of meat was drawn back over the taffrail, but could not hide the disappointment in his voice.

"Well," said Lambert, shaking his head, "I suppose it's salt beef for dinner then."

Chapter 13

DINNER with the officers and the Captain was, for Colyer, a rather pleasanter experience the second time around. Even after Malory sprang another surprise on her.

Fortunately, the main course had not turned out to be beef, salt or otherwise. A pig had been slaughtered and roasted and was served with the last of the green vegetables they had taken on board at the Cape. The only blot on the horizon was Spencer, who had laid charges against some men for insulting him.

Malory had declined to uphold the charges, leaving Spencer quietly furious that his authority had been undermined. Moreover, Colyer realised that the men knew Spencer had wanted to stop their grog, and the decision was no less unpopular for being overturned. She wondered if the incident would dampen the evening.

As it turned out though, the conversation was freer this time than the last, and the whole table, bar Spencer, merrily chatted away once the captain had started proceedings. Naturally, the subject that formed the basis of most conversations was the sea serpent and how they might subdue such a creature.

Malory had not mentioned Colyer's report, and the midshipman had long since come to the conclusion that he must have thought it a poor piece of work and not worthy of mention. When the pudding, a plum and raisin duff, arrived however, the first lieutenant broke into a natural pause in the flow of discourse.

"Captain, if I may? Midshipman Colyer has kindly conducted some research into our friend the sea serpent, and I thought you gentlemen might desire to hear some of his conclusions." Malory passed her papers back across the table to her.

She took a breath, and briefly went through the general points of her study, first about the ocean deeps, the conflicting theories, and the possibility that largely unknown creatures could form an entirely new ecology in the deeps. Then she went onto the specifics of giant sea serpents.

"Well, there have been several reports of creatures like the one we're pursuing, over the course of several centuries, although none has ever been recovered or captured. A German cartographer, Sebastian Münster, wrote a book in 1598. It's a sort of general description of the world, probably a commentary to his maps. But there's a section on the oceans. He says: "in the ocean one finds sea snakes, two hundred and three hundred feet long. They twist around the ship, harm the sailors, and attempt to sink it, especially when it is calm.

"The best description," she went on, pleased to find that the entire table was listening in rapt silence, "comes from a Danish scholar in 1741. He claimed to have seen a sea serpent himself, and reports a number of other sightings around the same time from others. He says: '... they saw a long marine animal, which slowly moved itself forward, with the help of two fins, on the fore-part of the body nearest the head, which they judged by the boiling of the water on both sides of it. The visible part of the body appeared to be between forty and fifty feet in length, and moved in undulations, like a snake.

"'The body was round and of a dark colour, and seemed to be several ells'—not sure what that is, I'm afraid."

"Forty-five inches," said the Captain, flapping his hand, "go on boy,"

"Er, 'several ells in thickness. As we discerned a waving motion in the water behind the animal, we concluded that part of the body was concealed under water. That it was one continuous animal we saw plainly from its movement. When the animal was about one hundred yards from the boat, we noticed tolerably correctly its fore parts, which ended in a sharp snout; its colossal head raised itself above the water; the lower part was not visible. The colour of the head was dark-brown and the skin smooth'."

A ripple of excitement broke out around the table, with each of the officers chattering animatedly with those around him. She cleared her throat theatrically, and felt a glow of satisfaction that they all broke off immediately and turned back to her.

"There are other descriptions which are actually remarkably similar," she went on. "Another is described as being, er, 'about six fathoms long, the body—which was as round as a serpent's—two feet across, the head as long as a ten-gallon cask, the eyes large, red, and close behind the head a mane like a fin commenced along the neck, and spread itself out on both sides, right and left, when swimming. The mane, as well as the head, was of the colour of mahogany. The body was quite smooth, its movements occasionally fast and slow. It was serpent-like, and moved up and down. These undulations were not so high that he..' a fisherman, this is, '...could see between them and the water.' The serpents were observed eating: 'squid, sharks and bony fish.'

"Good Lord, it's just the same! Absolutely remarkable," said Douglas to the room in general.

"Laocoön was said to have been eaten by two giant sea snakes," said Spencer, showing an interest for the first time that evening. Everyone ignored him.

"The important thing though is that science has not so far confirmed with any certainty the existence of this creature," Colyer concluded. "None have ever been captured alive or dead."

"Well, gentlemen," said Malory through a grin like a tiger's. "It seems we may be able to prove to the world the existence of a very elusive creature. Very good Colyer."

"Capital!" agreed Lambert.

They fell back on their plum duff. "But..." asked Lambert. "What can we do to draw it near enough to have a go at?"

"It clearly wasn't interested in the beef," Douglas agreed.

"Spencer, anything to offer?" asked Malory pointedly.

"Oh, *haud ignota loquor* as the poet said, you know how it is," Spencer replied moodily.

"I think I may have the answer," Colyer piped up, having let her enthusiasm for the subject run away with her somewhat. Once again the table fell silent. She gulped, but went on.

"Well, Hans Egede—the Danish scholar—mentioned it, and it might even be the reason why the creature was in the same area as us again," she postulated. "It wasn't interested in the beef, but perhaps it *was* following the fish that *were* interested in the beef."

The officers nodded and chuckled in understanding. "'Pon my soul!" remarked Douglas, after a brief pause. "The *sharks*."

"Exactly!" Colyer asserted. "It strikes me that after today's experience we ought to be able to snare shark, or possibly Albacore—something the creature might find more palatable than bullock. We just have to catch some. I hope the cook hasn't done anything with that beef yet..."

"Unless we can find any ancient Trojan priests nearby..." muttered Lambert, not quite *sotto voce*. Spencer glared at him, and looked for a moment as if he were about to speak, then sat back, glowering.

"We still need a way to snare the sharks *and* kill the creature if we can get close enough," cautioned Malory.

"Hmm," said the captain, who had been sitting in silence for some time. "Yes. Excellent. For the bait we have shark hooks, I believe, and I shall direct that the blacksmith and carpenter to fashion some more weapons that might be of use for the serpent itself. Like this." He motioned at the steward, who, as if knowing MacQuarrie's thoughts flitted into the sleeping cabin and returned holding...

"A harpoon!" exclaimed Lambert.

"Exactly so!" grinned the Captain. "I had this hung on the bulkhead—a reminder of my first command, escorting a whaling fleet to Greenland. We should be able to fashion a dozen or more before we catch up with the beast again."

Thoughtful murmuring burst out throughout the table. "I think this is an admirable moment," said the Captain, "to propose the customary toast, it being Friday. Gentlemen..." he raised his glass. "A willing enemy and sea-room!"

"A willing enemy and sea-room," the officers repeated enthusiastically, with the exception of a gloomy Spencer.

Chapter 14

As soon as the sun was up, the officers were keen to try to catch a shark or two—indeed, the captain had demanded that as soon as light permitted, efforts to snare a shark must be ready to commence. In truth, sleep had been difficult with the metallic *Tnk tnk tnk* of hammering on iron and the teeth-jarring screech of sawing wood floating through the fabric of the ship. After a night's activity the carpenter and blacksmith and their mates had produced the dozen harpoons demanded.

Lambert was officer of the watch, and Colyer midshipman of the watch. Quite naturally, she wanted to see what was to be done with the fruits of her studies.

Evidently she was not the only one—Malory and all the commissioned officers with the exception of Spencer, appeared one by one as soon as it was light, brimming with enthusiasm at the new task.

She was excited but apprehensive, hoping desperately first of all that they could snare a shark, and secondly that this would help them bring the serpent to them.

Before long, an animated debate was already taking place on the best way to catch one of the fearsome fish. No one was particularly keen to get close to a shark, after seeing the mess that had been made of a beef carcass.

"Shark hooks!" suggested Douglas. "Cook will have some, or they might be in the armoury. We can bait a few and sling them over the stern. Wait 'til we hook one of the bastards and pull it in."

"And try to bring it over the taffrail while it's thrashing around trying to get free?" said Lambert. "No, we need to tempt one of them close up and kill it with harpoons."

The lieutenants argued over their schemes, making point and counter-point until Malory held up his hand to stop them. "Gentlemen, we will attempt both ideas. Douglas's first, and if it doesn't work or I deem it to be too dangerous to proceed, we will try Mister Lambert's plan. Colyer, would you be so good as to fetch half a dozen shark hooks?"

She found them in the armoury and carried the large, gleaming, and fiercely pointed and barbed hooks back to the deck. After placing a large chunk of meat on each, they heaved a hooked line over each quarter, throwing a few fire buckets filled with food scraps and fishguts into the water for good measure.

They did not have to wait too long before they saw smooth, blue projectiles parting the water in the direction of the baited hooks. The sharks took turns to dart at the bait, but it seemed that they were merely sniffing at it, or trying to take tiny pieces, not willing to close their mouths around the hook itself.

"They'll have all the meat away before long!" complained Douglas. Lambert looked self-satisfied, but only for a moment.

Colyer leaned on the taffrail, watching the sleek shapes with a sneaking admiration as they dashed around the hooks, just below the surface, their fins carving trails of spray. At that moment, one of them seemed to jump bodily out of the water, its semicircular snout briefly pointing at the sky. It flopped back onto the water and began to flail violently.

"Look!" she shouted, unnecessarily as the others had heard the commotion and rushed back to the rail.

"We've got one, damn it!" yelled Douglas triumphantly.

"Capital Douglas. Don't we need to pull it in now?" inquired Lambert drily.

"Oh, heavens, yes," Douglas remembered. "Colyer, would you round some men up? Quickly please?"

It was as if they had forgotten how to do their jobs, she railed quietly to herself, while grabbing a handful of idlers who were part of the duty watch but unoccupied while the ship needed no alterations in course or sail.

"Haul away there," Douglas ordered, "handsomely now!"

The men hauled, but could barely pull in a foot of rope with each heave. The shark thrashed and twisted, resisting every inch that the rope could be hauled in and wrenching doggedly against the hook in its mouth.

After a strenuous effort from the men, the shark had been brought to within a couple of fathoms of the transom. It did not seem to have tired in the slightest.

"Primitive beasts," said a voice beside her. Colyer looked up to see Gilpin, who had evidently come on deck to watch the excitement. "Remember what I told you about transmutation?" She nodded. "Well, the shark there didn't need much of that. It's a simple creature indeed—a nose to sniff out prey, a fearsome set of teeth to savage anything it might meet, no brain to speak of. And the rest is a digestive tube wrapped in a perfect form-body. Better than anything Seppings or Slade have designed. And there have been sharks just like this one swimming the seas since before the flood, whenever that might have been. Oh, look, the rest have cottoned on to this one's plight."

It was true. The remainder of the pack had given up going for the bait and had started taking chunks out of their erstwhile fellow. By the time the men had got the shark to within six feet of the rudder, there were half a dozen predators worrying at it. By the time they had begun to haul it out of the water, much of the shark's body was missing. It continued to twitch and its tail thumped resolutely, bumping against the stern window as it rose.

"Oh Christ, the Captain," Douglas exclaimed and ran below to see if any efforts were needed to placate MacQuarrie. At that moment, a blue-and-white bolt erupted from the water and latched onto the finally-dead fish they had hooked. The black-eyed killer that had made the jump flicked from side to side and tore a huge lump from the sorry-looking catch. Just as the scavenger fell back, the line holding the dead fish gave way and the pair of sharks plopped back into the sea, hook and all. The men tumbled bodily backwards in a muddle of cursing, struggling to disentangle limbs from the mass.

"Blast!" snapped Malory, thumping the rail. The sea seethed behind the stern, and as the ship drew forwards, the foaming, bloodstained mass receded.

Douglas returned, red-faced. "Well, the old man wasn't happy at being disturbed but.... Oh, did we lose it?"

"'Fraid so, old chap," grinned Lambert. "It was a close-run thing but the sharks won."

Malory looked at Colyer with a suspicious looking shine in his eyes.

"Well, young shaver, any bright ideas?"

"We've still got my plan, Sir!" yelped an aggrieved Lambert until Malory shut him up with a glance.

"Mister Lambert has a point, Sir," she started diplomatically whilst searching for yet another nugget to impress the first lieutenant. She racked her brains. "If we could draw them in close and kill one or two quickly, we'd have a better chance of getting it up here before it was torn to pieces." She stopped, hoping someone else would take up the baton. But the others were looking at her, waiting for her to continue. What had happened to the days when no one listened to a word she said?

"...On the other hand, we need to have it secured so we can pull it in. The hook seemed to work all right, it was just too far to pull with the shark still alive and all the other sharks having a go at it."

"True. Continue..."

"How about we rig a boom over the side, dangling a line with a baited hook on it. And the line could be reeved through a block so we can haul it up smoothly without dragging over the rail."

"I don't fancy hauling one of those things up by the bulwark with it thrashing around like a stallion when the mares are in heat," argued Douglas. "What happens if it flings itself onto the deck still alive?"

"Well, as soon as we've snagged one," she responded as patiently as possible, "kill it with the harpoons, hoist it up and swing it aboard."

Malory laughed, a touch bitterly she thought. "You make it sound so simple. Well, we know they go for the beef, and we know we can snare one. It would take a harpoon right through the brain to kill it quick enough. I've never thrown a harpoon in my life. I'm sure I couldn't hit it the way they dart and dash around, never mind strike a killer blow. Could you?"

"Not if your life depended on it, Sir. But I know who might be able to."

"Very well. Let's repair to the wardroom while we discuss it, I'm in need of refreshment. Lambert, kindly see to the rigging of that boom would you?"

Chapter 15

LIEUTENANT Spencer's career was falling apart, and his life with it. He swayed in his cot with the motion of the ship, unable to sleep, recalling the mocking words of the sailors as they had worked. It was not his fault the ship had been caught in stays, he had acted to avoid a collision. And everyone knew the Leda-class corvettes were flighty craft and difficult to manoeuvre for all their great speed.

Being repeatedly humiliated by his superiors in front of the crew was both outrageous and unprofessional by any standards of the modern Navy. How had Captain MacQuarrie and his lackey Malory been able to maintain the ship for so long without disaster or mutiny? The state of discipline among the crew was clearly appalling. The midshipmen were not only allowed to run riot, but it seemed they were being positively encouraged to shirk their proper duties—even to think for themselves! And Malory was evidently practising quite abominable favouritism towards the low-class Colyer. He could not decide if the first lieutenant were more likely to be a predatory sodomite or a secret democrat, or indeed, which was worse.

He could not understand in the slightest why it was happening, but things had been going from bad to worse since he stepped through the doors at Marlborough College as a child. Just when he seemed to have made some friends, the lads would soon lose interest in what he had to say and even start playing cruel pranks on him. He managed to maintain a few acquaintances, and hovered on the periphery of two or three circles of friends, but was never able to form the sort of close bonds other boys seemed to have. He worked hard and did quite well at his studies, but never seemed to win the approbation of his masters the way the favoured boys did—those who were already being groomed for high office. He found himself reliving every snub and disappointment.

At the time he had brushed it off—indeed, not fully understood what had been happening throughout his childhood. He had never quite realised that it was those other boys who were seen as the future Pitts and Cannings, not him. Looking back, the signs were obvious.

As the youngest of three boys he knew he would not inherit his father's estates, but he would have a decent income and be given the best chances at a decent life, perhaps in the clergy or the military. The life that was eventually chosen for him was the Navy —at which he was delighted. The Navy was, after all, a band of brothers, and he saw himself renewed, as part of that wonderfully glamorous elite—the finest yacht club in the world. He could hardly wait to go to sea.

And yet it had not turned out in the least like that. His dreams of boarding an enemy ship at the head of a devoted crew, or taking over command when his Captain was wounded, had faded utterly. His career had been drudgery from beginning to end. The few opportunities for action had gone to other officers, some less senior than himself. He had been reassured, told his chance would come, but it never had. He had the right connections, he was undoubtedly skilled at navigation, he had an excellent knowledge of seamanship—on paper, at least. And, he mused, he was generally a very well read and educated man. What on Earth did he have to do to get a chance?

And then instead of the serious business of rooting the pirates out of Borneo, he was sent onto this outmoded ship on a highly speculative cruise with little prospect of action or glory.

Even so, he had tried to make the best of it and entered into the commission with every good intention. He had tried to help in the education of the midshipmen, and been shown nothing but ingratitude by that dried up old sailing master. He had tried to enter into serious discussions about the future of the service at dinner and been cut down to size. Everywhere he turned on the ship, the whole crew evidently had it in for him. But why?

He decided sleep was unlikely to come, and swung himself into a seated position on his cot. He was about to dress and step into the wardroom for a glass when he heard voices. It was Malory and that scrub Colyer again! What did the first lieutenant mean by bringing the midshipman into their wardroom yet again? It was simply not the done thing. He could not step out now and interrupt their conversation. Damn it all.

Now Malory was pouring drinks for the snotty from the wardroom's supply of claret. Was nothing sacred?

"Anything the matter, Colyer?" Malory was asking. "You're being even quieter than usual and the slight grain of humour commonly present among all your seriousness seems to have been extinguished."

"Sorry, Sir," the midshipman answered. "It's just...well, I'm deeply grateful for the invitations to the wardroom, really I am, but this is my first ship and there are other midshipmen more senior to me and they're starting to get resentful. Never mind Lieutenant Spencer, who I gather-"

What was this? Was the country quack's son about to insult him?

"Never mind Spencer," Malory laughed. "Spencer will never amount to anything and the sooner he realises that and slopes back to England the better it will be for all of us, himself included."

Spencer could barely believe what he was hearing. He was being impugned, slandered, and in front of a middle-class cockpit-officer! In his mind, he challenged Malory to a duel and shot the lieutenant through the head. No, the throat! He wanted Malory to realise what was happening as his life ebbed away.

"You should understand, Colyer," Malory asserted, as if lecturing a class full of cadets, "that the secret of efficiency is not the 'officer class', nor promoting fellows according to seniority, or even creating a naval college, though Lord knows it's a start. The secret of efficiency is *favouritism*. That means a fellow like me breaking through to the top and shamelessly advancing people of talent, no matter where they are on the ladder. During the great war it worked because those in charge of it all couldn't afford to be particular. And they certainly could not afford to run the Navy like the Army is run—an extension of public schools for the benefit of lordlings.

"The problem is," he went on, "the Navy became too successful. The service became glamorous, attractive, thanks to fellows like Broke and Hope, and glorious victory after glorious victory. Before you know it you have *this* member of parliament or *that* landed gent pulling strings to get his offspring onto the best ships. The whole thing has become an aristocratic playground.

"Well, it will stop when I am First Sea Lord. But it means when I choose to advance someone like you, young snotty Colyer, it means you must have absolutely no qualms about following your destiny as I set it out. And never mind those aristocratic shakings Johnson and Holford, they have their petty peerages and sprawling estates to keep them busy." He ran to a halt, almost angrily. Spencer clenched his teeth in fury.

"You can handle Johnson and Holford can't you?" he added, warily.

"Yes, Sir, it's nothing I can't cope with. And besides, I think they think if they bother me too much they'll have you to deal with."

"They're quite wrong. If you can't handle them you don't deserve my help. Look, you must see it's all about the future. The Empire is only as strong as the Navy which holds it together—and the Navy is only as strong as its men. There are other countries that would like to take Britain's pre-eminent place in the world but they can't challenge us without defeating this Navy. If we leave it to the natural order, some day we will lose the empire because it is some chap's *turn*. Some chap like Holford, or Johnson. Or Spencer."

"I'd better go and round up Panna, Sir," said Colyer. "I dare say they'll be ready with that boom soon."

"Do you think he can do it?"

"I've confidence in him. He says he got a fair bit of practice with a harpoon when he was out with the Greenland whaling fleet, but a whale is bigger than a shark."

"That's undeniable," Malory retorted. "Nevertheless, I suppose we're lucky to have a lascar topman as it is—how lucky must we be to have a lascar topman who can throw a harpoon? Well, let's get on with it."

Spencer heard the sound of chairs being pushed back, and the two of them leaving. He fumed inwardly, his tiny cabin seeming to fill with steam that built up until the pressure was enough to blow the walls out. This was a ship of layabouts, upstarts and jacobins, and the first lieutenant was the worst. People like that would wreck the country, wreck the whole Empire. It was up to Spencer to stop them.

With any chance of sleep utterly shattered, he sought as much solitude as he could find on a tiny ship packed with men. The disgruntled lieutenant pulled on his jacket and stomped on deck, before hauling himself up to the fore top and ordering the man stationed there to make himself scarce. He simmered in silence, watching the antics of the officers on deck, and wondering how he could bring them to account.

Chapter 16

AFTER half an hour or so the bosun and carpenter had rigged a sturdy tripod from an extra stunsail boom and various spare timbers, which projected over the port, lee bulwark where the hammock netting had earlier been removed. Granby slung a block onto the apex of the tripod, hanging above the streaming bow wave as it swirled along the hull. Half a dozen idlers had been dragooned in to hoist any shark they caught out of the water, and the men shuffled about uncomfortably. Colyer wasn't sure whether their awkwardness was due to their assigned task or the fact that several officers were close by.

With luck they won't be the only fish out of water, thought the midshipman.

Or perhaps, it was apprehension at the scale of the task ahead. While they had been trying to catch sharks, there had been a couple of unconfirmed sightings of the sea-serpent itself. Naturally, there were now lookouts posted at every available spot —fore and aft, port and starboard, fore, main and mizzen tops and even a frozen topman clinging to the cross trees near the very tip of the mainmast. Colyer was unsure whether the serpent was feeding off the sharks that were attracted by their bait, or whether the men were simply convincing themselves that every bit of floating debris or unusual reflection was their quarry.

The captain had ordered that he be called as soon as there was a sighting, and the fact that he had been dragged on deck twice with little to show for it had not improved his mood. They all felt the need to get on with the next part of the plan in the feverish hope that it would all work.

Daedalus and The Deep

From the block hung the second shark hook, on which a sizeable chunk of beef was now being impaled. The bait was hoisted to the block, ready to lower into the sea. Colyer picked up one of the harpoons, and wandered to the forecastle where Panna was relaxing among the skylarking off-watch hands.

"Your weapon, whaler!" she grinned, tossing the harpoon, which he caught with a flourish. The nearby men raised a ragged, amused cheer as the lascar strode aft, harpoon in hand.

He inspected the tripod from all angles, while tying his hair back. Silently, he fastened a few fathoms of log line onto the end of the harpoon, then did the same to three more of the projectiles which he lined up against the bulwark. "Hey, Carson?" He yelled to a nearby sailor, "Pass these up to me when I call, yeah?"

The seaman scuttled over, with a gap-toothed smile. "Aye, jus' sing out thar, Ranoo."

The lascar grabbed the first harpoon, hopped up onto the main chains and made the line fast below a deadeye.

The hook was lowered into the water, and it was not long before white trails began to appear in the green water, racing towards the meat. Panna hefted the harpoon, and raised it, the barbed tip hovering by his right ear and pointing down into the water.

The first shark reached the hook and nibbled at the meat, swerving away after a moment. The next did the same, while the two following started tussling with each other and broke away before even reaching their target. The next, though, rushed in directly from the bow, and turned on its side, mouth gaping as it lunged for the flesh. Colyer found herself taking a reflexive step back away from the side.

The shark's jagged rows of teeth were briefly visible before its mouth snapped around the meat. It tried to pull away with whole chunk of beef, and plunged the point of the hook deep into its jaw.

Exactly as had happened earlier, the trapped beast began to thrash, but Panna's arm had already extended and the harpoon speared, utterly straight, at the shark's head. The point lanced into the side of of the beast in front of its gills. It thrashed even harder than before.

"Harpoon!" called Panna, almost calmly under the circumstances. Carson tossed a second weapon up to the topman, who tied off the line, and almost nonchalantly, took aim. The shark had shaken itself into a vicious blur amid a maelstrom of foaming water and blood.

"Come on..." Malory muttered under his breath as another shark was already hurtling in from the beam. Panna drew back his arm and smoothly cast the harpoon. It sailed across the gap and sliced into the centre of the ensnared fish's head, buried up to the wooden hilt. The shark fell completely still in an instant.

"Heave away, now!" shouted Malory, and the men yanked the line. The dead shark sprang out of the water, up to the block, in a shower of spray, while the second animal that had been approaching raised its shovel head and took a semicircular lump out of the captured fish's tail.

Panna slung a line around the shark under its scimitar-shaped pectoral fins, tied the bight off and passed the end to the men on deck while he hopped back over the bulwark. Together, they manhandled the body, harpoons and all, across the rail and down onto the deck.

A cheer erupted from the foredeck and the off-watch hands began chanting *"Pa-nna! Pa-nna! Pa-nna!"* The lascar smiled warmly and raised a spare harpoon in embarrassed triumph. Then it was back to work.

"Excellent!" said Malory, clapping his hands in satisfaction. "Now, let's see if we can snare one or two more, and then we can have a go at bringing in the sea serpent."

Using the same method, Panna was able to recover two more sharks. In fact, a third had fallen prey to his harpoon but had not been caught well enough on the hook and fell back into the sea to provide food for its primeval compatriots. Each time Colyer saw the sharks tear into the flesh of their own kind with such furious gluttony, she could not suppress a shudder. On one occasion Panna had narrowly missed becoming a meal himself while trying to recover a harpoon stuck obstinately in the flank of a dying shark.

The officers once again fell to discussing the best means of using the sharks to snare the sea serpent. All agreed that some variation on the shark-catching plan seemed to offer the best possibility. They decided that a long boom rigged from the cathead, trailing a dead shark, would bring the serpent alongside the vessel and give the men a chance to strike at its body with harpoons. They did not want to bring it too close, but equally not too far away that the harpoons would be ineffectual. At its first sighting the beast had seemed unconcerned about approaching the ship to within twenty or thirty yards, but a fatal blow would need to be struck closer than that.

Malory ordered Panna to select some more men to train in throwing the harpoons, and suggested Colyer supervise. They picked out a selection of idlers, and borrowed a fender to use as a target. Colyer, as politely as possible, ordered the off-watch men to clear the forty feet aft of the bowsprit to use as a 'shooting range'. It would not normally have been a popular move, but today the men accepted it—there was much out of the ordinary to keep life interesting at the moment. Anything that broke the monotony of forecastle life was to be welcomed, and the newly recruited harpooners' target practice provided opportunities for predicting winners and losers, cheering on messmates and even the odd illicit bet.

The men Panna roped in had already separated themselves into their natural groupings, gun crews, waisters and topmen. The gun crew men were, to a man, stocky and muscular, their powerful torsos and thick limbs developed over years of hauling heavy cannon into position. The topmen were, by contrast, spare and wiry, with the waisters' physiques somewhere between the two.

The gun crews were the most powerful, able to drive their harpoons right through the fender, when they were able to hit it at all which was around half the time. The topmen were not able to throw their harpoons with the same force, but were invariably able to place their harpoons on the target. The waisters, less powerful than the gun crews but no more accurate, were quickly discounted.

After a thorough competition, Panna, with Colyer's assent, chose the two most accurate gunners and the four strongest topmen, and, with a proud smile, handed them each a harpoon. The spectating idlers cheered, laughed, slapped backs and turned their attention to the work taking place around the port cathead to rig a boom—in effect, a giant fishing rod for a sea serpent. Colyer had a sudden notion of how ridiculous this all was, a thought quickly replaced by mounting excitement.

They were about to go fishing for a *sea-serpent*! She could have laughed aloud at the romance and adventure of it. The 'blue devils' which had permeated the whole ship from mainmast truck to false keel looked to have been banished completely with the pursuit of a quite different monster.

CHAPTER 17

FROM the foretop, Lieutenant Spencer regarded the proceedings with contempt. With luck they would stop this ridiculous pantomime soon enough and the ship could return to its proper purpose. Better yet, they might sight a sail, which they would be duty-bound to investigate and then have no choice but to end these antics.

They had sailed quite unforgivably far off station. Since sighting the 'sea serpent' they had progressed on a generally South Westerly heading, while they should have been heading North. They were by now in danger of sailing on, deep into the Southern Ocean with its huge seas and high winds. Further still, and they would encounter great islands of ice floating in the sea. Probably a thousand miles away from any slaver or pirate, who would be free to pursue their illegal trades with impunity. It made Spencer's blood boil.

At that last thought, he looked down to leeward. The sea was a vast sheet of blue-green. Near to the ship, the waves forming the surface could be made out, but beyond that, the ocean appeared as endless, flat and unbroken. It was the same to windward, ahead and aft. The ship below seemed small beyond possibility. He floated among the ship's great spread of canvas, completely alone.

When he had come up on deck, the other lieutenants had been fiddling about with a tripod rigged over the beam. There had been an increasing amount of noise and racket drifting up from the spar deck in the last few minutes, and he looked back to see what on earth those fools were doing now.

Daedalus and the Deep

It seemed they were sporting with a topman and encouraging the man to catch sharks. No doubt all in an attempt to indulge the captain in his risible obsession with hunting the sea serpent.

If that was what passed for entertainment in this ship he wondered how the vessel had not been lost with all hands long ago, or the company condemned, to a man, to Bedlam.

A shark was hauled over the side, accompanied by cheering and whooping from the idle hands and off-watch crew. The officers were being shockingly familiar with that lascar and the common midshipman. He curled his lip at the appalling spectacle, and rolled onto his back, unable to look at it any more. Instead, he stared up along the topmast, watching it sweeping, port to starboard and back, against the wispy clouds.

By and by, he turned his gaze back to the deck, to see that the activity had moved to the bow. The low-born snotty seemed to be holding some kind of spear-throwing competition on the forecastle. Unsurprisingly that savage, Panna, was at the forefront. Maybe that was it—the ship had gone native while out in the East.

At the same time, Lambert and Malory were supervising the carpenter to rig a spar extending from the port cathead. Spencer huffed to himself. These games were all very well, but the ship had serious business to attend to. The captain and his lickspittle officers were guilty of dereliction of duty. With a private grin he resolved to report everything to the Admiralty.

Spencer turned away again, unable to look at the scene any more in his scorn. At that very moment, as he gazed out to windward, he saw a disturbance in the water several hundred yards away, and to his astonishment, the sea serpent's head shot vertically from the water, something large and flapping in its jaws. Just as suddenly, the serpent disappeared, sliding silently back into the sea with nothing to show it had ever been there.

He leapt up and looked below and aft. No one was reporting the creature. He realised with all the activity going on below, the lookouts were not paying attention. He slumped back to a seated position, chuckling to himself. It was another mark of the unprofessionalism of this dreadful ship. He toyed with the idea of showing up the lookouts by reporting the sighting himself, but decided against it. He would probably end up being sniped at by Malory in front of the men again, and besides the creature was now nowhere to be seen. Almost gleefully, he kept his silence.

It was by now late morning, and the hands were piped to dinner. The off-watch seamen trooped to the lower deck, leaving the upper deck relatively empty for the first time since sun-up. The officers left the structure at the cathead and strolled aft to take a sighting of the sun for midday. He let out his breath in a long sigh. All he could hear was the sea, sloshing round the bows and running along the corvette's flank. Spencer decided to stay put. It was the first time in his naval career he had missed a shooting of the sun. He doubted he would be missed. He was not due on duty until the next watch, so he stretched out on the base of the foretop and went to sleep.

Spencer awoke around half an hour later to the sound of a rough coughing. The lieutenant opened his eyes to find a topman crouched by the shrouds. He cursorily tapped a knuckle against his forelock. "Beggin' yer pardon, Sir, but this is me post. L'e'tenant Lambert ordered me up 'ere."

"And if I ordered you down again?" snapped Spencer, rubbing his eyes. The topman looked confused and conflicted, but Spencer huffed and added, "very well, you may keep lookout. I'm going to bed. Mind that you keep a close eye for any sail, whether it be Navy, merchantman, corsair or slaver and sing out as soon as you sight one."

"Mister Malory said to keep our eyes peeled for the beastie."

"We have a job to do, damn your insolent hide, and it involves ships, not sea serpents!" snapped Spencer, leaving the topman looking thoroughly bewildered. The lieutenant swung himself into the rigging and climbed down at a leisurely pace. The boom rigged from the bow now had a block frapped to its outer end and from that a dead shark trailed through the water, swerving gently from side to side in the bow wave.

A loose line of men was spaced out along the bulwark. Still bleary from his nap, he asked one what was going on.

"Waitin' for the beastie, Sir," grinned the man, gesturing at the harpoon leant up against the bulwark beside him. "When it turns up to grab that shark, we'll stick 'im, like."

Spencer harrumphed and stomped below decks. Exhausted and still feeling somewhat lethargic after his doze on the foretop, he collapsed into his cot fully clothed and did not wake until shortly before the end of the afternoon watch—roused by some infernal racket on deck and the sound of running feet. He was due to take over in the first dog watch, so he called the steward and demanded some food be brought to him, as he had missed luncheon.

The steward had an insolent look in his eye, but did not complain and brought the lieutenant some hard tack and a little cold meat. The wardroom was otherwise empty. He did not consider this particularly strange given the other officers' febrile interest in the sea serpent and their tinkering with the ship to tempt it near.

He jumped to the sudden sound of a *thok! thok!* reverberating through the hull. This was followed by a sound something like frightened horses screaming. What on earth was going on now?

He finished his meal, pulled his uniform together as neatly as he could (which was not very neat at all) and sauntered on deck.

...To be confronted by the giant sea-serpent, hard beside the ship, contorting wildly and screaming with its long, pointed jaws opened wide. Its head towered above the deck, waving drunkenly, while its tail thumped against the tumblehome of the hull. A gaggle of men clustered by the rail yelled and hurled harpoons at the creature, then ducked and jumped away as the creature's head swayed in their direction.

It was a sight and sound that was so utterly unearthly that Spencer bolted below deck, scuttled to his cabin and leapt onto his cot, drawing his knees up and wrapping his arms around himself. The world had gone quite, quite mad.

It was some minutes after eight bells had rung at the end of the watch that he shambled on deck, to receive a flea in his ear from Lambert and a lecture from Malory about his behaviour. He listened dumbly to his admonishment, dimly aware that he was once again being dressed down in front of the whole ship.

CHAPTER 18

THE creature was even bigger than Colyer remembered. She was alerted to its presence by a shout from the masthead, which caused every unoccupied man to crowd to the rail. She heard a man next to her muttering "Hello, Beastie!"

The creature was a little off to leeward, and behind the stern, but catching them up steadily. Once again its pointed snout was raised above the water, its frilly mane catching the wind and streaming outward down each side of its neck. It cut the water smoothly, and for a moment the midshipman thought the sleek creature made the fine-formed corvette seem like a hulking transport by comparison, thumping gracelessly through the sea.

For a moment, everyone stared, awestruck at the approaching beast. "You men," shouted Malory, breaking the spell. "Anyone with no business at the bulwark, clear away now!" The group melted away as quickly as it had formed. "Where the hell is Spencer?" she heard someone mutter. Malory sent a goggle-eyed Gower to fetch the captain, and dispatched Lambert back to the quarterdeck where, as officer of the watch, he should have been. A few minutes later they saw MacQuarrie emerging from the aft companionway and, for a moment, staring slack-jawed before composing himself and moving to the windward side of the quarterdeck with a heroic, patrician pose.

"Stay down," the first lieutenant hissed at the harpooners, "Don't move until I give the command. Then I want a good, even broadside. If you miss, pull your harpoon straight back in on the line. If you hit, grab another harpoon and wait for the command to hit it again."

Daedalus and The Deep

The harpooners readied themselves, crouching along the deck behind the low bulwarks. The officers and Colyer were now alone standing to their full height on the quarterdeck and gangway as the serpent drew up towards them. Colyer found once again that she was holding her breath, and the sound of her blood thundered in her ears.

The serpent pulled in alongside them, its narrow black eyes playing over every inch of the ship and its rigging. She heard Johnson muttering *"Christ, Christ, Christ..."* Douglas was feverishly sketching the serpent and making notes in a notebook, but Colyer could see his hands trembling.

The creature was now fully level with the ship, sunlight glinting from its glossy flanks. It dipped its snout into the water, throwing up a twin plume from its divided mane. Its single crescent-shaped nostril drew up to the dead shark, tentatively, until it was almost touching the bait.

"Stand by, men!" hissed Malory. The serpent cracked its jaws open, revealing its swept-back teeth and over-hanging upper jaw. Colyer could barely stand the tension. The creature suddenly threw its mouth wide open and lunged for the shark. As the jaws clamped shut over the fish, Malory raised his arm and shouted "Fire!"

The seven harpooners leapt from their hiding places, and slung their weapons in a rapid ripple down the side of the vessel. Five struck home, and three went in deep. Quickly, the men grabbed new harpoons or reeled in their previous weapons on the retaining lines, but the creature had already started to buck. Its fluked tail smacked twice against the hull. A scream, the like of which Colyer had never heard in her short life, rent the air along with a spray of fragments of shark flesh.

The serpent started to pull away from the ship but the harpoons stuck in its flank started to pull on the lines that tied it to the rail. The beast screamed again, raising its jaws high in the air, but slewed slightly closer to the corvette again, slackening the lines slightly. Each of the officers was rooted to the spot. Colyer once again had that sense of her insides turning to liquid, and feeling a compulsion to run. She stayed still, willing her muscles to obey her brain and not her fear, promising herself that if any of the officers fled, she would follow them.

None did, though Douglas had dropped his notebook on the deck. In the few seconds since the harpooners first struck—which had seemed like minutes—they were ready again. "Fire!" yelled Malory a second time, and a second time the seven men threw for all they were worth.

Only another two hit their mark this time, as the beast was veering and flexing from side to side. Nevertheless, the serpent uttered its terrible cry a third time and, daring a step closer to the rail, Colyer saw that a dark, viscous liquid was seeping from the wounds along its side. It plunged its head back into the water, then raised it again and shook its mane, showering the officers and men with spray. She had a quick sense once again of Panna, his resolute presence imposing serenity on the men beside him.

In amongst her useless fear she felt a wash of sympathy for the creature. Its behaviour seemed to be becoming desperate, anguished. She quickly hardened her heart—how on earth could she know how this creature felt? Besides, surely it was nothing but a dumb brute, capable of feeling pain or the urges of biology but nothing more? Its eyes were opened wide, almost round.

The harpooners were slower to recover this time. Malory was just about to order a third strike when the serpent swerved in towards the ship and butted the bulwark with the side of its head. It drew its neck back slightly, then lunged again and clamped its jaws around the bulwark.

The officers, in unison, stumbled back and Colyer tripped on a carronade slide. She skidded along the deck on her backside, scrabbling with her feet to stand again, expecting any moment to see the monster looming over her, mouth gaping. Her mind for some reason flicked back to that moment in Borneo where she had waited for the cannon fire to hit her, convinced that every second she would be torn to a pulpy mass, even though the moment had never come.

...But by the time she had recovered herself, the serpent had only worried a few lumps out of the rail and then pulled its head back away from the ship.

"Steady, Colyer," Malory said, "it doesn't do to fall over in front of the men, you know." She looked at him, incredulous, but he was smiling gently.

"Sorry, Sir, that slide's a menace," she retorted, desperate to display some *sang froid* in the heat of the moment. At that moment she noticed that most of the harpooners had leapt back as well, and were only now recovering themselves.

Daedalus and The Deep

The creature turned its attention to the boom which had trailed the dead shark, and with a few snaps of its jaw and shakes of its head had splintered the structure into a formless tangle.

"Fire!" yelled Malory a third time, but all seven harpoons plunged uselessly into the swirling gap between serpent and ship. The serpent was once again pulling away from the corvette and with a single, mighty effort, it peeled itself away from the tormenting vessel. The harpoons embedded in its flank one by one ripped out of the creature, each carrying a small chunk of dark flesh, apart from the aftermost harpoon where the line securing it twanged and broke. The beast swam on a diverging course, one harpoon trailing from its tail. It flicked and flicked its after half, tearing the wound wider, and eventually the harpoon came free and slid into the sea.

Just then, the serpent began a determined whipping of its body in that peculiar vertical flexing motion they had noticed before and pulled ahead of the corvette once more. The officers gathered once again at the leeward rail of the quarterdeck.

"Report!" snapped the Captain to Malory.

"We snared it with harpoons but it pulled itself free," Malory responded patiently, even though the situation must have been obvious. "It must be badly injured though. It has a number of harpoon wounds in its starboard beam. It has drawn ahead again although it seems to be needing to make a greater effort than before. I would estimate it is doing 12 knots, and once again heading Sou' West." He stopped to catch his breath.

"Very well," said the Captain suspiciously. "We will of course pursue. Lambert? Shake out the royals and haul your wind."

As Lambert carried out the orders, Malory looked at his watch. "Damn," he cursed, "eight bells has gone and we haven't rung the bell. And where in God's name is that wastrel Spencer, he's supposed to be taking the watch. Will someone ring that bloody bell?!"

Finally, Spencer appeared on deck looking haggard and wan. Colyer wondered if he was ill.

"Poor show, Spencer, very poor," Lambert sniped as Spencer took the deck from him.

"I expect better of my officers!" thundered Malory. "I demand the highest standards, and frankly punctuality is the minimum requirement of the dullest, least promising officer in the corps. We are in pursuit of the serpent and if you lose track of the beast, God help you, because no one here will!"

Spencer took his dressing-down in silence and his abject appearance soon reduced Malory to silence. Any hint of insolence or an attempt to explain would have the first lieutenant lecturing for hours, but such passive acceptance drew out only Malory's contempt. Soon it was so apparent that Spencer was beneath his notice that the first lieutenant let him off with taking the last dog watch in Gilpin's place so the sailing master could enjoy dinner in the wardroom.

In truth, the serpent was not hard to follow this time. It was clearly visible against the green sea most of the time, and there was a distinct trail of blood to follow as well. It was even possible to detect a peculiar brassy scent from the blood on the water when sitting in the beakhead. Even Spencer should be able to manage.

"I hope the sharks don't come back for it with all that blood in the water," worried Lambert.

"They may not be attracted by its blood," Gilpin suggested. "It smells like no creature's blood I've ever come across. It may even drive the sharks away for all we know—it made short work of them before and who knows what that creature might be capable of when wounded?"

It was a sobering thought, and not just for the sharks.

Colyer strolled down to the gangway to thank Panna for his efforts. The lascar was gathering up the remaining harpoons, and if he had been affected by his experience, he didn't show it.

"Good work today, Panna," she said, conscious not just of her own gratitude but the convention that a good officer should always recognise a task well completed. Panna gave her his best reassuring smile and a surreptitious pat on the shoulder, and got on with his work.

Malory invited Colyer to dine with the officers in the wardroom that evening, and the camaraderie of the 'Royal Navy's finest sea-serpent hunters' made it an enjoyable, if sometimes raucous occasion. Even failing to secure the creature that day could not dampen their spirits, as they felt it was now only a matter of time before they triumphed.

That evening they ate shark for the first time—which Lambert declared the only fit meal for such men capable of taking on a sea monster and living to tell the tale. Colyer couldn't claim to have enjoyed it particularly but it was nice to have something relatively fresh to eat as a change from meat from a cask and vegetables from a can.

Chapter 19

THERE was a palpable sense of relief throughout the ship at first light when the lookouts announced that the serpent, or 'beastie', as the men were now calling it, was still in sight. Douglas was officer of the watch and kept asking for reports to see if they were gaining—if he didn't make a report to the captain every half hour or so, he knew there would soon be a testy demand coming his way.

Despite their efforts, the distance remained about the same, probably half a mile or a little under. Every so often the serpent dipped beneath the waves for up to a minute, but always returned to the surface in roughly the same place relative to the ship.

It must be weakening, thought Gilpin with a momentary sense of sorrow. He had no doubt that the creature had vast amounts to tell man about the vast and trackless oceans of which he had literally only scraped the surface. But how much more could one learn by observing it in its natural environment than from a battered corpse?

"Morning, Mister Gilpin," said a youthful voice behind him, and he turned to see the young mid Colyer approaching, fresh faced and brimming with enthusiasm for the new day. Well, whatever the dubious morals of their current 'mission', it seemed to have done wonders for this lad, who had really come out of himself.

"Good morning, Colyer," answered Gilpin, about as brightly as he felt this morning.

"Do you think we'll catch the serpent today?" the cadet asked.

"We seem to have no trouble keeping up with it now," Gilpin thought aloud, "and it could easily outpace it when first we encountered it. I've no doubt the harpoons caused it some pain even if they did no lasting damage."

"You think we didn't hurt it mortally?"

"Difficult to say. Your man Panna isn't the only fellow on this ship who has done some whaling," Gilpin went on, "and in my experience it takes a lot more to kill a creature of that size. With a whale, you can run it down, tire it out so it doesn't fight when you come in to deliver the fatal blow."

"Still, a whale has layers and layers of blubber and thick skin, this serpent doesn't seem to have much between skin and its vitals."

"No, but it's so long who knows where its vitals are?"

Colyer frowned. "That's true. So how do you think..."

At that point, MacQuarrie appeared with Malory and Lambert in tow, and gathered the officers, Gilpin and Colyer together for a conference on the day's tactics.

"I suggest we should sail it down until it runs out of energy," offered Lambert when the captain asked for suggestions, "and finish it with the harpoons."

"Mister Gilpin suggested that as the creature is so long, we can't guarantee to hit it somewhere that will kill it," said Colyer, "and what's to stop it seizing men off the deck?"

Interesting, thought Gilpin. *Clearly unwilling to pass another man's ideas off as his own and concerned for the crew as well.*

Malory considered for a moment. "It's my opinion that we'd be lucky to get near enough to use the harpoons again."

"What about muskets?" Douglas suggested. "The marines are itching to have a pop." Kane, Lieutenant of Marines, nodded enthusiastically at this.

"I'm not sure they will do enough damage, and certainly not at this range," Malory replied, deflating both of them.

"But when it tires and slows?" Kane tried again.

"No guarantee of that, Mister Kane," Gilpin interjected. "There's one thing that doesn't make much sense to me. This creature isn't like a whale to my eyes; it doesn't need to come to the surface to breathe. Have any of you seen it spout, even once?"

They shook their heads.

"In fact it looks like it has been dipping below the surface to breath. Something's keeping it up here, possibly something to do with the wounds it has sustained, but I'm not rightly sure for the moment.... Anyway, if it recovers it could dive deep. Or it could wait for a squall and dip beneath the ship, and by the time we come out we wouldn't be able to see it."

"It has not done so thus far," Malory reminded him, "even through the night."

"No, but equally I don't think we can rely on it sailing on a constant heading until it expires from exhaustion either."

"True, true..." replied Malory and they all fell silent again. Gilpin inwardly berated himself. If he had backed Lambert's plan it could have allowed the creature to escape, and he believed fiercely that it deserved to survive. But at the same time the service had been good to him, and he owed it his loyalty. The officer corps was tentatively becoming a scientific body of men, growing away from the tyrants and adventurers of the past. He wanted to encourage that growth as much as he could. And if it meant sacrificing this glorious creature...

"I expect ideas and a plan of action," snorted MacQuarrie, reminding them of his presence. A few more suggestions were made and as quickly dismissed.

"Good grief, we'll be firing broadsides at it before long," muttered Lambert.

"Well why not?" Colyer piped up. "Do we have any spider shot? Something like that could wrap around its neck—could kill it without blowing the body to smithereens."

"That's not a bad idea," Lambert responded, sounding a touch disappointed he had not quite thought of it himself. Malory smiled.

"Not bad at all," continued MacQuarrie. "I dare say we'll have some spider shot somewhere, and if we don't we can get the blacksmith to make some up. Some lengths of chain joined into a star-shape, and balls from langridge cases welded onto each end. It could work."

"Crosbie will be overjoyed," said Malory drily. "By your leave, captain?" MacQuarrie nodded. "See to it will you, Mister Lambert," he continued. "Right, let's heave the log and see if we can wring another half-knot out of her."

Gilpin took charge of the log, while Colyer saw to the glass. The wooden quadrant dropped into the sea and the thin line immediately started running off the drum in Gilpin's hands. "Turn!" he said as the first mark on the line crossed the rail. The glass measured 28 seconds precisely, and Colyer called the instant it ran out. Gilpin nipped off the line and took a reading. Just shy of nine knots. He pulled on the chord that turned the wooden drogue from a parachute into a flat dart that could cut easily through the water. They repeated the exercise twice more and Gilpin took an average of the readings. Nine knots dead—not bad at all for a reach with the wind somewhere ahead of the beam and a slightly confused sea.

Gilpin discussed trim with Malory, and they sought MacQuarrie's permission to have the forward two 32-pounders moved to the aftermost gunports to lift the bow slightly, and to have the hammocks taken down from the netting and stowed in the lower deck. After the heavy cannon had been manhandled the entire length of the gun deck, the ship's motion was slightly, but noticeably, easier and with the hammocks with their netting stowed below decks there was less parasitic drag over the deck from the wind. They streamed the log three times again, and the average was now distinctly nearer ten knots.

MacQuarrie looked grimly satisfied and retired to his cabin, but the first lieutenant decided more was possible.

"We'll rig a fire hose up to the t'gallants and give the sails a good soaking," he ordered.

"Aye aye, Sir," Gilpin responded dutifully, and after a flurry of activity with tackles and line, the sound of pumps began rattling from below. In moments, water began squirting across the sails, dampening the cloth to smooth the airflow and stop some of the force escaping through the weave.

Malory sent Colyer into the foretop once again to check the relative positions of the ship and the serpent. Gilpin was pleased to see him take his sextant, with which he could take precise angles. After a little under half an hour, the midshipman returned to the deck with a couple of pages torn out of his journal, which were covered in scribbled trigonometric calculations, half of them crossed out and redone.

"Catching it slowly, Sir," the midshipman puffed, catching his breath. "At seven bells it was nine-hundred-and-sixty yards away, fifteen minutes later it was around nine-hundred-and-thirty, give or take, and a moment ago it was more like nine-hundred yards, a little over perhaps.

Eight-bells sounded, at the beginning of the forenoon watch. It was still only eight o'clock in the morning. Douglas handed over the deck to Spencer, who looked even more haggard than he usually did. Shortly afterwards, the Captain came on deck, and asked for a report from Malory. The first lieutenant set out the plan of attack.

"Hmm," considered MacQuarrie. "Very well—I'd rather the thing was cut about a bit than we miss it altogether, but do try not to damage it too much."

"Thank you, Sir," Malory agreed. He turned to Gilpin."Sailing Master, I'd appreciate it if we could work up to windward somewhat. The creature may yet realise he can escape us simply by turning directly into the wind, and I'd like to close that route off if we can. The weather-gage was never more important."

Lambert reappeared, and made his way to the first lieutenant. "The gunner says we have a small supply of spider-shot, Sir," he reported, "and the blacksmith can make some more up to our specifications. I thought longer chain and fewer arms would serve our purpose in this respect."

"Indeed, very good Mister Lambert. See to it if you please."

"Erm, excuse me, Sir," Spencer interrupted, who had evidently overheard. "Is it wise to use up our spider-shot in this way if we don't have much of it? It is after all ideal for hampering smaller sailing vessels without damaging them too much, and is just the ticket for slavers and the like once we get in close enough."

Malory looked a little taken aback at being challenged in this way, and by an officer who would have surely done well to keep his head down to boot. Gilpin waited for the explosion and the now-routine public rebuke, but it never came. "Your attention to duty is...*admirable*, Mister Spencer," Malory said very deliberately, "but in any case academic. We have sighted no sail since leaving the Cape."

Gilpin moved across to the wheel and bade the helmsman play the wind-shifts and ease up to the Northward whenever the direction of the breeze veered slightly. He called Colyer over to demonstrate.

"You see, the wind is very rarely constant in direction and depending on the atmospheric conditions, tends to swing between half a point to a point." Colyer nodded, and started writing a note or two in his journal with accompanying diagrams.

"When the luffs shiver like that, we're as close to the wind as we can be with the sails set thus." It was true—the forward edges of the sails caught the wind like the leading edge of a bird's wing, and the slight flickering of the boltrope at the edge showed the sail was on the very edge. Too much and it would back, but Gilpin's experience and skill was not about to let that happen.

"Now the luff stops shivering and the sail is completely full. The helmsman may ease the ship to windward..." the helmsman cautiously allowed the wheel to unwind to port a bit at a time and the bow of the corvette swung by tiny degrees to starboard, until the luffs of the sails were ever-so-slightly trembling. After another couple of minutes, the trembling began to increase in amplitude. The helmsman pulled the wheel back and held it with the brake against the tendency to point up into the wind.

"We can gain a little ground to windward therefore without going to the bother of swinging the yards," Gilpin explained. "Every time we do that, although we gain in the long run, we lose a little ground. This way we can just play the natural tendencies of the conditions to our advantage. That's it," he encouraged the helmsman, "keep her full-and-bye, just so."

After a while, in this manner they were able to steadily climb to windward of the serpent and by two bells instead of the creature being directly ahead of them, it was moving in the same direction but diagonally across from the ship's bow.

Spencer, however, kept eyeing the shivering luffs with anxiety —Gilpin remembered he had been taken aback a few days ago, and was no doubt nervous about repeating the accident. "Kindly keep the sails full if you please, Sailing Master," he chided.

"Belay that," growled the captain from the windward rail. "I want her dancing on a knife-edge and ready to try a broadside as soon as you can." Spencer glowered but said nothing.

Just at that moment, the watch was startled by a hail from above. "Sail!" came the cry from the maintop. "Port quarter!"

Lambert dashed into the leeward rigging and hooked himself on with the crook of his elbow while aiming his telescope with his free hand. "Schooner. Looks like a fast ship."

"Slaver?" asked Spencer, of no one in particular.

"She's hull down, crossing our course, heading West, perhaps West-Nor'-West. Wait, she's hauling her wind, heading North. She did that as soon as she saw us, I'll be bound! Must be a slaver, bound for Brazil or Chile."

"Sir, permission to alter course in pursuit," called Spencer.

"We have our quarry Mister Spencer, and it is headed South West," replied the Captain mildly, "Maintain course."

"Sir, our orders state we are to pursue and apprehend any-"

"I am familiar with *my* orders, Mister Spencer, and am overriding them in the greater interests of the service." MacQuarrie's tone had hardened, but he ignored the admonishing tone. They were letting him get away with a lot this morning, Gilpin thought, but surely he'll regret it later.

Almost unbelievably Spencer had not finished. He clenched his teeth. His face had darkened. "Captain, I really must protest. There are discovery vessels which are responsible for the pursuit of natural history, while as a ship of war I believe we have a duty-"

"LEAVE THE DAMNED SLAVER, DAMN YOU!" thundered the Captain with such rage that Gilpin jumped an inch off the deck. "LET! IT! GO! AND MAINTAIN! YOUR! COURSE!"

"YOU'RE NOT FIT TO COMMAND!" Spencer screamed back. The entire ship fell silent in an instant. "We have a DUTY to take PRIZES. We..." he broke off, sobbing. "When we get home I'll have you cashiered," he burbled, "you're a disgrace!" He turned, first to the officers, then to the crew, staring from the gangways. "This SHIP is a DISGRACE!"

Even Malory was in a dangerous situation at this point and Gilpin thought he looked like a man walking a tightrope over a chasm. The captain had gone a shade of indigo and was trembling volcanically. His bushy whiskers rippled on his temples as his jaws worked the muscles beneath—it would have been comical, the sailing master thought in a detached way, if he did not have the power to kill them all there and then. Spencer had subsided into a quiet grizzle.

"Sir, with your permission," Malory said finally, "I will have Lieutenant Spencer removed and confined to quarters."

"You will not," said the Captain with a voice like the edge of a razor. "You will have *Mister* Spencer removed and placed in the bilboes to await punishment."

Daedalus and The Deep

Spencer's eyes widened with fear and disbelief, yet he said nothing more. Malory's thought-processes almost seemed to be external, Gilpin thought. He could follow the dance the lieutenant was leading himself to manage the situation.

"My man there, master at arms, and you, Granby, take him below," ordered Malory, buying himself a little time. "Captain, Lieutenant Spencer may as an officer wish to opt for a Court Martial. I believe...."

"Yes! Yes! Court Martial!" Spencer shouted. "I'm entitled to-"

"NOTHING!" the Captain interjected. Then, calmly, to the quarterdeck, continued, "he is entitled to nothing. I am stripping him of his commission, and turning him before the mast. He is no longer Lieutenant Spencer, he is Ordinary Seaman Spencer. His pay will be amended to reflect this. And tomorrow, he shall be subjected to six dozen lashes."

"Six dozen...?" exclaimed Malory, shocked speechless despite himself. Spencer started weeping again, and Gilpin noticed, with some sympathy, a stain spreading on the lieutenant's white trouser front.

"Very well, four dozen, out of respect for his father," answered the Captain. "After all, Lord Godalming's a decent enough fellow, and he has to live with the fact that his son is such a low and filthy creature." Almost cheerily, he turned to address the hands, who by now were as rapt an audience as any Drury Lane actor could hope for. He clapped his hands and rubbed them together.

"You hear that, you fellows? I am, on this quarterdeck, *GOD THE BLOODY FATHER!* You would do well to remember it. Now, back to your posts."

In storms, combat and pursuit of a possible prize, Gilpin had never seen "man o' war's men" move as fast as the crew of the *Daedalus* did just then.

Chapter 20

COLYER, along with the whole ship, was a little shaken at the treatment of Spencer, so her heart was in her mouth when she was called before the captain shortly after the lieutenant—the *former* lieutenant—had been led away.

However, it turned out that the brief appointment was simply to inform Colyer that she would now be Acting Fourth Lieutenant once again. The captain barely sounded more enthusiastic about it than he had the previous occasion all that time ago off Borneo, and there was an added lecture about discipline and loyalty which she had to endure. Lambert lent her a spare hat to replace her midshipman's cap.

But soon it was back to business. Malory gathered the officers and informed them that the captain intended to beat to quarters, and fire on the sea-serpent with spider shot when the ship had worked into a position where its broadside guns could be brought to bear. Colyer would retain her post in the foretop for now—there wasn't time to prepare one of the other midshipmen, and besides, Malory didn't trust them enough.

The swivel guns mounted on the fighting tops would be supplied with both grape shot and half-pound round shot. The guns would come into play if the serpent attacked the ship, or they were able to put the ship alongside the beast as if boarding a hostile ship. Colyer didn't think the small weapons would be much use to them if the creature got that close, but it felt better to have something to fire at it. After having seen Panna's aim throwing harpoons, she was doubly pleased that he was sharing her post.

In addition, the entire ship's company of marines would be stationed around the deck fully armed with muskets. Finally, as a last resort, the master at arms had issued any seamen not occupied working the guns or the ship with pikes and cutlasses. It was a bloodthirsty appearance that the *Daedalus* took on as they prepared to meet the creature again.

They had definitely gained on the beast. Even with their efforts to gain ground to windward, they had pulled much further alongside too. Both serpent and ship now sailed on a near-parallel course, with *Daedalus* to windward. The ship's boats had already been swung out and were currently trailing in a line behind the corvette like a brood of ducklings swimming after their mother. MacQuarrie decided to clear for action but wait until the gunner had got the range and bearing right before beating to quarters. After the dull hours they had spent at their posts to absolutely no purpose when chasing the slaver in the Indian Ocean, Colyer was grateful for that.

"Come on Colyer," said Malory, "let's see if your idea works." They moved to the rail. Beneath them on the gun deck, the gunner was preparing one of the 32-pounder broadside guns. It was loaded with a 'spider'—a five-armed star made out of chain, with each arm tipped with a small iron ball. When fired from a cannon it would whip through the air, tangling and tearing any cordage or sails. If it could be made to wrap around the long, narrow neck, could it kill or injure the serpent sufficiently for them to recover it?

The foremost gun boomed, and Colyer briefly saw a blurred, rapidly rotating shape swirling through the air. It skipped on the water throwing up a little puff of spray, somewhat short of the serpent. The creature did not respond to the shot—its neck could be seen poking out of the water, down to leeward.

There was a further pause—evidently the gunner was raising the cannon's elevation and tweaking its bearing. After some minutes, the gun boomed out again. The spider still fell short. The acting lieutenant heard the captain snarl in annoyance, and Malory shifted awkwardly next to her. There was precious little of this specialist type of shot to waste throwing it into the sea. Although they would normally expect more than two shots to find the range and bearing of a distant target, the fact that the first efforts had been so far from the mark did not augur well.

Midshipman MacLeod emerged from the gun deck and trotted over to the captain. "Mister Peddle's compliments, Sir, and he inquires whether it is possible to close the distance. He says that the...windage?...of the spider shot is reducing its range, Sir".

With a few orders passed between captain, first lieutenant and sailing master, the helmsman put the wheel up and for around ten minutes the *Daedalus* bore down gradually on the sea-serpent. Colyer sneaked a look at the creature, noticeably closer now. It was still ploughing on, forging through the waves in the same constant direction. She wondered idly if it was migrating to spawn—there had to be some purpose to the ruler-straight course it had maintained since they had first encountered it? She committed the thought to memory and made a mental note to share the theory with Gilpin when this action was over.

The gunner tried again, initially deliberately aiming behind the serpent—evidently he did not want to scare it with splashes ahead, though surely the creature knew what they were about since the episode with the harpoons?

The next test shot fell directly in line with the serpent's course, and a little behind where they estimated its tail ended. There was a pause for a few moments while the gunner was apparently moving along the gun deck beneath her feet, laying each gun individually.

Midshipman McLeod reappeared and informed the captain, "Mister Peddle sends his compliments, Sir, and wishes to inform you that he is about to fire the first broadside, which will be composed of standard spider shot from the armoury and the new ammunition made to Mister Lambert's specifications, Sir."

"Very well, thank you, Mister McLeod. Malory!" the captain shouted, "Hands to quarters."

"Aye aye, Sir," acknowledged the first lieutenant, "Beat to quarters!"

A long drum-roll from the two marine drummers announced that the crew was to assume battle stations. Colyer scaled the foremast rigging once again, shortly followed by Panna who had brought the powder and shot for the swivel gun. She noticed he had already lashed a harpoon to the post in front of the mast doubling, clearly wanting to leave nothing to chance. They chatted for a while companionably, waiting for the first broadside.

"I was happy when I heard you got your step, Sir," he said genuinely.

"Thank you, Panna," she smiled, "but I think it had more to do with Spencer disgracing himself."

"Reckon you deserve it. You do twice as much as them le'tenants and the mids don't do nothing at all."

Daedalus and The Deep

"Don't let any of them hear you say that, Panna," she grimaced, pleased nonetheless. "Else you'll be flogged again instead of Spencer."

He looked thoughtful at that, then sceptical. "Don't reckon the lads would stand for that," he said. "Not about me that is, I mean not seeing Spencer flogged. Ain't every day they get to see an officer beaten."

She was surprised at that. Were they really so bloodthirsty? "Do they hate officers that much?" she asked.

"No, just the bad ones!" he chuckled. "If a ship's got good officers, means it runs smooth like, plenty o' food, prize money sometime. And some of the men likes to see a flogging now and then, s'long as it ain't them."

She raised her eyebrows. This could be a violent world, for all the beauty and freedom.

"Don't care f'rit meself though," he said gently, looking out to sea. "I know what it feels like."

The first broadside roared out, to be followed by a strange, receding *whip-whip-whip* noise as the spiders cut through the air. A row of white feathers sprang up on the water, and were carried away by the breeze. She pulled her telescope out and looked across to the spot where the sea serpent had been. It had raised its pointed nose to the sky and seemed to be waving its head about, but looked unharmed. She kept her gaze on it and saw that its course had started to diverge from their own.

"Deck there!" she called. "Serpent altering course two points to the South!"

Her report was acknowledged, and she felt the ship begin to swivel beneath her to stay on a parallel track, while the waisters adjusted the trim of the sails. Below the top, she heard the foreyard creak round on its parrels.

"Reckon you'll make a good officer, pardon my boldness le'tenant," Panna said a little nervously. She did not know what to say, so remained silent. "You cares about the men, but you knows when to take risks."

"Really?" she answered, surprised. "I think I just...do what it looks like I need to do."

"Thass it, Sir," he said.

A second broadside rang out, and Colyer saw the deadly spinning chains slingshot towards the serpent. At least two spiders struck the water right above where she estimated its body must be, but its neck had been missed by the projectiles. A stripe of turbulence in the water revealed that the serpent's long form was now undulating powerfully beneath the water, and it seemed to be drawing ahead slightly once more. Perhaps it had not been so badly hurt by the harpoons as they thought.... She reported the change to the deck once again.

Then a third broadside ripped out, and one of the long 'Lambert Spiders' (as Douglas had teasingly taken to calling them) struck the serpent full across the neck, four feet below its head. The iron balls wrapped the chain several times around the throat like a bolas.

Through her telescope she could make out the creature whipping desperately. A good third of its length must have been out of the water, and it flexed so hard it had become a blur of motion. For a moment, every man on the ship that had a clear sight line to leeward watched, anxiously. For thirty seconds, the creature twisted and lunged in all directions.

My God, we've throttled it! thought Colyer, for a moment willing the serpent to break free before remembering which side she was supposed to be on. She noticed Panna had slipped the string of beads out of his pocket once again and was silently mouthing something.

There was a sound like a pistol shot.

Colyer saw fragments of something flickering in the sun and arcing away from the serpent's neck, causing a pattering like rain in the sea around it.

It had broken the chains like rotten string.

The serpent shook its head and looked right at the ship. Then it pointed its snout to the sky again, threw open its jaws and howled.

If the sound they had heard when they had impaled it with harpoons was a scream, this was a roar. It turned in the ship's direction and began thundering towards them.

She heard Malory yelling. "Master, haul your wind! No, belay that, there's no time. Hit it again! Not the spider-shot, ball, chain, bar—any bloody thing you can load!" She could see frenetic activity through the large central coaming in the spar deck which opened up to the gun deck below—guns being run in, cartridges passed round, gun to gun, shot pulled from garlands. Kane, captain of marines called, "Marines, form line! Load muskets!" from the spar deck. The bow and stern chasers were being hauled onto something like the right path and hastily loaded.

And all the time, the creature was forging in their direction, eyes glittering, mane flowing in the steady wind.

A broadside crashed out, and Colyer felt the vibration up the mast of the ten 32-pounders, some of them double-shotted, firing almost as one at minimum elevation. The sea tore up into a ragged welter of spray. And through the curtain of pummelled water as it rained back into the sea, the serpent swam, as if immune to their shot. The two 56-pounder deck guns fired independently, adding to the cacophony and the hail of shot.

"Reload with case-shot, grape and cannister!" shouted Malory clearly, recovering a little of his famous composure.

"We should get the swivel gun ready," Colyer remembered, but Panna had already begun to load it with a cartridge and grapeshot.

The sound of the 32-pounders thumped out in a cascade along the ship as yet another broadside was fired. This time the case shot raised a barrages of tiny splashes as the shrapnel and musket balls were flung into space. The serpent seemed to dodge between the shots, almost dancing on the water, its neck bending this way and that to avoid the worst of the storm of sharp-edged destruction.

"Boarding pikes and cutlasses!" shouted Malory. Idle men who had until moments before been stock still, eyes wide at the sight before them, picked up some weapon or other they had been issued with but never thought they would need to use.

Still the serpent came on. There was an intelligence to its movements, and a determination that chilled Colyer's heart. It was now no more than a couple of hundred yards off, but that meant point-blank range for the cannon. She looked on with horror as the grapeshot ripped into the serpent's flesh. It screamed out, and was knocked back several yards each time a blast of hot gas and flying shrapnel battered it, but recovered and continued to thunder towards the corvette's flank.

Someone was trying ball shot, and the heavy, solid projectiles pounded into the waves around the creature, but trying to hit such a small target even at this range smacked of desperation. Perhaps the guns were running low on ready-use case shot? As if in confirmation, the distinctive whirling shape of bar-shot could be seen skimming away from the ship during the next broadside.

"Stand by to tack ship!" yelled Malory after a swift conference with MacQuarrie. Colyer's jaw dropped. This was high risk. If the ship was caught in stays again, they were done for. But she understood: they wanted to switch to the starboard battery—the men of the port battery were evidently tiring.

The *Daedalus* staggered through the eye of the wind, and for a few horrible minutes the ship's momentum fell away, losing ground to the onrushing sea serpent. Over the sound of the sails clattering round onto the port tack, the serpent could be heard screaming again, angrily, as it swerved to meet the ship's new course.

The men of the starboard battery, kicking their heels until that moment, eagerly began their own rapid-fire, getting in two tight, closely-bunched broadsides before the serpent had regained the distance it had lost after the tack.

By now she could see the wounds criss-crossing the serpent's flesh where pieces of case shot had gouged it. Dark fluid seeped from a hundred cuts, and its once-proud mane was shredded in places. It was moving more slowly now, and its head seemed to hang. But still it pushed towards them.

One more broadside pounded along the flank and when the smoke cleared, the serpent's head towered over the deck. The marines raised their muskets, and behind them a ragged line of sailors brandished pathetic-looking hand-to-hand arms. Kane shouted "Aim!"—but the serpent had not pounced. Instead, its head began to sag, and after a moment, was tumbling towards the sea as the creature's long neck unfurled. With a hollow smack that sent a feeble ripple lapping against the hull of HMS *Daedalus*, the sea serpent fell back into the water and lay motionless alongside the corvette.

A tired cheer rose up from the men on deck, and was strengthened by those on the gun deck as soon as they realised what had happened. Wisps of smoke floated dreamily away on the wind, and the dark stain in the water by the serpent's head started to dissipate.

Colyer breathed a deep sigh. The pursuit was finally over. She felt no triumph that the sea serpent had been killed—just relief that an arduous task was over, and the next stage of their voyage home could begin.

Daedalus and The Deep

"Get that thing secured before the sharks get a sniff of it!" yelled the captain, and after a series of instructions passed around by the bosun and sailing master, soon men were rushing about the deck with coils of rope, oars and boathooks to start the business of pulling the serpent's body up out of the water. He turned from the bulwark, and raised his arms dramatically.

"We did it, boys!" he called. "Double rum ration for all men as soon as the beast is secured!"

A louder cheer rang around the ship, as the men rushed to do what they could to bring the serpent's inert bulk aboard. She smiled to see the bosun and sailing master in earnest discussion as to how it could be stowed—the bosun even gestured a circular motion, as if the serpent was nothing more than a giant cable to be coiled down on deck!

Fore and aft, and at the waist, men began working looped lines over the form of the sea serpent, which was now completely still apart from a slight ripple imparted along its length by the gentle swell. The men leaned out to begin to draw the lines tight. Then...

Seemingly without any pause to tense muscles or gird itself, the sea serpent flicked its entire length, scattering the men working at the rail, and threw its front half onto the gangway with a mighty, creaking crunch of protesting timber.

In that time the creature had already grabbed one seaman whose back had been turned at the moment it sprang back into life. The creature crunched down on the sailor's body, and shook it almost casually, before opening its jaws slightly and letting the shredded mass fly. The bloody corpse smacked into a group of men that had been backing away, knocking three or four to the deck and leaving dark red stains splashed on the holystoned planks.

This broke the spell and a welter of pistol and musket fire rattled out. Kane had started bellowing orders, trying to get the line of marines re-formed. But the creature had moved so quickly it was hard to take in. It was darting with insect-like speed and agility, completely at odds with an animal as long as the largest whales. It didn't seem to be troubled by the few shots that came anywhere near it, as it flopped and thrashed across the deck, crushing the bulwark, ripping rigging lines loose and stoving deck planks in.

Most of the weapon fire was barely aimed—some was not aimed at all, and as men tried to fire and retreat, Colyer heard a musket ball ping off the mast within feet of her, and another crunch into the fighting top's planking directly beneath her feet.

At that moment, Panna let out a yelp and his right arm flew upwards spasmodically. He had been aiming the swivel gun and something had smashed his hand against it, the ship trembled and he crumpled sideways, sliding over the edge of the platform.

Colyer yelped too as she threw herself at the edge. She would have missed him but as he tumbled he had grabbed hold of the rim of the wooden platform.

She grabbed Panna's wrist just below where his hand had clamped onto the lip of the platform. He swung slowly, the mangled remains of his free hand releasing a red spatter which tumbled wetly into the air. His eyes looked back into hers, big and wide and dark. Not a sound escaped his lips. She tried to pull at his arm but with his weight against her strength, she could not move him by the tiniest fraction of an inch. "Try to get your other arm up!" she pleaded. He just looked at her. She saw he was bleeding from a wound in his head as well.

"COLYER!" A yell from the deck. She wrenched a look down, not loosening her grip on Panna. With a shudder she saw the serpent had shuffled halfway up the foremast rigging behind her. Its flanks, dark and wet as rotting leaves, pulsated as it wriggled higher. The ship groaned and started to lean under the weight.

"SHOOT THE BASTARD THING! SHOOT IT!!" Malory's voice was a shrill knife through the air. The speaking trumpet made it a howl. "NOW, DAMN YOU!"

She looked at Panna once more, her grip tight as ever.

And then, seemingly without having moved at all, she was standing at the swivel gun, training it down into the creature's face, her fingers sliding on Panna's blood where his hand had been against the breech.

The serpent looked back up at her, its dead eyes brimming with cold malice. It opened its long mouth slightly, revealing ranks of small teeth like darts. She tugged at the lanyard.

The packet of pistol shot burst and ripped into the creature's muzzle and eyes at near point-blank range. It immediately jumped free of the rigging, emitting a thin whine, twisted its great length like a salmon leaping a rapid and speared into the water. The foremast quivered horribly with the load suddenly released—the midshipman leapt back across the fighting top but Panna had already gone. The lascar's limp form pinged away from the platform, and she had time to see him crack the fore-yard and spin toward the waist coaming, which he hit with a liquid thud.

Colyer stared, catatonic, as the figures of Panna's shipmates rushed to the inert form lying twisted on the planks below.

Chapter 21

THERE was damage to repair, and wounded men to see to. There was even a man to bury. But, no sooner had the rig been put back into some form of working order, and those with light injuries returned to duty, than the captain ordered the ship hove-to, and hands mustered to witness punishment.

Gilpin at first thought he had misheard, but the shocked expression on the faces of the other officers revealed that he had not.

Malory cleared his throat, somehow making it sound apologetic. "Might I post additional lookouts, Sir? Just in case the serpent should reappear?"

"You may not," the captain replied haughtily, "if the beast should dare to trouble us during punishment, it is clearly more savage than an Irishman, and I do not believe such a thing to be possible. In any case, I doubt it shall come back so soon after the narrow escape it had. No, we shall catch up with it in due course."

Gilpin wondered if the captain had been watching at all during the recent engagement. He did not think it was the *serpent* that had had a lucky escape. For that matter, he wondered if the captain realised where the quarter of his crew with distinctly Hibernian accents came from...

While a grating was being rigged in the waist, Malory discreetly approached several officers and warrant officers who would be stationed at various points around the ship, bidding them keep a weather eye open lest their adversary return.

Spencer was brought up. Since his outburst on the quarterdeck he had been confined on the lower deck, his feet locked into the iron brackets attached to the deck, known as bilboes. He had not even been let out during the last battle with the sea serpent, and Gilpin could only imagine the effect that could have had on even the strongest-minded.

As the former officer was led to the grating, Gilpin reflected on how the scenario usually went. Some ranted and raved and tried to wrench away from the guards, some accepted their punishment quietly but their heads held high, a very few sobbed and wailed. But never had he seen someone with so little will as Spencer seemed to possess at that moment. His spirit had not just been broken—it had been expunged.

His shirt was stripped off and he was lashed to the grating without resistance. The drum roll began, and the lashes started. They were counted out, and after the first dozen, the first boatswain's mate handed over to a second. After the second dozen, the cat was changed. Gilpin glanced at the captain and saw a burning intensity to his gaze that chilled the sailing master—a feeling that increased when he saw the same, hungry glare on the face of each seaman.

Horrified, he though, *this isn't a punishment, it's an invocation. Or a sacrifice.*

After the third dozen, Gilpin could see Spencer's ribs glinting white through the torn muscle and shredded skin.

He had not uttered a sound since the flogging began.

The surgeon's assistant and a loblolly boy held the punished man up by each arm as he hobbled off the deck. The hands still had that bloodthirsty look, but were looking a little bewildered at his silence. Perhaps they had wanted tears or for him to call for his mother. He wouldn't have been the first.

"Like 'ow that feels do ya, ya sod?" came a shout from somewhere in the ranks.

"Silence there!" bellowed Malory.

Spencer had almost reached the companionway. "Bear up Spencer," said Lambert brightly as the man was carried past, his wrecked back uncovered for all to see, "*legum servi sumus ut liberi esse possimus*."

"What *does* that mean?" Granby muttered to Gilpin out of the side of his mouth.

"Eh? Oh, I believe it's something along the lines of '*we are slaves of the law so that we might be free*'. I think Spencer said it to Colyer after the poor lad was beaten when he tried to stand up for Livock."

"Did 'e now? What a snivellin' little bastard. Flogging's too good f'rim."

"You know, I honestly believe he meant it *kindly*," said Gilpin. "For it to be a comfort of some sort. I think when he came aboard he meant well. He just had no idea how to go about it."

The bosun snorted sceptically. Now Gilpin thought of it, Colyer seemed the only one apart from himself who had not been seized by the mania of Spencer's punishment. The acting lieutenant had worn a glazed expression, seeming to be looking at something in the distance.

As soon as Spencer had been taken below, the sailing master expected that the hands would be dismissed and they would continue on their way. Instead, the captain kept the men in place and gleefully read the articles of war in full, paying particular attention to that lengthy list of offences that could have fatal consequences. The spark in MacQuarrie's eye every time he repeated the line "...*shall suffer death*!" sent a shiver through Gilpin.

Once the ship was underway once more, Gilpin ducked below to see how Spencer was doing. He did not care especially for the former officer, but he felt for him, and it seemed that no one else on board held the man's welfare to be the least bit important.

He waited outside the sick bay while the surgeon conversed with the loblolly boy. "Give him some rum for the pain, here's the bottle," Owers was saying. "Give him as much as he'll take, then lay him on his front. We'll wait for the blood to dry before dressing the wound, otherwise it will stick."

Owers emerged from the space, and noticing Gilpin, muttered that he would be back in a few moments, then hurried away. Gilpin sat on a cask and waited.

"Ere's some rum," Gilpin heard the loblolly boy (actually a man in his 20s or 30s) say, before adding, "but the men *drinks too much*, I sez, and it'll do yer good for me to stop your grog, *Ordin'ry Seaman* Spencer. There's a few lads forrard who deserves this more'n you. Now, down on yer chest in yer 'ammock, we wouldn't want any more 'arm to come to that nasty wound now."

After a moment, the loblolly boy stepped out of the sick bay, bottle in hand. He saw Gilpin and looked him in the eye for a moment, challenging. When it was apparent Gilpin didn't mean to stop him, he ducked past.

Gilpin entered. Even in the dim light of the sick bay the effect of the whipping was still horrific, and the little room smelt of iron and salt. Spencer would be confined to the sick bay for some time. On the other side lay the poor, expiring Panna. The topman still breathed, but there was little anyone could do for him now.

Spencer was laying in his hammock—which he had had to buy from the purser after his banishment to the ranks—on his front with his arms hanging over the sides. Gilpin knelt down so his face was at the same level as Spencer's.

"Spencer, it's me, Gilpin," he whispered lamely. "I know it's bad, but...well, it will feel better soon enough."

Spencer's eyes seemed to gleam with recognition, but without saying a word, or changing his expression, brought his arms inside the hammock, formed a pillow with them, and turned his head away.

Gilpin waited for a few minutes, but started to feel a bleak hollowness that made him creep out of the thick, heavy air of the sick bay and scramble back to the quarterdeck.

"Mister Gilpin," said the captain when he had returned to his post, "I wish to continue Sou' West for a day or two, to see if the sea serpent has the nerve to reappear. If he does, I shall not be denied this time. If not, well.... Our supplies will not last forever and as *Seaman* Spencer was so keen to remind us, we *do* have orders. I shall simply have to bring another ship to these waters. Sou' West Mister Gilpin then, if you please."

Once the course was laid in, Granby sidled over to him.

"You know that saying *'below 40 there's no law, below 50 there's no God'*?" the bosun asked. Gilpin nodded.

"I think the Captain might be a few degrees further South than the rest of us, if y' know what I mean."

Gilpin could only agree, tacitly of course. It was only later that he remembered the last line of the expression.

'Below 60 there's no hope.'

PART 3

THE BATTLE

INTERLUDE

THE *pain was incredible. She had no idea that fighting the creature would be this difficult. Not for the first time the thought crossed her mind that it was too difficult, that it was beyond her. And not for the first time she dismissed the notion completely. Too much rested on her victory. The ancient rules no longer served her people, other than a tiny, corrupt elite. This was the only way she could bring about change. She must fight and defeat the giant creature or die in the attempt.*

She had known it was big. After it had caught and trailed the sharks as all-too-convenient bait, she had known it was clever. In fact she was beginning to believe that the tiny creatures that infested it were not parasites but symbiotes. She was not just challenging a creature, but a colony.

Even so, she was sure that she had got the better of it after it had attacked her with the stabbing prongs. It had hurt—oh, how it had hurt, but she had persuaded the creature that she was weakened. She had even thought it was time to deliver a killer blow, when again she realised how badly she had underestimated her foe.

Indeed, it was only when she had experienced the roaring, flame spitting teeth along its flanks that she realised just how fearsome this creature was besides its size and its brains.

It had flung spinning strands of some hard-edged but flexible fibre that had all but throttled her. It had spat heavy, hard rocks that she felt the force of as they thumped into the water near her.

It had expelled clouds of sharp, tearing fragments that had sliced her flesh and embedded there, so it hurt every time she moved. They were working their way out, but each one was a glowing jewel of agony. And when she had received a blast of tiny pellets in her face after trying to climb up the creature's spines, the agony.... It was like being bitten by a shark so fast you never saw its jaws.

How did it do that? Did it ingest rocks and stones to expel at some attacker? Did it retain the crunched-up bones of sea-beasts it had digested so it could later spray them out?

She put such questions out of her mind. For now, the hunt was on, and it was all that mattered. Both creatures knew there would be no quarter. She was slower now, and her great agility had been blunted by the fearsome onslaught of the beast's spitting fury. It was able to keep pace with her as she swam away, heading doggedly for the heights above her own kind's home.

But she now knew the creature's weakness. It was a beast of the upper air, of space. Never once had it dipped below the threshold into her own atmosphere. It could not hurt her there, and she could exploit the depths below.

Moreover, she could disrupt those creatures that crawled over its body in their mysterious business, even if she could not hurt the beast itself—yet. Maybe it would have to use up energy incubating new symbiotes, or would be unable to function as well when their numbers depleted.

She could feel the turbulence rising in the thin gases of space, through the effects it was having on the waters of her atmosphere. Through the heavy heave of the waves, she could sense a building fury in the gaseous ether above—far, far away but getting gradually closer.

And she would make sure that when the time came she trapped the creature in that turbulence. Perhaps it could not sense such things as she did, and by the time it did it would be too late to flee. With luck her knowledge of the deep might mean the difference between victory and defeat here in space.

Chapter 22

THE lascar topman Panna was still not dead three days after falling from the fore top. The young acting lieutenant, Colyer, had taken the accident terribly hard and spent most of his time off-watch with the lascar. The man would die, there was no question of that. It was just a case of when the broken spring inside him finally wound down. Of course no one was saying that in anything other than a whisper. It didn't seem fair to their shipmate.

His head had taken a serious blow on the foreyard and then again on the waist coaming, which he had connected with as he landed. The skull had virtually collapsed, and his face was a ruin, now wrapped almost entirely in bandages. Gilpin supposed this was as much to save the feelings of his messmates and Acting Lieutenant Colyer than for any healing purposes.

The patient could only be given small amounts of food and drink, and those could only be applied with a funnel and tube down the man's throat. He had also broken his left arm and leg, and the left hand was pulp. It even seemed that the man's wounds had not all been caused by the fall—the surgeon had dug a musket ball out of the ruined flesh of the topman's head and another from his hand.

The worst thing was that the lascar appeared to be conscious some of the time. He couldn't move or speak of course, but his eyes opened and appeared to look around the room. Colyer had demanded to be informed whenever that happened, and when the acting officer was not on watch, rushed to the patient's bedside and spoke reassuringly to him until his eyes fluttered closed again.

It was hard to ignore the presence of the sickbay's other resident. Still, whenever Gilpin had visited, Spencer had barely uttered a word. He seemed to ignore the presence of his replacement completely.

This was just as well. Gilpin had heard tittle-tattle from various sources that when he had begun to heal from the initial shock of the flogging, Spencer had been heard ranting and raving. He had supposedly accused the first lieutenant of all kinds of improprieties, some professional and some...personal. He even seemed to be blaming Malory for perceived slights years ago, which could not be correct—to his certain knowledge, Malory and Spencer had never crossed paths at all until the junior lieutenant was transferred aboard from *Agincourt*.

Gilpin kept an eye on the youth Colyer as much as he could, but the ship still needed repairs which absorbed most of his attention. The fore-mast had jumped partially out of its step when the serpent had climbed up the rigging and then sprung off, overloading it and releasing the weight too quickly. This was not to mention the damage it had done to the shrouds which held the mast upright. He had made a representation to the captain to find land as soon as possible so they could make proper repairs to the step. The charts and his notes showed there was land in the vicinity—Cook had sighted the tops of mountains in the last century and named the island or islands 'Sandwich Land'.

There was no inhabited land for hundreds of miles, possibly thousands. Some sealing and whaling took place in these waters, but it was not really the right time of year for that, and Gilpin was little surprised that they had not sighted a sail since they entered these latitudes. Not much was known about the land in these remote waters, other than the fact that some existed and it was somewhere to their South and West.

Naturally the captain was pushing for the ship to be back to full working order as soon as possible and First Lieutenant Malory was absolutely of one mind with him—although Gilpin wasn't at all sure that it was for the same reasons. He was uncertain if the ship was going to be thrown into another head-to-head fight with the sea serpent, or lick its wounds and begin the long voyage home.

Whichever of those possibilities would triumph, the ship was still heading uneasily South-West under easy sail. As if mirroring the atmosphere on the ship, the weather had over the last few days become dull and uncertain. A smooth, unbroken grey cloud overcast the sky from horizon to horizon, while the wind had dropped to a constant force two, according to the newfangled

Beaufort Scale, and the sea settled to a gentle swell. The whole world around them seemed to be waiting for something to happen.

It was getting colder, to boot. Not so long ago they had been sweltering in the tropical heat of Borneo—and today the men's cold weather clothing had been broken out of the hold.

Malory decided to bury the man who had been killed by the serpent, in the full knowledge that they would likely have to go through the whole rigmarole again in a day or two when Panna died. It seemed that he did not have the heart to appear to Colyer to be waiting for the lascar to expire. Or perhaps he felt that any positive action was better than passively waiting for circumstances to change around them.

Every man was scrubbed, shaved, spruced and turned out in his best clothes. The ship hove to, pitching lazily on the long waves as the sounds of the funeral service drifted over the waters. At least, Gilpin reflected, this felt like it should—the captain taking his role as the father of the crew, healing their wounds and allowing tragedy to bring them together.

MacQuarrie reached the verse from Philippians that inevitably brought a lump to Gilpin's throat. The poetry of the words was as beautiful as the hope they expressed.

"...Christ our saviour, who at his coming shall change our vile body, that it may be fashioned like unto his glorious body, according to the mighty working whereby he is able to subdue all things unto himself. Amen."

The crew muttered "amen" in response, and the body, wrapped in sailcloth and weighted with shot, was committed to the deep.

Later that day, Panna finally expelled his last breath. Colyer was evidently trying hard not to show how much the man's fate had affected him, but Gilpin could see in his eyes that he was crushed. He learned that on the day Panna died, Colyer had approached the topman's messmates to find out if any of them knew anything of Panna's family.

Evidently the men knew very little—this seemed genuine to Gilpin, and not the impenetrable forecastle wall of silence that could sometimes descend between officers and men.

It seemed that forlornly, Colyer had asked to look through Panna's effects. These were pitifully few, and Gilpin doubted that the acting lieutenant would find much enlightenment there.

Gilpin knew Panna from this cruise and the last—knew him to be a steady, reliable hand who was popular, but did not speak

Daedalus and the Deep

much to anyone. It was a surprise to hear that he had a family at all. He knew Panna and Colyer had shared a post in the foretop and had evidently struck up a close friendship. It was always hard the first time you lost a friend in the service, especially now they lived in more peaceful times than when Gilpin had gone to sea so many years ago.

For the second time in two days, the men were turned out, the ship was hove-to, and the captain read the funeral service. When the reading was finished, the men tipped up the plank on which the lascar's shattered remains sat, and the sailcloth-wrapped body slid gently, almost tenderly over the side and into the sea. Gilpin could not bring himself to look at Colyer.

The sailing master scanned across the horizon. It occurred to him that this distant corner of an ocean that spanned the entire Southern Hemisphere might never have seen a burial at sea, and may never do again. Panna's mortal remains might sit on the floor of these remote, Southern depths, undisturbed until the end of time. He did not know whether the thought was comforting or saddening. Suddenly, this expanse of unremitting grey above and below felt a very lonely place. Gilpin had never felt as incongruous in this world in all his years at sea.

The crew felt the tension as well. After the immediate rush of work following the serpent's attack, and the emotion of the two funerals, there was relatively little for most of the men to do. There were numerous false sightings of the sea serpent, which increasingly angered the captain and the first lieutenant. They had beaten to quarters twice to no purpose before MacQuarrie warned the lookouts that they would be flogged if they reported seeing the serpent without being completely sure.

Malory in particular was impatient to effect repairs to the foremast step. The damage meant they could not set much sail on the foremast, which in turn prevented setting full sail on the mizzen or the rig would be impossible to balance. The light winds and limited rig caused the corvette to slop uneasily through the water, displaying none of the tautness and poise that normally made it such a joy to sail.

Gilpin had rarely known as much relief as when the lookout at the mainmast crosstrees shouted that land was visible to the South East. Joyfully the helm was put down and the corvette limped toward the cloud-capped cone that poked smoothly out of the sea many miles distant.

Chapter 23

THE atmosphere aboard the ship was tangible at the best of times. It had not taken Colyer long to realise that even with the separation between officers and men borne of centuries of practice and social structures, it was generally possible to feel a single emotion that characterised the dominant feeling of everyone aboard.

When the sighting of land was announced, and cascaded from mainmast truck to keelson in seconds, that feeling was palpably, childishly joyful.

When the corvette drew close enough to see from the deck what this land was like, that mood ebbed away like a Solent tide to be replaced with something apprehensive, superstitious as only sailors can be. This was a world that appeared to be dead, empty. The island could have been the physical manifestation of Colyer's mental state.

The island rose, smooth-sided out of the sea. From a few miles out, the silhouetted shape transformed slowly into a barren, volcanic rock with little or no vegetation. The soil was almost black, against which thick steam clung permanently. White cloud spilled lazily from a giant, tilted crater which hung, lopsided from the mountain's peak. Patches of snow dotted the upper slopes, the only visible water.

Gilpin had consulted the charts and announced, with some certainty, "this is Sandwich Land, or part of it. We're a little further North than Cook's recorded latitude," he continued, scratching his head, "but I suspect what he saw was a chain of islands, and perhaps only identified the Southern end, as his record speaks of thick fog and generally bad visibility. I estimate we are three hundred or so miles East of the island of Georgia, and the Falkland Islands are a further eight hundred miles beyond."

"No land known here?" asked the captain.

"Not precisely, Sir, no," answered Gilpin, perplexed.

"Very well. It shall be marked in the log as MacQuarrie Land," he stated, in an offhand manner. The officers stared at him.

The captain and Malory elected to circumnavigate the island tentatively, at a distance of a mile or so in case any hidden rocks lay closer in, before trying to find an anchorage. Colyer stood at the rail taking the sight in. The Western flank of the island was by far the steepest, and the huge, leaning crater made up the upper third of the slope. She imagined that at some point in its history, a cataclysmic eruption had blown most of this half of the island away. The other sides of the island declined gently, curving away to form a kind of plain that skirted the Western mountain before sliding gently into the sea. The island was around three miles in length, and a little over a mile and a half wide.

There were no trees or animal life visible on the Western slopes—indeed, the slanting black-brown face looked as if it suffered frequent rock slides and was surely too steep for trees to cling. As they skirted around to the Eastern side of the island to observe its hidden expanses, Malory called out to her. "Mister Colyer, would you be so good as to ascend to the maintruck and look out for anything out of the ordinary? It would be most useful," he added, "if you could identify any areas of woodland, watercourses or signs of animal life."

She saluted, acknowledged the order, and scrambled up the main ratlines, round the futtock shrouds and into the very highest reaches of the ship's rigging. As she scaled higher and higher, she felt some of the care of recent days lift, but then a wave of guilt that brought it all rushing back.

She reached the peak of the topmast and sat down on the capping, astride the topgallant mast, looping her arms around it and pulling out her telescope. The island struck her as a relic of geology rather than a piece of living, breathing land. Slabs of rock on the shattered Northern face, carved vertical by the sea, revealed layers in their substance like rings in a treetrunk. In other places the island rose uniformly from the sea, appearing as nothing more than a vast seabed mountain that happened to penetrate into the air at its very tip. Large blocks of ice floated in the smaller bays. There was no line of surf suggesting the presence of a shelf or reef, as there had been around most of the islands they had encountered in the East.

As they continued to progress around the land, she saw a shiny black mass writhing and swirling on the lower slopes. She recoiled in horror. What new ghastly freak of the natural world was this? She forced herself to look back, carefully focussing the telescope. The mass resolved into a vast flock of black and white birds, crowding across the empty, treeless plain. Oddly, she could only see one or two birds flying around the island, and they were large sea birds, some way off the coast. From the colony, not one bird took off, nor did any arrive and land.

That huge colony was the only sign of life. She could see not so much as a twig of plant life, and no animals other than the black and white birds jostling around the coastal areas. The only water visible was locked in the snow around the higher slopes of the mountain, on the opposite side to the crater.

With a lingering sense of regret, she left her perch high above the world and scaled back down to the deck. She reported her findings, including the huge crowd of birds, and the fact that none were in flight.

Gilpin laughed. "Penguins!" he exclaimed. "I dare say this is a colony of penguins. Ross reported several different Southern species, some rather large."

"Who?" inquired the captain, somewhat abruptly.

"Captain James Ross," answered Gilpin, seemingly insensible to the captain's rudeness. "He led an expedition to the Antarctic regions which returned shortly before *Daedalus* left for Borneo. He discovered incontrovertible proof of an Antarctic continent." The captain merely grunted.

"I wish to represent," Malory suggested, "that we look to anchor in the broad bay on the South West side of the island. I think we should approach under jib, taking soundings all the way in. There's no sign of any reef or rocks beneath the surface, but there's no survey of the area and we should take no chances."

"Indeed," MacQuarrie answered, his mind evidently elsewhere. "See to it, would you, Malory?" He took his leave and disappeared below.

"I'd like to send a party ashore," Malory suggested to Gilpin, "and will seek the captain's assent to do so. If what Mister Colyer says is accurate, we won't find any useful wood ashore, maybe even no streams or springs. Nevertheless, we may be able to top up our water from snow melt if we can reach the upper slopes. Equally, if we can catch some of those birds it could be useful for fresh meat."

"Aye aye, Sir," agreed Gilpin. "I'd like to go myself but the ship requires my attention. Might I recommend the bosun?"

"Very well, but make sure his mates know what is required of them." He looked thoughtful for a moment. "And Mister Colyer should go, he's proved himself resourceful on detached missions in the past." He turned to Colyer. "You would of course be in nominal command, Acting Lieutenant."

"I'll make sure I consult with Mister Granby on all matters, Sir," she responded —she had no intention of doing otherwise. "Mister Gilpin, I'd be grateful if you could spare some time to discuss the arrangements of the shore party when it's convenient," she added.

Gilpin agreed, and Colyer was grateful. It would be good to get off the ship for a while, even if it was only onto this blasted rock. At least now she was an acting officer she needn't worry about putting Holford's and Johnson's noses out of joint, or the potential consequences. Not that she would have cared if they had sulked or played their silly games. There were more important things in life, as she had discovered lately.

They were making their approach now, with a single jib flying out over the bow and a man in the forechains port and starboard.

"Nooooo bottom, noooooo bottom with this line...." the call drifted out until they had reached well into the little bay. Eventually, the leadsman hit the sea floor, which the tallow on the end of the lead revealed was rocky, and the bed began to rise sharply.

Malory decided this spot was adequate, and ordered the best bower dropped. It fell with a reassuring rumble and clank, a sound Colyer felt she had not heard in a very long time. The anchor bit, and the ship fell to silence, or at least as close to silence as the soft lapping of waves, thud of the anchor cable and rap of ropes against the mast would allow.

They would not set foot on the island today. There was too much work to do getting the repairs in hand and it was already mid-afternoon. She retired to the relative calm of the wardroom to think and make some notes about the expedition. It wasn't easy— the sight of Panna's broken body lying on the deck kept creeping back into her mind. Every so often she would find that instead of running through lists of equipment and stores they would need, she was listing the things she could have done to prevent him from falling.

After some ten minutes of attempting to write a single line, she concluded she was unlikely to make much progress this way. She threw her notes and books into her cabin and went to find Gilpin and Granby to discuss arrangements for the shore party.

The sailing master was not on deck. According to Gower, he was forward, seeing to the damaged foremast step with the carpenter and the smith. The entire forward half of the ship was a mass of ropes, spars and activity. The sudden release of tons of weight from the foremast had led to the entire structure twanging like a violin string, and this had caused the heel of the mast to work out of the huge timber that it normally sat in. The 'partners'—wooden chocks that secured the mast at each deck had also sprung free, and could not be replaced until the mast was properly back in its step.

Gilpin and the carpenter had rigged various tackles and connected them to the capstan, which a gang of seamen were now noisily turning. Colyer stayed out of the way, but eyed the proceedings with anxiety. If the heel did not follow the correct path and jumped off the step altogether, it would plunge straight through the hull and sink the ship in minutes. In all likelihood no one below the gun deck would survive.

The men grunted and hauled, the rope creaked and protested, and with a series of thuds and bangs, the huge stub of the foremast crawled the distant inches towards its proper seat.

Mercifully, the tapered foot thumped down into the step, sending a shiver through the fabric of the ship. The men straightened and stretched, the sweat running off them in streams.

Gilpin moved away from the centre of the activity, and spotted Colyer.

"Anything I can do for you Lieutenant?" he asked. He was clearly relieved that the operation had been a success as his mood was lighter than Colyer had seen it for days.

"Just trying to get things ready for the expedition," she replied. "But you appear to be busy!"

"I always have time for you, Mister C," he grinned. "Now I have avoided sinking the ship, I can start to devote my thinking to other things. Shall we ascend to the spar deck?"

"Yes, let's," she replied. "But...I don't mean to presume but shouldn't we have...I don't know, sent everyone on deck who wasn't needed down here?"

"Possibly," he mused. "But the water's freezing around here, no one could live on that island, and there's three hundred miles of the Southern Ocean between us and the next remotely habitable land. Which is Georgia, itself a relatively barren place. I've seen what happens to men in those circumstances. No," he concluded, "better to go quickly."

She retreated into silent wonder. This voyage was becoming stranger with every passing day, and yet each new strangeness just had to be accepted, and come to terms with.

The foremast rigging had slackened somewhat once the heel had been re-seated, and the next task was to bring the shrouds into tension, equally so the mast did not bend to one side or the other. Or so Colyer thought.

"We ought to inspect the mast again to make sure it hasn't sprung," said Gilpin.

"Haven't we already done that?" Colyer asked.

"We have, but a mast under tension can hide cracks and splits. Now it's back in place we should go over it again. I'd rather not have to fish it if we can avoid it, but better that than merrily sail off with a split foremast."

Colyer could not but agree. It was her post when in action, and she did not feel like going into battle with a suspect mast beneath her.

"Would you help me check it?" Gilpin asked. "With two of us we can work up each side, it won't take as long."

She spent the next hour hanging from a bridle under her arms, scrambling up the mast a bit at a time, checking for cracks, splintering and splits. Gilpin ascended the opposite face of the mast. Both of them were suspended from ropes reeved through blocks attached to the fighting top, which led back to two groups of stout gun crew men who took their weight as they ascended.

When they had painstakingly reached around thirty feet off the deck, Gilpin cleared his throat. "I gather you took the death of

Seaman Panna very hard," he said conversationally, hidden by the mast. "How are you bearing up?"

That question came like a slap to Colyer. She had carried her grief within her until that point. It seemed like no one else's business. But Gilpin clearly did not mean the question unkindly, and he was a man she felt she could talk to, up to a point. She took several breaths before deciding not to deflect the enquiry.

"I let him fall," she said simply.

"I don't believe that to be the case, Mister Colyer," Gilpin replied. "From where I was standing, it appeared you tried to save him even with the serpent crawling up the rigging toward you."

"I.." *It wasn't as simple as that.* "He saved my life. A few days before. I was falling and he saved me. When he was falling…"

"He was a good seaman," Gilpin broke in. "And I think if faced with the same circumstances you were, he would have done the same thing."

"But…"

"I've lost shipmates before," the sailing master interrupted, "and you always go over everything in your mind—everything you did, everything you could have done differently. That's well—it means that next time you might be able to act quicker, or think of another alternative. Or you might not. But you can't change the past."

"I know, I know…" Colyer admitted. "But…there are…he told me he had a family in Ceylon, and I don't know how…. They might never find out what happened to him."

"That's another fact of life in the Navy, I'm afraid," Gilpin sympathised. "Men might leave some note about their next of kin behind, and they may not. They know what naval life is like, that they could be gone in a moment even in fair conditions. I know Seaman Panna had sailed with this ship on two successive commissions, and he had come straight from another ship."

"That's right, and he'd been a whaler before that."

"So he hadn't seen his family in a long time. I dare say there's reasons for that too."

"He said…" Colyer recalled the conversation in the foretop, not yards from where she was now. The pain on Panna's face. "He had done some things in the past. I think he was trying to make up for them."

"That's not an uncommon thing for us sailors either. The ocean is a big place, plenty of places to escape, and always room for a man who can pull on a rope."

"No. I know. But..." She dragged the thoughts out. How would her family feel if she died on this ship? The chances were that they would never find out. She pictured Panna's wife and child, knowing he had run from all his responsibilities, not knowing where he was in the world or whether he had spared them a second thought. She just wanted to tell them what he was like, what a...*decent* man he was. That he never put himself before anyone else. "He died before he could...I don't know—put things right, I suppose."

"Hmm," considered Gilpin. "Do any of us ever really tie up all the loose ends? It's a rare man that leaves nothing undone. But you say he saved your life?"

"Well, yes."

"He saved another man's life. That's an achievement for anyone—'greater love hath no man'. Something to weigh in the scales?"

"But I'm not..." she cut herself off.

"Not what? Not *worth it*?"

She smiled wanly. It was hard not to be swayed by Gilpin's relentless reasoning, even as she had nearly slipped up.

"Look," he went on, "we can look in the ship's books before we get home, and it could be that he left an address, or something we can follow up. You may get your chance to do right by his family. Now, we'd better go over that section again, I think."

She took several breaths. "I think you're right," she responded finally.

Chapter 24

"Pull...pull...pull..." The *Daedalus*' gig and pinnace both rowed steadily into the bay followed at a distance by the launch, the corvette dwindling behind them. They rowed gently, placing no needless exertion on the men, even though the state of the sea was calm and only a moderate breeze blew. In fact, the island now masked them from the prevailing Westerly wind, though the gentle conditions they had experienced since sighting the island were not what anyone expected from the Southern Ocean. Most of the men expressed the belief that by the time they were ready to return, they would be pulling through a six-foot swell and force eight winds.

The penguin colony could be heard from the ship as a sort of low buzz, but as the boats approached, it grew and grew in intensity. The sound became a squawking chatter, then a barking roar. Although the thickest concentration of birds was on the plain beyond the shore, it was apparent that there were still hundreds, if not thousands, of birds on the beach.

The boats approached, and Granby gave the command to toss oars, letting the low waves carry the pinnace the last few yards onto the shore. Casting a glance at the lieutenant's boat, he saw Colyer had done the same in the gig. Men in the bow jumped into the foaming backwash and held the boat. He ordered the others out, and to drag the heavy craft as far as they could up the black sand of the beach.

The launch, following shortly behind, disgorged a party of men into the surf who began manhandling a number of heavy water casks out of the boat, which then backed off and turned back toward the ship. The midshipman in command raised a hand and Granby acknowledged it as the sailors waded out of the sea.

He looked around. On the other side of the island, the volcanic mountain poked lazily into the sky. Fluffy, white puffs of steam had drifted over the peak and wreathed the mountain top. From this distance, with the great plain stretching away in the intervening space and perspective reducing its height, the mountain looked innocuous enough; not the dominant feature that it was from the sea.

He surveyed their immediate surroundings. There was nothing on the beach to secure the boats to, so they would have to use the anchors. Colyer's crew was already doing that, stretching both of the gig's anchor cables over the sand and driving the flukes as hard into the soil as they could. In a while they could bring the boats properly up the beach, out of the reach of the tide or high waves.

On the beach, small clusters of penguins stood, regarding them and uttering their strange chattering call. They did not look pleased, nor did they look in the least bit scared by the men and their boats.

"Will I start clubbing a few a' they birds?" asked a seaman, incredulous that their prey should just stand and watch, conveniently awaiting their fate while the men secured the boats.

"Not yet, Palmer," Granby decided. "They ain't scared of us at the moment but if we go wading in they might clear out. No, we'll let 'em get used to us first. P'raps we can bag a few of 'em tomorrow."

"Ah, a'right," Palmer agreed, clearly disappointed. "If yer think they'll still be 'ere."

Granby could have split his sides at that, but controlled himself. The thought that a million or more flightless birds might find a way to absent themselves from a three mile long island in the space of one night was laughable. He took a closer look at the birds. They were around two feet in height, a deep, glossy black on their back, which switched abruptly to white, or very pale grey, on their front half. From a distance they appeared to be smooth-skinned, but closer up it was apparent that they were covered in a short but dense fur. They had a distinctive black strip under their chins which gave them the impression of wearing a black hood tied tightly to their heads. Most of them simply stood still, but occasionally one would choose to move from one loose grouping to another, and its waddling, side-to-side walk with its stunted wings outstretched for balance was nothing short of comical.

They rigged some canvas shelters along the top of the beach and pulled the boats above the tide line. Now it was time to explore. He approached Colyer to form a plan of action, picking his way along the beach between clusters of verbose penguins, which uttered their sharp, staccato call at him as he passed.

"I'd recommend dividing the party into three groups, Sir," suggested Granby raising his voice above the cacophony. "One to remain and finish establishing the camp, a second to work around the coast and a third to strike out across the plain towards the mountain."

"That sounds sensible," Colyer responded. "How would you advise we divide the party up? I'd like to take the third group," the officer quickly added, unable to fully mask his enthusiasm.

"Aye, I thought y'might, Sir," the bosun smiled. "All right, in that case I'll volunteer to lead the second group..."—Colyer nodded in agreement—"and we can leave Woodman in charge o' the shore party."

"Agreed. If I might suggest that the priorities for the plain group are to look for water and, unlikely as it may sound, any trees or animal life," offered the young officer. "The coastal group can look for driftwood and any other creatures that might dwell on or around the beach." His tone was firm, but Granby noticed a questioning glance from the lieutenant, giving him the chance to offer advice if he had seen something Colyer might have missed.

"Aye, Sir," Granby nodded in response. It was refreshing, the bosun thought, to come across an officer who was willing to accept his experience and take it at face value. There were those, he considered, unwittingly bringing Spencer to mind, who felt that the very fact of seniority of rank conferred upon them a greater knowledge and skill in every area than those below them in station.

"By the way," the lieutenant added, breaking into his thoughts, "what sort of creatures do you expect we might find along the beach?"

"Seals I 'spect, if anything," Granby replied. "Why d' you ask le'tenant?"

"Well, I brought along a few of the harpoons we had made up for the serpent," Colyer said. "I wondered if they would be any use to you. I'll take one, but I can't imagine we'll need more than that."

"Good, that'd be helpful, Sir, thank you. Well, we might as well make a start like. If y'd like to pick which of your boat's crew you'd like t' go with you and which to stay with the shore party, I'll do the same. Likewise with the men who came with the launch."

"Very well," Colyer agreed. "We'll divide supplies and aim to set out within the hour."

The officer started to gather his things to leave, but Granby cleared his throat. Colyer looked up.

"What did you have in mind about keeping the parties in contact?" he asked, adding "and signalling if we needs any support?"

The lad coloured briefly before recovering his composure.

"Er, well...three evenly spaced shots if we need any help?"

"Aye, Sir, that should do it. And we'll aim to be back at camp...?"

"Rendezvous no later than..." Granby watched the boy thinking. The ship's bell might not be audible at any great distance, and none of them had watches.

"No later than sundown," concluded Colyer, looking pleased with himself.

"Aye, Sir," answered Granby with a wry smile, knuckling his forehead.

It was indeed less than an hour before the groups of fifteen men under Granby and Colyer set out, the acting lieutenant's group striking out into the empty interior of the island carrying a number of small empty water and rum kegs, and the bosun's party following the line of the shore carrying harpoons and clubs.

As the bay curved to the North and East, the men found themselves walking out of the greatest concentration of penguins. There were still substantial pockets though, which Granby estimated must number in the thousands. The noise had certainly not abated.

This pattern continued for the next half hour or so, until Granby estimated they must be approaching the Eastern extremity of the bay. Some way ahead of them, they could make out a spur of rock that thrust into the Southern Ocean. Before they reached this, however, the group of penguins just ahead of them started squawking louder than ever, and attempting a waddling run up the beach.

Without any other warning than the penguins' sudden movement, a dark shape the size of a man burst out of the sea and flopped onto the dark sand. The shape roared and started to shuffle rapidly up the beach, pushing itself awkwardly with flippers on its shoulders and flapping its stubby tail as penguins scattered away from it. It snapped its jaws at the birds, but they were all now out of reach.

The men of Granby's party had started as one at the eruption from the sea, and had automatically assumed defensive positions, brandishing weapons.

"A sea-leopard!" the bosun exclaimed. The large seal was slate-grey across its upper surfaces, with a pale-grey throat spotted with dark blotches. It spotted the men and roared at them, its wide-open jaws lined with long, sharp teeth. The penguins were forgotten—the seal might not know what the men were, but it took them for competitors.

"Move round behind it!" hissed Granby at a couple of the seamen, one of whom was carrying a harpoon. He took another harpoon from a man standing nearby, and moved gradually towards the sea-leopard, jabbing its barb towards the animal's head. The rest of the men began to creep into a cordon around it.

The sea-leopard snarled and bared its teeth at Granby. He continued to prod his harpoon in the direction of the seal, which hunched itself down but did not retreat.

"Now!" he shouted, and the sailor who had moved into position behind the seal thrust his harpoon hard and fast, shoving the barbed tip down through the back of the animal's neck. The sea-leopard screamed and flailed, snapping its jaws at any of the men it could see. Blood poured out of its mouth, but it continued to threaten, trying to drag itself down toward the sea.

"Again!" shouted Granby, moving in himself. After a feverish few minutes of stabbing with the harpoons, the bloody corpse of the seal lay still, its blood seeping freely into the dark grey sand.

In that manner, they killed another four seals, which they left high up the beach, under canvas and protected by a single sailor, to collect on their way back. Presently though, the beach ended and the coast became a bare, rocky series of tongues thrusting into the ocean. They picked their way along the rocks, moving a little inland as the going became more difficult.

There was little that Granby could make out between the territory around the camp and the land they were traversing now that was different. After a while, however, they saw the heartening vision of green on the plain beyond them. It turned out to be a thin growth of wiry grass and moss, but it was plant life nonetheless. Nothing they could eat though. The rock had been shaped by the wind into an expanse of ripples and grooves. Any soil that formed, Gilpin saw, would immediately blow away, other than in the deepest crevices. Even for the grass and moss, it was a tenuous existence—but at least it meant there should be some fresh water to be had. Colyer ought to have been able to find enough to add to the ship's dwindling supply.

There was little sense in continuing with his own party, Granby thought, trying to separate his suspicion of this strange, isolated land from the requirements of the service. The terrain had not revealed anything new, and it appeared that there was a ready supply of food to be obtained from the beach in the vicinity of their landing. He had no idea if penguin was edible, but at least they should be able to top up the ship's supplies with seal meat.

With a certain relief, he turned his party around and began the walk back to the boats.

Chapter 25

COLYER'S party had found little in the way of life, but they had found water. After some hours walking, the gradient had increased distinctly, and they had noticed a number of tiny trickles running across the rock. Later, they found a larger stream, running down the mountain in a deep runnel in the rock. The number of small streams surprised Colyer. Surely there could not be so many springs on this arid slope? It was only when she looked further up the mountain that she concluded that the water was melted snow or ice from the vast white cap that capped the summit of the peak. The water must trickle down in tiny rills that steadily joined to form streams, only to evaporate or seep into the rock further down.

The water appeared clean, so they started to fill the kegs from the larger watercourse. It would do for their own supplies, and they could come back later to top up the ship's supplies in earnest.

When the containers were full, she gave the party a short rest. Looking out over the island, their vantage point seemed higher than she had imagined—the shallow increase in the slope had masked just how far above the coastal plain they had climbed. The rocky apron stretched away on all sides except immediately behind, where the mountain continued to rise. She could see the penguin colony only as a dark, slightly-mobile mass down by the sea. Beyond, the ship floated as a tiny speck, its masts only just visible, on the grey sea.

It was an impressive view. She knew if they climbed to the shoulder of the mountain, they would be able to see much further, and possibly into the volcano's crater as well. It was getting late though, and she wanted to be back before dark. She made some notes in her journal, roused the men and started the journey back. When she caught up with Granby again, she would try to persuade him of the benefits of a sortie to the edge of the mountain.

Back at the landing point, it was clear that both parties had been successful. Meanwhile, the master's mate, Woodman, had overseen the completion of the camp so they would all be able to spend the night under some cover.

"We should send the carcasses and water back to the ship tomorrow morning," Colyer suggested, "and collect some more empty casks."

"Aye, Sir," said Granby. "P'raps we should try one of the seal carcasses this evening though—just to see whether it's edible like, and if it's worth killing any more of 'em."

"Good idea," Colyer agreed, tempted by the prospect of fresh meat. "Tomorrow we can try again if the seal is palatable, and perhaps bag some penguins as well. Seals won't top the stores up fully, if the number we've seen so far is any guide."

"Right y' are, Sir," said Granby. "If the birds is edible too, we should be able salt enough meat down to see us to Gib."

The seal was edible and, indeed, quite pleasant, with the blubber particularly fine. During the evening they planned out the following day's strategy. A hand-picked sealing party would set out along the beach, while another group would ferry the stores gathered so far back to the ship and then turn their attentions to slaughtering penguins. Colyer was not relishing that. She had become quite fond of the little creatures once she was used to the racket they made, but Granby and his party already had experience of tackling the sea-leopards so she conceded that it made perfect sense for him to lead that party. She had found it relatively easy to wring out of him an agreement to take a small party of men to the other side of the mountain. In fact, he agreed to come too, if slightly reluctantly. When they had finished their work, they would spend half a day on a quick exploration.

Colyer went to bed feeling, if not happier, then at least more purposeful than she had since Panna died.

...And jerked awake from a deep slumber, one hand already on her pistol before she remembered where she was. It was the dead of night, not even a glimmer of sunrise. By the quiet of the camp she sensed it was many hours from morning. Why had she suddenly awoken? Had she heard something? She pricked up her ears. Even the penguins were quiet at night...

Granby was stirring awake a few feet away from her. She heard a muttered "*what in be-jesus was that?*" from the next tent.

And there it was again—a long, low, unearthly moan. Perhaps more of a howl. However it could be described, it was a noise the like of which she had never heard from any animal, and which she could imagine no earthly creature making.

And again there it was, starting high, almost like a whistle, and swooping to a low thrum. It did not sound like the kind of noise that was made with a mouth or throat, but by some other means entirely—like a musical instrument compared to a human voice. She threw off the blanket, trying to ignore the cold, and pulled her jacket on.

Outside, she found the man who was keeping watch.

"Did you hear that, Woodman?" she asked.

"Bloody right I did at that, Sir," the mate swore. "Nigh on jumped out o' me skin."

"Did you see anything?"

"Not a thing. It's black as a...begging your pardon, Sir, it's black as pitch."

"Mister Colyer?" It was Granby, emerging from the officer's tent. The last syllable of her name coincided with the first note of the haunting call, sounding out again. They listened, alert, for a few seconds. When no repeat came, Granby said, "I s'pose it could be a whale. Sometimes you hear them through the hull o' the ship. It could be near the surface, the sound carried by the wind like?" He did not sound convinced of his own argument.

Over the following two days, the party collected more water. In addition they successfully slaughtered enough seals and penguins to keep the ship going for months, to bolster their dwindling supplies of salt beef and canned vegetables. Several times a day the launch had put out from the ship to carry their supplies back to the corvette and bring more empty water casks.

Colyer had found slaughtering penguins to be heartbreakingly easy. The little creatures were not afraid of anything that wasn't a sea-leopard, it seemed, and stood by squawking confusedly even while their neighbours were clubbed insensible. She tried to make sure it was done as kindly and quickly as possible—it seemed even the men had begun to find the penguins endearing, and took no pleasure in the work. Killing sea-leopards, she understood, was almost gladiatorially heroic by comparison.

Daedalus and The Deep

On the fourth day, the whole party struck out across the plain bearing empty water kegs to fill up with water one final time. When they had reached the streams, Granby, Colyer and two men would continue while Woodman supervised the filling of the small barrels, returning them to shore to fill the larger casks before coming out again and continuing with the arduous task until the exploration party returned.

Colyer felt a touch guilty that she would be avoiding the heavy, dull work, but as an officer it would not be proper for her to lift and carry anyway. She reasoned that she was only taking a few men away and the benefits of a little more scientific exploration could not be dismissed.

The acting lieutenant, bosun and two seamen strode out following a curving, upward path around the side of the volcano. They skirted upwards for more than two hours after which, finally, the Western slopes of the island were visible, as was the ocean, stretching onwards in a succession of huge, swelling waves that in some measure had travelled unbroken from Cape Horn. Below them, the land fell away, until it stabbed into the sea in a jumble of sharp-edged rocks.

To their right, the mountain continued, until it was interrupted by an immense, bowl-shaped depression, which was half-filled with fluffy white cloud. They decided that it would be unwise to continue any closer to the crater, but Colyer examined it with her telescope and made some sketches. Granby gazed out to sea, observing the sea birds' behaviour.

After a while, Colyer asked him about the birds. "They're petrels of some sort I think," he outlined, "but a bloody sight bigger than any I have seen before. See how they clip the wave tops and spin into the water when they see a fish," he pointed. She looked through her telescope, following one as it drifted about, its wings poised into twin V-shapes, until it suddenly flipped onto its back, plunged into the water, and emerged a few seconds later with a fish in its beak.

"Oh look, Mister Colyer," shouted one of the men almost in her ear, "an albatross!"

It was unmistakeable. She gasped with surprise and delight. The bird was immense—or rather, immensely disproportionate. Its body did not seem markedly bigger than a large gull or the brown petrels that were darting about the waves. Its wings, though, were magnificent. Impossibly long, and swept to a pointed tip, they bore the bird about as if it were floating.

They watched in awestruck silence. Colyer felt a swell in her chest from the pure grandeur of it all.

"I 'ope it don't start following us," the man said under his breath. A sea-serpent and an albatross following the ship—that would be bad luck indeed. The rest of them ignored the thought.

"I would have thought him quite over-canvassed even in this wind, yet he bears it so easily," she remarked. "I can't help feeling *Daedalus* would need a reef or two."

"Aye, Sir, right enough," responded the bosun, a mildly crestfallen tone entering into his words. "Makes our big sheets o' canvas look a bit clumsy all right."

The albatross swam in the air, borne by the slightest current. It circled gracefully.

"If we could ever make a sail after the pattern of an albatross wing," she suggested, "I reckon we could make to windward with the loss of, what, but two or three points?"

"You sound like Mister Gilpin, Sir," Granby chuckled. "How you goin' to support the mast?"

They fell back into overwhelmed silence, watching the albatross scudding on the rising wind.

"Blast!" exclaimed Granby after a while. "Beggin' your pardon, Sir, but the weather! We ought t' make sure we can still get t' the ship all right." The seamen who had accompanied them suddenly started at that, roused from the enjoyment of their rare spell of idleness, and began to pay attention.

Colyer scanned her telescope slowly across the waters. The waves had increased in size somewhat over the course of the morning but conditions were still fair enough for them to make the gap across to the ship. *What was that?* Something had stabbed up through the water almost right where she had been looking.

She found the spot again, and her heart lurched. *It was the sea serpent*—and it was still with them. The creature had just killed a seal, seemingly by spearing up from beneath it and pitching it twenty or thirty feet out of the water.

"Look!" she shouted at Granby, pointing. "Out there!" It had swum over to where the crippled seal lay flapping on the water and bit right into it. The serpent finished its meal and swam on, this time heading almost due West.

"So it followed us?" breathed Colyer, in shock.

"It could be that, p'raps," Granby responded mysteriously.

"What d'you mean?" she asked, realising that she already knew the answer.

"Well, I doubt there's only one of 'em. And we tracked that creature sailing almost due Sou'-West all the way from St Helena. Reckon it had a good reason to come here. Mebbe this is where it lives."

Colyer exhaled lengthily, as they watched the serpent champing on fragments of seal. The men were muttering to themselves. They quickly packed and hurried back down to the watering party.

CHAPTER 26

CAPTAIN MacQuarrie felt that he and his ship had reached a turning point. After they had retreated tactically following the last encounter with the serpent, everything had seemed to be running away from him. The damage to the foremast had caused them to limp away when they should have been giving chase.

He knew that the serpent had taken a battering, and its attack on them had been the last throw of the dice of a desperate creature. He had half wondered if it had crawled away to die after the encounter, so was enthused to hear that it had been sighted once again, and not four miles from where they were anchored.

The repairs had been completed. The ship's stores had been restocked better than he could have hoped with water and fresh meat from the island. The shore party had now returned with all their equipment, and there was nothing to stop them slipping their anchor immediately. In fact, it was only after a conversation with Malory that he decided not to simply cut the cable and leave the best bower lying on the sea floor.

The only problem was that they were now so far South that the winds were prevailing Westerlies, and that was precisely the direction the serpent had been seen heading. They would have to beat to windward to follow the creature. So be it. Though the wind seemed to be building, it was still surprisingly light for this part of the world—a moderate breeze only, for now at any rate. At least they would not be forcing their way into the teeth of a typical Southern Ocean force 10.

The *Daedalus* drifted out of the bay, still masked somewhat from the wind by the land, and when the ship had reached a distance of half a mile or so, hauled its wind and passed the island to the South. Gilpin tacked ship shortly after they had cleared the land which allowed everyone on the ship a good view of the gaping maw of the island's Western face.

There had been a force three blowing, which allowed the ship to make around six knots through the water—although of course their speed to the West was less because they had to zig zag so as to sail into the wind's eye. Rather than building as expected, the wind now showed signs of dropping away.

Soon the island had receded to a faint mass on the horizon, and then a smudge of cloud, and then it had gone, as if swallowed by the sea which once again surrounded them in all directions without respite.

"Muster the men in the waist, Mister Malory," the captain ordered. Soon, the crew was gathered across the central part of the ship, on the gangways at either beam and standing in the open middle of the gun deck.

"It's been a hard cruise so far, my lads," he began. There was a low mutter of agreement. "And Lord knows there's been little enough to show for it. No prizes, no slaves freed, no pirates run down. Even when we struck land it was naught but a barren rock." The crew nodded furiously, then looked hopeful as if some consolation for hardship was about to come their way. Well, he would give them more than that.

"You are a good crew," he went on. "You've not complained or jibbed at anything that has been asked of you, and for that you have my thanks." The men looked shifty and said nothing in response to that. "We now set out on an endeavour that will reap a true reward for all of you." The assembled seamen pricked their ears up at that. "I promise that once we have completed our task, it will be a feat that every man and boy can look back on in days to come with a sense of pride in himself, his actions, and his shipmates. Well, not long ago we fought a sea-beast that's never been tamed nor captured nor even proven to exist," he declaimed. "We ran it close and we came within an inch of taking it. It eluded us then. It will not elude us again."

The crew members looked at each other in surprise, and again said nothing. MacQuarrie continued. "You may have heard that yesterday the beast was sighted once again. Those reports are true. It is heading West and we are in pursuit."

A burst of chatter rang out from the waist. Excitement no doubt, and perhaps concern about what the prize money would be and how it would be divided. "Silence there!" shouted one of the boatswain's mates.

"I can't tell you what prize money there will be for a sea serpent, lads, or even if there will be any at all," he said, taking up the unasked question. "But the world of science and advancement will be forever grateful to you Daedaluses. And you can be proud as I am that the men to finally bring this creature to the world's attention will be British. You will be performing a service to Britain by showing the world that whatever challenge the men of our great nation pit their efforts against, they will surely overcome! And though our orders tell us we should go home after our cruise, who among you would crawl back to your families with this challenge unmet?." The men looked bewildered. Well, it had been a long cruise—bodies and minds were tired. He tried again.

"I say we should follow this serpent round Cape Horn if we have to. We should not—*will* not bear up until we have given our all in this struggle—what man could do more? What man who calls himself a man could do less?"

There was a stunned pause from the crew. Then, from somewhere in the waist, a thin voice said, very deliberately, "three cheers for the captain," and a ragged, tired cheer went up three times and died away quickly. A boatswain's mate snarled something inaudible.

"Dismissed!" said the Captain with a flourish, and the men shuffled away, the level of chatter rising steadily then falling as they dispersed throughout the ship.

"Good to get the men behind you on something like this," MacQuarrie asserted to the officers around him. Malory merely stared. Clearly he had a lot to learn, prodigy or no. The captain was about to dispense more wisdom about the management of ships and men, when the sailing master asked permission to tack again. Reluctantly, MacQuarrie agreed as he did not want to get too far off the track that the serpent had last been seen on.

The ship broke into activity once more, as the yards were braced round and the ship's head swung across the wind, onto a new angle where the sails would fill and drive them in painstaking zig-zags to the course they ultimately followed. The gentle breeze finally puffed out the sails on their new tack and the corvette gradually gathered way.

DAEDALUS AND THE DEEP

It was only later that he realised that the man who had called for three cheers was the former officer whom he had disrated and turned before the mast, Spencer. The Captain huffed. It would take more than that to win back his favour.

Chapter 27

It turned out that even Malory had not been entirely sure what the captain intended until he had announced it to the whole company. The first lieutenant was close to tearing his own hair out, but even his persuasive manner with the captain had not weakened MacQuarrie's resolve in the slightest. The corvette's orders had been exceeded to a considerable degree, and all of the officers stood to face consequences if the captain's gamble did not pay off. The wardroom was nervous.

It was equally clear that the men were unhappy. Several times Colyer had come on deck or walked into the mess area to see little knots of men hurriedly dispersing. When she finished her watch that evening, she stepped through the companionway and down the ladder—to see a gaggle of men who were muttering in low tones. They had their back to her, and did not look in her direction as they filed forward. She followed at a distance, as quietly as she could. The men descended the forward companionway, onto the berth deck.

As she padded softly down the steps she heard the sounds of the group fumbling their way between the rows of slung hammocks of the port watch. Out of the gloom she heard one of the resting men shift at the disturbance and mutter, "give us a tug could yer shipmate, I've got wood like a bleedin' spanker boom."

The tension rose up in her and broke like a wave. "Punishment for buggery is death, in case you weren't listening to the articles of war!" she barked, "so shut up and sleep or I'll shoot you myself!"

The gaggle of sailors making their way aft whipped round, shock visible on their faces despite the dim light from the companionway. She coughed theatrically, and said as bravely as possible, "I hope this isn't a *combination?*"

The men shuffled awkwardly and she caught sight of Spencer, seeming to leer in the half-light. "No, Sir, just 'avin a chat like," one of them protested.

"Funny place to have a chat, wouldn't you say?"

"We was just going."

"Indeed you were!" she declared, hands on hips, heart thundering. She tried to keep her breath under control until they had dispersed, then hurried to the wardroom to find Gilpin.

After she reached the master's cabin, she confided her fears about the men. Gilpin shrugged knowingly, rubbing sleep from his eyes.

"They're not happy, and they're scared, though there's none of them will admit to it," he said. "Unfortunately I don't think there's much we can do—just keep an eye on things, stay vigilant and try to calm things down wherever we get a chance."

"You don't think they'd actually *mutiny* do you?" she asked, whispering the evil word as if to lessen its malign influence.

"There's every reason they won't," Gilpin reassured her. "They're all professional man o' war's men, volunteers. It isn't as if they were pressed or sent from the prisons. They know if they stepped out of line they'd lose all their pay and probably end up hanged. But we're all out of our knowledge now, and that's never a comfortable place to be."

She was about to turn in to her own cabin when she remembered Spencer's presence in the group she had run into.

"That *is* strange," Gilpin scratched his head. "The impression I had was that the men couldn't stand him. I thought they were ostracising him. If I'm honest I was more worried they would do him violence."

"Still, a man doesn't become an officer for nothing, and he's been humiliated by the Captain," she suggested. "Perhaps the tide has turned now the Captain's committed them to months more in the Southern Ocean?"

"Who knows what really happens in Jack Tar's mind?" Gilpin shrugged. "Nevertheless, my guess is that they'll calm down once the shock has passed. But keep your eyes open and talk to me quietly if there's anything worrying you."

He smiled as comfortingly as possible, and asked her about the expedition. They had had little time to talk since getting underway again. She mentioned the petrels and the albatross she had witnessed from the mountainside.

"Transmutation, Mister Colyer!" Gilpin responded dramatically. "A magnificent bird which has striven to fly longer and longer, further and further, and its wings have mightily outstripped those of the common gull."

She nodded soberly. It had been a fascinating spectacle.

"It's thought they don't touch land for months at a time," Gilpin went on. For years and years they stretched a tiny bit further and a tiny bit further. Reaching for the heavens by infinitesimal degrees. A noble creature. By the bye, did you know discipline in the Royal Navy is improving all the time? The number of floggings has halved in two or three years. Man can be like the albatross, Mister Colyer, when he wants to be. It will turn out right, you'll see."

Despite Gilpin's apparent confidence she left with her worries unabated. The next morning she withdrew a pistol from the ship's armoury with the intention of keeping it with her at all times, though she resolved to draw the powder and shot when she turned in. Later that day she checked the axe that was permanently lashed in place on the foretop, her action-station. The tool was intended for cutting away rigging in an emergency, but she reflected there could be other kinds of emergency than those created by the weather. She took the axe to the blacksmith and had him sharpen it to a wicked edge before restoring it to its place, wrapped in new oilskin.

After three days of beating to windward in failing wind, the ship had made less than 100 miles. The frustration in both the forecastle and the quarterdeck was palpable, though the regular tacking did at least keep the men busy and reasonably tired out. The wardroom dinners were strained, with the officers dancing around the subjects of the sea serpent and the tinder box that was morale.

On the fourth morning she rose early and went on deck. It was hard to sleep now the fear of a foredeck uprising was never far from her mind. The wind was around force two on the scale created by Admiral Beaufort, which, recalling her seamanship texts, she ascertained from the flag flapping limply at the head of the driver. The sea had transformed into a long slop of a swell on the starboard bow, making the motion deeply uncomfortable, and suggesting it was blowing hard somewhere miles away. She climbed up to the main mast crosstrees and surveyed the scene all around, looking for any land ahead of her. Of course there was not so much of a even a smear of steam on the horizon from the island they had left, but the lack of any break in the expanse of sea made her feel oddly flat.

She fell into a reverie, allowing the sense of being above the whole world to take her into an unconnected series of daydreams. She was snapped out of it by distant shouting below. She looked down at the quarterdeck to see what was going on. It looked like there was a line of seamen advancing towards the stern. The officers seemed to have gathered into a knot. What on earth was going on? The word *mutiny* jumped back into her mind, and for a moment she felt silly and jumpy. Then she thought twice and began scrambling downwards—before, after a moment, coming to her senses and creeping down the rigging. It would not do to attract undue attention if there was indeed a mutiny in the offing.

The man in the maintop's full attention was taken by the drama below. She dropped lightly onto the platform and jabbed her pistol at the lookout. "What's going on," she hissed. He whipped round in surprise and jerked back when he saw the pistol. She raised a finger to her lips, and he nodded wildly.

"It's Spencer!" the lookout whispered back. "Him and a bunch ae' others are tryin' tae take the ship. But I din't know nothin' about it! Most've us don't!"

She looked back down. Captain MacQuarrie was lying by the rail, and she thought for a horrible moment that they had killed him, but there was a man standing over him with a boarding pike pointed at his head. Spencer had a hanger pointed at Malory's throat. That was an officer's sword.... She realised he must have reclaimed his old weapon from her cabin and felt sick at the thought that he had invaded her only private space.

There were six mutineers in all. Where were the marines? She could only see two on deck, and they had both dropped their weapons—each had a seaman standing behind with a knife at his throat. Presumably the mutineers had got the drop on the rest of the small company below decks...

Spencer had started yelling. "I am RETAKING this VESSEL in the NAME OF THE QUEEN!" he howled, flourishing his cutlass in time to the words. "I CALL upon all LOYAL men to join me in

RELIEVING the CAPTAIN of his command, along with his BAND of LICKSPITTLE *officers* and...CATAMITES, who are GUILTY of GROSS DERELICTION of their duties."

Silence greeted this outburst, and eventually Malory said something which she could not hear, but which had Spencer raising his cutlass as if to slash downwards through flesh and bone before one of the other mutineers shouted at him to stop-being-such-a-bloody-idiot. The mutineers facing Lambert and Douglas jabbed their cutlasses and pikes, demanding the officers surrender their pistols. They lowered them to the deck carefully to make sure they could not go off by accident.

Fortunately it seemed the mutineers had no firearms—all the muskets and pistols not with officers had been locked down the previous day after Gilpin had had a quiet word with the first lieutenant. Only Malory had a key.

But all the mutineers were now facing aft, their attention taken by Spencer and Malory.

"This is an END to your FILTHY, *DEMOCRATICAL* ways Malory, you ghastly SODOMITE," Spencer spat. "One more WORD and I'll RUN you THROUGH!"

Once again entreating the lookout to remain silent with a gesture, she shoved her pistol into her belt, threw off her jacket and shoes. She lowered herself noiselessly through the lubber's hole and scaled down a halliard, hidden from the men forward by the thick mast, and behind the backs of the men aft.

She dropped onto the deck, padding along in her socks. A few of the seamen who had not taken part in the embryonic mutiny saw her but said nothing. She felt a stab of relief—the men were still loyal, and essentially Spencer's uprising had failed. He could still take some of the officers down with him though. She stopped, twenty feet from Spencer, eased the hammer back and pointed the barrel at his head.

"Anyway," Spencer snapped, his sword still pointed at Malory, "ALL those LOYAL to the CROWN..."

She pulled the trigger.

The pistol went off with a roar of powder and a jet of smoke. Spencer pitched forward, gurgling. The ball had caught him in the neck. He spasmed from head to foot, once, twice, then lay still.

"*Jesus Christ*!" she heard someone say, somewhere a long way away. There was a clatter as someone dropped a sword. Then all of the mutineers dropped their swords and started pleading for clemency.

Colyer did not move. Had she *meant* to fire? She swayed on the spot, watching but not seeing the lights shifting in the shiny, dark pool that was radiating from Spencer's corpse. She only registered after a couple of moments that a tall, frilled form of a reflection had swum into the red puddle.

The reflection opened its mouth.

Chapter 28

THE first Gilpin knew of the attack was when a scream rent the air from forward. The brief, small, stupid mutiny had just come to an abrupt end after Colyer had appeared on the quarterdeck in his socks and, shockingly, shot Spencer in the back of the neck.

Had the mutiny been any better organised or larger, the young lieutenant would have been killed where he stood, but the uprising had been a fragile thing and the single shot had shattered it. Spencer had evidently persuaded a few of the more gullible members of the crew that the Captain and officers were no longer rightfully in charge. That only they were truly the *loyal* ones, and had a duty to return to the duties the ship had been ordered to perform by the admiral back in Cape Town. Most of the men had evidently still been too cowed by the captain's earlier behaviour to risk challenging MacQuarrie's authority, and Spencer had only involved men he was sure of.

Gilpin moved over to Colyer who had stood, stock still since he fired the shot, took the pistol and put an arm around his shoulders. The youth stared at the deck with dead eyes, but then jumped back, yelping.

It was then that a horrible scream rose from the vicinity of the bow. Men rushed forwards, grabbing anything to use as a weapon, fearful of a second outbreak of disloyalty.

It was much worse than that.

An impossibly long, impossibly huge head emerged from behind the main course, a flailing seaman trapped in its jaws. The man was yelling with inarticulate horror, his blood spraying the bulwark from a dozen wounds.

DAEDALUS AND THE DEEP

"Somebody bloody shoot it!" Malory yelled. Douglas and Lambert scrabbled about the deck for their pistols. "The marines is all tied up!" someone else shouted. At that point, the creature crunched down on the sailor, who whined pitifully and fell silent. It dropped the bloody mess back on the deck and dipped below the surface, leaving only a lazily spinning vortex and a patch of red.

Finally, a gaggle of marines burst on deck, in a state of disarray, running to the side with hangers and one or two hurriedly loaded muskets. Some were missing their breeches, others their boots. The spectacle would have been comical at any other time. They were about to discharge the few firearms into the water, but Malory stopped them and ordered the ship cleared for action.

It was probably the slowest that *Daedalus* had ever reached action stations, but after five minutes or so, both batteries were able to fire if called upon, a line of marines stood at each rail in something like proper order, and the topmen stood ready to take in or shake out sail if required. The two bodies, Spencer and the seaman killed by the serpent, were taken below and thrown into the gundeck scuppers. The Captain—still unconscious—was removed to the sick bay, as his cabin became part of the gun deck when the corvette cleared for action. He had evidently taken a heavy crack across the back of the skull from the hilt of a hanger, and half his head had swollen and turned purple.

Silence descended over the ship. The *Daedalus* stood on, continuing the tack that took it North West by North.

After an interminable two and a half hours in this state, Malory tacked the ship and had the hands piped to dinner by divisions. It was a way of stalling the inevitable, when they would have to go into action or stand down. The first lieutenant called the officers to him.

"We need to be ready at a moment's notice to fight back," he asserted, "but of course we cannot remain at action stations indefinitely. After all, it's not like a sea battle where you generally have a degree of notice that an enemy ship is coming at you."

They murmured their agreement. "Suggestions please, gentlemen," Malory demanded.

"Could we clear for action for certain times of the day?" Lambert suggested. "We always used to beat to quarters at dawn as a matter of course. We could do the same at noon."

"Doing so first thing is not a bad idea. But what if the creature strikes when we are not at quarters?" Malory asked. "Also, I believe if we did that too regularly the men would lose their concentration, it would just become a routine. Anyone else?" Gilpin saw him look to Colyer, but the acting lieutenant remained silent, not making eye contact with anyone.

"Why not add duty gun crews and marine parties to the watch rota?" Gilpin suggested. "We could maintain, say, three gun crews at readiness at all times and a file of marines, so we can at least start to get some shots off and give everyone else a chance to get into action."

"That sounds more like it," Malory answered. "Very well, we'll try it for a couple of days. While the weather is calm we can load and run all the guns out. The duty crews can fire whichever are pointing the right way. It's not ideal by any stretch but we'll see how it works."

"There's the question of our heading, Sir..." Douglas said, delicately.

"No there isn't," Malory snapped back. "Captain MacQuarrie ordered that we stand to the Westward, and we must continue to do that until there is a good reason to do otherwise."

"But the captain's incapacitated," Douglas protested.

"He could wake up this minute," Malory fired back. "And what would you say to him if he asked why we weren't doing as he had ordered?"

They all nodded, dejectedly at that. It was up to Malory to carry out the captain's orders to the best of his ability. To turn for home now would be just as much a mutiny as Spencer's ill-fated uprising in the eyes of the Admiralty.

"If we reach the Falklands," Malory added, reassuringly, "and the captain still hasn't recovered his senses, then we'll look at the situation anew. There might be a ship with a senior officer there and we can be justified in changing our course of action."

Gilpin was not surprised—Malory was in a tenuous position. The captain had a tendency to defer to his first officer in many things, but he was still the ultimate symbol of the law on board. If the captain was dead or permanently incapacitated, Malory could take whatever decision he thought was in the interests of the ship and the service. Until that time, he was bound by the last orders Captain MacQuarrie had given. It was ironic. When conscious,

Daedalus and The Deep

Malory could generally bend the captain to his will. Unconscious, there was no persuading him to amend his orders.

The trouble was that the orders were obsolete. The Westerly track had been set to follow the sea serpent—a creature which had evidently doubled back and taken a man off their very deck. Then there was the question of whether they should even be tackling the creature at all—Gilpin was under no illusions that they were the ones being hunted. It seemed the captain did not share that view.

The *Daedalus* seemed to have sailed into a kind of limbo. The failed mutiny had nipped any larger scale indiscipline in the bud, but the crew were just as unhappy as they had been. The reasons for carrying on to the West, trying to chase the serpent, had in many cases been rendered irrelevant, but until the captain regained consciousness or circumstances changed markedly, they had no choice but to continue West into the wind. The sailing master had no doubt Malory was working on some plan to break out of the straightjacket, but it would take care and skill as well as the first lieutenant's abundant nerve.

Gilpin sought out Colyer. He was sitting at the wardroom table, in a daze. The youth looked slowly up at Gilpin, and his eyes did not show any sign of recognition for a good five seconds.

"It's all right lad," Gilpin said, putting his palms down reassuringly. "You stopped them. The mutineers have all sworn loyalty and accepted punishment."

The lieutenant looked down. "I killed him."

"Good thing you did."

"I could have avoided it." His voice was flat. For a moment there seemed to be a gulf inside where the young man's heart should have been.

Gilpin swallowed. "It needed to be stopped quickly. With a shock. Any warning and Spencer would have killed Malory."

"There were only a few of them," Colyer went on, as if he had not heard Gilpin at all. "Only a handful."

"They could never have taken the ship," Gilpin agreed, "but if they'd panicked there would have been *much more* blood shed."

Colyer looked up at him, disbelief in his eyes.

"I've seen these situations before," Gilpin pushed on. "They're born out of *desperation*. Desperate men do stupid, bloody things. You took one life to save many—and you restored order to the ship."

"Order?" Colyer gasped. "What does *that* matter?"

"Look," said Gilpin, sitting down opposite Colyer. "Say Spencer and his men had started hacking away with those swords and pikes. They'd have killed five or six men, maybe more, and they would have been killed themselves. The officers, or the marines, or loyal men—someone would have had to kill to stop the mutiny.

"That would have bred discontent in the forecastle. Those men who were killed on both sides would have had friends. Those friends would bear grudges. The thing gets blown up and blown up until we don't have a mutiny—we have a bloodbath. You did what you needed to do today. You did what was necessary. And you were the only one who did, up to that moment."

The young man met his gaze again, eyes moist. "You can't ever say with certainty that you saved a life, can you?" he asked, softly. "But you will always know when you've ended one. Or two."

"No," Gilpin said tiredly. "You can't ever really know. And you can't keep a tally either. You can only do the job that needs to be done with the tools God put in your hands."

Gilpin rose, and put his hand on the young man's shoulder. "This is the life we lead," he said. "Every day is a struggle with the wind, the waves, the men and ourselves. And as officers we have men's lives in our hands all the time. But I'm confident, Lieutenant Colyer, that you are doing well with that grave responsibility. You're made from the right fabric, I'd wager. But what's more important, you're working to carve the best character you can from it."

The lad looked desperate. "It...Doesn't...Help," he almost sobbed. Gilpin could have laughed.

"Of course it doesn't. You're a good man, Colyer. What you did —what you *had* to do—will stay with you. It will change you. Do your best to let it change you in a way that makes you do better. Keep doing better. Find alternatives to killing if you can. And accept it if you can't."

Colyer almost smiled. "Transmutation, Mister Gilpin?"

"If you like, Mister Colyer," he replied, warmly. "Keep striving. Like the Albatross."

Colyer looked puzzled.

"The Albatross didn't want those great wings to make his life easier, did he?" Gilpin explained. "He worked to give himself those great wings so he could fly further, higher, longer. In stretching out into those cold wastes, not touching land for years, he made his life much harder. But he's become glorious for the struggle."

A look of desolate understanding passed across the boy's face.

During the forenoon watch, Malory and the warrant officers worked out the arrangements for the standing gun crews and marine detachments. In the afternoon, the first lieutenant stood the ship down and began the implementation of the new watch pattern.

The wind continued to drop, and the first wisps of mist began to drift down from ahead.

CHAPTER 29

THE ship was virtually becalmed, but Malory was keen to deal with the punishment of the mutineers. Colyer thought the first lieutenant probably wanted to get it over with while the captain was still unconscious so as to present MacQuarrie with a *fait accompli*. There was no telling quite what the captain might do to mutineers. He would undoubtedly demand the death penalty—but men sentenced to death had the right to demand a court martial, and MacQuarrie had overridden the rules on that score once already.

Who could say what effect hanging six men from the yard-arms would have on an already traumatised crew? And there would undoubtedly be courts martial for the officers that allowed things to reach such a head.

In fact, Malory had taken steps to play down the seriousness of the incident. The morning after the standing defences were implemented, Malory gathered the lieutenants and Gilpin together on the quarterdeck where he had had a canvas screen raised to mask the space from the rest of the ship. A dramatic touch perhaps, but justified by the greater privacy afforded.

"I mean to give each of those men involved two dozen for insubordination," he said in such a way that made it clear this was not a discussion. "Two counts each. I will write the log up to reflect that the men refused to take certain orders and made insulting remarks to senior seamen. I want to be quite clear that this was not an organised mutiny, nor was it an attempt to take the ship. Mister Colyer!"

"Sir?" she responded through the daze that had been upon her since she pulled the trigger.

DAEDALUS AND THE DEEP

"As you will recall, Mister Spencer had stolen a weapon during the—ah, *protest*, and was about to kill me. You shot him to prevent that happening."

"Yes, Sir," she answered mechanically. It was true, for the most part.

"Very well. I need you to write your report, making all of that clear. You need not refer to any other men who might have had weapons, nor should you need to touch upon any violence that might have been done by any man other than Spencer. Is that clear."

"Yes, Sir," she answered. So she was not free of it quite yet.

"Beg pardon, Sir..." Douglas coughed, "But the captain? He will know something was up—someone cracked him over the back of the head, after all."

"Yes indeed," Malory responded. "You will recall that it was Spencer that struck the Captain."

Clever, she thought. You can't hang a man who has already been shot in the throat, and bled his last onto the decks. The captain would be further cheered by the knowledge that Spencer's body had been pitched over the side without ceremony—literally tossed overboard without a word, denied the usual rites. Colyer had already heard several versions of the assault on the captain. It seemed that the attack on MacQuarrie was the first anyone knew that there was a mutiny—or a *protest*—in progress, and in the confusion different people had seen different things. No one seemed to think Spencer was responsible though—he had more than likely made straight for his nemesis Malory, and arranged for some other fool to incapacitate the captain.

It did not matter. He was guilty. And he had been punished. Colyer felt grubby for a moment, that her act had been used by Malory to tie the loose ends up so conveniently.

After making plans to carry out all of the floggings as soon as possible, Malory dismissed the officers. As they were moving out of the screened-off area, she heard Malory say "Mister Colyer? I desire you to remain for a moment."

She turned and waited. The last of the other officers, Gilpin, slipped through the flap in the screen—she just had time to see him nodding reassuringly to her.

"I have not had time to speak to you privately after the...incident," he started, uncertainly. Unwittingly, she raised her eyebrows. This was unlike the lieutenant. Indeed, he almost looked like a different man. She suddenly realised how young he must have been. Perhaps 23 years? The moment passed quickly, and in the blink of an eye, it was the imperious, immoveable Malory who stood before her once more, his full lips pressed together in determination.

"You saved the ship, and quite possibly my life," he stated, levelly. "It was your duty as an officer, of course, and I would expect no less. Nevertheless, had the task fallen to a less capable or less lucky individual, circumstances might have fallen differently. Therefore as first lieutenant, and as a man, you have my thanks."

She coloured, quite involuntarily. He stood before her, his piece said, calmly awaiting a response.

"As you said, Sir, my...duty. I...." she tailed away. Would she never be allowed to forget? The trigger pulled, the explosion of powder, the spray of blood...

"Well, we should attend to the punishment," Malory said after an interminable moment of silence had passed. "You are dismissed."

"Thank you, Sir. I only wanted to keep...the ship safe, Sir," she faltered.

A flicker of smile played around that mouth for an instant.

"Of course, Lieutenant," he said. "Your post, if you please?"

She saluted clumsily, shoved her hat under her arm and fled from the quarterdeck.

The sky had turned grey and dark, like a muttered threat. The growing mist reached up from the sea, obliterating the horizon, trapping the ship in a closed universe made of tones of grey. Malory ordered hands mustered for punishment. Under normal circumstances the ship would be hove-to for this. However, the full spread of sail hung limp from the yards, and not so much as a ripple could be detected streaming back from the bow, betraying the corvette's utter motionlessness.

A grating was lashed upright in the waist and the first of the miscreants brought out.

The first man was walked to the grating. Incongruously, he appeared almost cheery. Colyer thought he must realise he was lucky to have avoided the death penalty, and then to be met with only a light punishment, all things considered.

The men seemed to be hurrying with the knots. The marine drummers began the long roll, and Colyer thought the drumming sounded faster than usual, though that was absurd of course. A boatswain's mate delivered the first two dozen without ceremony, and the seaman was marched away. The second man was strapped to the grating, and another boatswain's mate took over with the cat. Colyer glanced over at the men. Usually the expressions on the faces of the men ran the gamut of emotions from resentment to fear to blood-lust to hatred to relief. Today, every man-jack wore the same bearing—a sort of jumpy apprehension. It was as though they couldn't wait to finish the punishment and get back to sailing. It didn't seem to matter that they were stuck in a flat calm, with no chances of going anywhere.

The second man was cut down, and the third put up for his punishment. The drummers began again. With a ghastly sound of chords swiping through the air and then connecting with increasingly bloody flesh, the strokes of the cat were counted off.

The mist had closed in since the punishment began, and the light was now no brighter than twilight. Colyer caught sight of Malory sneaking a glance at his watch.

The fourth man was tied, spread-eagled, to the grating. His two-dozen counted down. Then the fifth man. Colyer realised she was holding her breath, and released it slowly. The mist was billowing up around them now. The lashing finished. Thank God. Only one to go. Men started to untie the knots. The punished sailor stepped back from the grating. Colyer instinctively glanced towards a large shape that was looming in the mist to her right. An instant later, the form resolved into a pair of massive, sharp-toothed jaws attached to a vast head, darting into the waist. The punished man whipped into the air, a kind of voiceless whine issuing from his mouth, his torso clamped in the sea-serpent's jaws as it wrenched its head back, away from the ship.

"Marines...FIRE," Malory spluttered among a cannonade of expletives, and a ragged volley of musket fire crackled into the fog. The duty gun crews had hurriedly assembled around three of the starboard 32-pounders, and the first boomed uselessly, its shot flicking unseen into the misty atmosphere.

"Cease firing, CEASE FIRING!" Malory yelled. Silence fell over the ship like a solid mass. "We need to wait until we can see the bloody thing," Malory hissed to the officers. Colyer remained silent. The whole situation was completely unreal. "Beat to quarters! What the hell did those lookouts think they were playing at?" he stormed. Granby got a mouthful of foul language and the lookouts were accused of watching the punishment instead of attending to their duty.

Then, he dragged Kane over and dressed him down, furiously, for the marines not being more vigilant.

"I'm sorry, Sir," Kane apologised, and shuffled awkwardly. His usual impassive expression had not changed but his eyes betrayed a horrified disbelief that he had failed so utterly in his role, and so soon after the mutiny he and his men had been unable to prevent. It was probably the first time in his career he had felt derelict in his duty in any way, and now the whole world was falling apart.

Malory let the silence hang, before exploding. The first lieutenant tore into the marine, telling him to attend to his sanguine duty, pull his gory head out of the visceral bilge and apply some arterial intelligence when following the crimson orders he had been given.

In different times, this would have been an experience almost too humiliating to bear. Now, no one much cared. The sound of a voice suddenly impinged on Colyer's consciousness, and she realised it had been speaking for the last few minutes. It was Lambert, muttering "What the hell do we do? What the hell do we do?" over, and over.

"Right!" Malory shouted, gathering the officers to him. "Boats. We're going to get out of here. We'll swing the boats out and tow the *Daedalus* into some blasted wind."

He gathered Holford and Gower to pass the messages on to the master and mates, to prepare the boats for towing the corvette. She noticed the dead look in their eyes. The boys were beyond fear.

The largest boat, the launch, had already been swung overboard, and was currently bobbing listlessly behind the stern, as it was normally stowed on beams across the waist. A team came aft to haul it alongside, while two more teams came onto the quarterdeck to lower the gig and pinnace from their davits. The men had a nervous, twitchiness about them. They worked professionally, but Colyer noticed hands shaking, clammy sweat on foreheads and arms.

Malory had evidently noticed it too. "I want an officer in each boat!" he added to his previous instructions. The lieutenants all looked up as if their heads were connected to the same string. They looked to Malory. Colyer saw the calculation on his face—who was expendable? Finally, he broke the silence.

"Lambert, you will man the launch. Johnson, as senior midshipman will take the gig. Colyer? The pinnace for you."

She felt a great emptiness deep in her stomach. Out in an open boat with nothing between her and the sea serpent but a few thin planks. As the launch was brought to the entry port for the crew to board, she looked to the others who had been chosen for the task. Lambert was attempting to joke with Douglas, but his face was somewhere between white and green in colour. Johnson was sobbing openly, until Colyer saw Gilpin give him a talking to, and he seemed to pull himself together.

After a period where the boats were loaded with their crews, and cables passed through the hawse-holes at the bow, the three boats began to row. Colyer took her place in the sternsheets and started her boat's crew pulling slowly, building gradually to a faster speed. *Daedalus* weighed more than a thousand tons, and there was no point wearing the men out before any momentum had been built up. She glanced across to the other boats. Lambert was doing the same, but over to starboard, Johnson was urging the gig's crew to a furious pace.

For a moment, she felt like following his example, fear rising with the energy of the rowing, and forcing the men to drag away as fast as possible. She knew it was useless though. The serpent could swim faster than the corvette could sail even in the best possible conditions. The best hope was to find wind, and that might take hours.

She attracted Lambert's attention by waving and jabbed a finger at Johnson. He looked over, then nodded to her in understanding. "Hi! Johnson—slow down!" he instructed the boy. "Follow my stroke." Colyer heard the midshipman respond with a surly "Aye aye, Sir", and reduced the speed of his men's stroke.

Initially, the boats could have been trying to drag the Portsmouth Spit Fort. The oars dragged heavily through the water, foam piling against the blades seemingly to no effect. After a few minutes though, it was possible to feel slight movement of the boats through the sea. After a few more minutes, *Daedalus* had even developed a slight bow-wave for the first time since the wind had dropped away completely. Colyer's heart rose slightly. Surely it would not take too long for them to find enough wind to become masters of their own destiny again? The steady, rhythmic stroke of the oars was almost relaxing in itself. It was almost possible to forget the huge, vicious sea serpent that was stalking them.

Almost, but not entirely.

The easily-driven hull of the corvette gathered speed surprisingly quickly. The three boats with their full crews rowing hard produced a certain amount of momentum. It was never going to be possible to reach any great speed, but a couple of knots was attainable. The fog was not clearing but the movement raised the mood among the men in the boats and the ship itself. Colyer allowed herself to hope.

She heard a hollow thump a few feet away, and looked across to the other boats. "What was that?" she called to Lambert. He was standing rigidly, then he began looking all around, his eyes darting across the narrow strips of water between the boats, and back toward the *Daedalus*. "What *was* that?" she repeated, a strident tone creeping unbidden into her voice.

"Something hit the bottom of my boat," he yelped. The lieutenant paused, as if in feverish thought. Then "It could have been anything. Carry on."

They continued for several more minutes. Then, Colyer heard the hollow thump under her own boat and felt something dragging on the keel for a moment or two.

"Something hit *my* boat just now," Colyer called to Lambert.

"We have to go back!" Johnson whined from over in the gig.

"Shut up!" Lambert snapped. At that moment, something round and smooth broke the water for a second, before dipping slickly below the surface again. A barrage of involuntary expletives and intaking of breath rippled through the normally-disciplined men.

"Christ, that was the sea-serpent alright!" Lambert shouted. "What do we do?"

"Ahoy boats, why do you slacken your pace?" came a distant call from the *Daedalus*. They ignored it for the moment.

"Back to the ship!" Colyer responded, "we can't fight the serpent out here."

Lambert seemed to freeze for a moment, but then shook himself. "Yes. Yes. Johnson!" he directed at the midshipman in the gig on his far side, "Back to the ship, make for your davit straight

Daedalus and The Deep

away, cast the lines off. Ship there! The serpent's here, we're coming back in!"

Colyer ordered her crew to stop rowing, then when the line to the ship slackened, uncleated it and let it fall into the sea. "Port side back oars, Starboard side pull," she ordered, turning the boat round. At that moment the sea erupted on the far side of the launch where the gig was turning, in a towering spray of water, flailing seamen and splintered sections of boat. Through it all burst the sea-serpent, shooting vertically out of the melee. It hung in the air for a moment, before toppling sideways back into the sea with a mighty thump. Colyer grabbed the gunwale of her boat as a sudden wave bodily picked the hull up, then let it down. A rain of spray pattered on the men's heads.

"Pick up survivors!" She yelled to her boat's crew, automatically before quite realising what she was doing. The beast must have surfaced right under the gig. Most of the men were swimming for the launch, which had backed oars to wait for them, and in a few seconds, the pinnace had reached the scene.

A few men scrambled over the gunwale, but Lambert was already shouting, "That's everyone, Colyer, make for the entry port, get most of the men off before you get the tackles rigged." She heard Johnson howling like a baby, wailing without restraint until a seaman socked him over the back of the neck.

She saw Lambert was making for the starboard side, so she took the boat back along the port beam. The rowing was ragged and she steered the boat right into the side of the frigate by the midship steps. It banged against the paintwork, an offence normally worthy of punishment, now drawing not so much as a remark. The frightened and soaked sailors who had come out of the water scrambled up the handholds and over the side. Colyer motioned to the aftermost rowers that they could go too.

Malory's head appeared over the rail.

"Sir, do you want to take the boats in tow?" the acting lieutenant cried, hoping not to have to spend a moment more exposed in this way.

"No," Malory answered, "we'll take them back on board. We may need them, I fear," he added, ominously. Colyer and the remaining sailors took the boat back under the port quarter davit, and with shaking hands, they hooked on the tackle that had been lowered to them.

"Up the falls," she ordered the sailors, and with mutters and guilty nods, they scaled the ropes to the relative security of the deck. "All fast!" she shouted to the deck, where someone responded "Haul away!" and the pinnace began to rise. Her hopes rose with it and in less than a minute she was back on the deck.

Malory strode up to her. "Damnation!" he spat, at no one in particular. "That blasted creature has us in chains!"

"I think Lambert was right to order the withdrawal," she started, but he batted her justification away with a wave of his hand.

"I know, damn it all, we can't stand to lose more men and the boats to boot. We're stuck here until the wind picks up, and Lord knows what that thing can do to us while we sit here..." He tailed off, raging silently. He stood for a moment, obviously deep in thought. Colyer waited, forgotten but not yet dismissed.

"Well we'll give it something to think about anyway," he uttered eventually. "Lambert, Douglas, here if you please! Can someone call Mister Gilpin? And someone shut that snivelling snotty up or throw him over the side!" Johnson had indeed begun crying openly again. A boatswain's mate knocked him to the deck, evidently delighted to strike a superior without any consequences. The midshipman looked mortified then humiliated. He scrambled onto his feet and scuttled away. The officers gathered around Malory.

"It's almost dark now, but we'll maintain as keen a watch as we possibly can," he explained when the senior crew had all arrived at the quarterdeck. "Tomorrow we will run out the guns, port and starboard, place divisions of marines fore and aft, and reinforce them with topmen. It didn't like being stuck with those harpoons either, so if there are any men spare without weapons, they can bear one of those, or a boarding pike. I want no man unarmed or unoccupied. We will feed the hands at their stations. We will wait, and wait, and wait, 'til the crack of doom if necessary and either we get a breeze or we fight that beast when it comes 'til we can fight no more. One way or another I mean to be rid of it."

CHAPTER 30

THE *Daedalus* sat slopping in the swell, stationary but for the slack pitch and roll that caused a sickening corkscrew as the sea undulated beneath. The limp sails thwacked against the masts, mocking the crew below. The swell had built gently during the night and by first light was heavy and uncomfortable. For a while, Malory attempted to swing the ship's head into the sea using the rudder, to make the motion easier. But, with no wind to act on the sails, the corvette stubbornly fell away each time until it was taking the swell on the port bow.

Gilpin had experienced enough years at sea for such conditions to be familiar, but there was still something unsettling in trying to move about the deck. With any wind at all, the sails tended to stabilise the ship, bracing it against the waves and the natural roll. Furthermore, the wind generally broke up the peaks somewhat, except in areas like the Southern Ocean where the wind could build up waves that ran uninterrupted for hundreds of miles. Today's rolling undulation was smooth as glass. It didn't run into the hull only to be shouldered aside—it picked the vessel up bodily, rolling it around like flotsam.

He felt a stab of sympathy for the three youths sent into the mastheads as additional lookouts—Gower in the mizzen, MacLeod in the main and Lieutenant Colyer in the fore. They must be bouncing round like India-rubber balls by now. Then there was the stress of being a lookout in those circumstances—unable to stop concentrating for a moment, quartering an ever-moving sea for something that might only be visible for a moment.... His stomach twanged slightly at the memory, still fresh after decades. The rushing sloop in the far south which would smash its bows and sink in moments if no one saw the lump of ice they were about to run into.... The cruiser in the midst of the Pacific running low on supplies, men facing starvation if a lookout missed the peak of an island peeping faintly over the horizon...

It was no task for the unreliable. The oldsters, Johnson and Holford, could only be trusted as messengers, he was sad to agree with Malory about that. Holford had become quietly embittered, ignored and sidelined. Johnson was near catatonic following his experiences in the boat. Usually both situations would have caused him a deal of concern. These were not usual circumstances, even for a navy that prided itself on being ready for anything.

In fact, he was half hoping one of them would cause trouble so he could have them mastheaded anyway. Malory would not decline the punishment.

He felt some sympathy for first lieutenant too. The first real taste of command, which the lieutenant seemed to think was his destiny and right, and the situation had spiraled out of control. He did not envy the officer his hard lesson in human fallibility. But it was no doubt a valuable lesson, which all aspiring commanders should learn and too few did.

Gilpin returned his attention to the rolling waves. The feeling was unspoken, but the old sailing master sensed it rippling through the more experienced men. A sea like this only meant one thing—there was a high wind blowing somewhere. A gale, perhaps.

He realised he had avoided raising it with Malory out of a kind of superstition—and with a jolt, he understood that he was willing the gale on them. Did he really think that by mentioning it he would jinx the wind and leave them becalmed forever?

This ran against everything he knew as a seaman—the superstition was ludicrous, but even then, *wishing* for a wind like that was senseless. Even with the sails reefed and the hatches battened down it could lead them into serious trouble. Perhaps even fatal. *Daedalus* could be crank in a sea, like all ships of her class. Mishandled she could easily broach to. With the full rig from courses to royals she had on her now, a sudden blow could haul the sticks out of her.

But it could also carry them away from that...thing. The sailing-master bridled at himself for that. This was one of God's creatures. If only it had not the appearance of being so persistent. So driven. Try as he might, he could not think of the sea serpent as just a dumb animal. He sensed an intelligence driving its actions. That was foolish, surely? A conceit.

No, he had to talk to Malory. They had to prepare for what was coming. Sea serpent or no, it would do them no good to be caught unawares by a storm. The skies had started to clear, but great piles of cloud had followed the dissipation of the haze. Something was happening—changing. He was the sailing master, and it was his responsibility to see the ship prepared. He started to make his way aft.

Gilpin found the first lieutenant on the gun deck. Malory had been seeing to the preparations to defend against the sea-serpent. Malory looked up as Gilpin approached, and bid him help him check the guns. They walked together along each battery, inspecting tackles for wear, looking to see if there were too few or too many cartridges laid by, if the supply of shot was adequate.... They decided on chain shot and langridge to start with.

Each gun was loaded and run out. The men stood by, in their positions. Those that could see from their posts peered out of the gunports, trying to see anything at all. The gundeck settled into an uneasy silence.

With those preparations complete, the two men made their way back to the quarterdeck. The bow and stern-chaser cannon were set at minimum elevation, pointed as close to directly fore and aft as they could bear and loaded with grape. They then saw hand arms distributed, placed at strategic points around the deck. eventually, there was nothing more to distract from the weather.

"Fair swell now, Sir," Gilpin remarked.

"Indeed," replied Malory. "It's blowing a hooley somewhere all right."

"Yes," agreed Gilpin, pleased that Malory had taken the hint. "To the West I'd guess."

"That's no surprise. It's been too damned calm for this far south. The glass is all right though."

"It wouldn't fall necessarily—I've been hit by sudden storm fronts with no warning before, though usually in the tropics. I think we should be ready to take some canvas in."

"I agree," answered the first lieutenant. "What would you recommend?"

"To be frank, Sir, everything. Furl all the light weather sails, hoist storm trisails, strike down the t'gallant masts if we have time."

Malory exhaled steadily, and stood motionless for several moments. "Take in courses and t'gallants, strike down t'gallant masts but close-reef the topsails. I understand about the trisails but that's a big task and there isn't time to start bending new canvas now. It would be just like that infernal beast to set upon us in the middle of it, and we've been caught with our breeches down one too many times for my liking. At least setting the t'gallant masts down might ease this God-damned rolling. Give the word, if you please."

"Aye aye, Sir," Gilpin responded, before chancing his arm with "may I rig preventers too, Sir?"

Malory growled, but agreed as long as all could complete in double quick time. Gilpin informed the warrant officers. A chain of instructions cascaded through the ship. Trimmers broke away from their gun crews and topmen swarmed up the ratlines. Within a few minutes, the corvette's full suit of sails had been brailed up against the yards, with only the narrow rectangles of the triple-reefed topsails remaining set. Shortly afterwards additional backstays had been rigged up and tensioned. The rhythmic crashing from aloft immediately abated, which was some relief at any rate. The men scuttled back to their guns.

As they had agreed the day before, the remaining detachment of marines were divided into columns fore-and-aft. Hardly columns, Gilpin observed—eight men in each plus the sergeant and lieutenant, Kane. The officer was evidently determined that the marines would atone for their earlier disgraces, having been completely caught out by the serpent on previous occasions and to cap it all, allowing themselves to be disarmed by a gaggle of mutineers. Kane bellowed at the bow column to keep their eyes peeled, then mercilessly drilled the stern column. When he seemed reasonably content with them, he stood them to and drilled the bow column.

As this was happening, Gilpin noted the master-at-arms handing harpoons to the few men that could be spared from the guns—loblolly boys, the purser, even the captain's clerk. He smiled wanly at the incongruous appearance of these unwarlike men poised around the rail, weapons in their hands, fear and disbelief in their eyes.

For the rest of the men, there was nothing to do but wait. Eight bells rang, signifying the start of the forenoon watch—a meaningless symbol of meaningless time with everyone at their posts and likely to stay that way until this ended, one way or another.

The excitement of beating to quarters, shortening sail and generally readying the vessel for a fight soon wore off, to be replaced with a mixture of tension and boredom. The corvette slopped uneasily. Every so often, a man would slope sheepishly over to the rail and vomit into the sea.

The stink of it hung around the deck, as ship and crew awaited the inevitable.

Chapter 31

COLYER forced herself to maintain a strict lookout procedure from the foretop, working clockwise in quadrants six points across, from horizon to gunwale. Mercifully, the mist had thinned into haze, which itself had begun to clear. Even the cloud seemed to be breaking up. As the minutes passed into hours, and she lost count of the visual circuits she had made of the sea, brighter patches in the sky became wispy, and eventually broke into blue, though the long swell still spoke of stormy weather somewhere around.

Time seemed to expand, and Colyer reached the state of not knowing whether she had been searching the sea for minutes or hours. She heard a soft cough to one side, and a hand emerged through the lubber's hole. A wooden tray appeared beside it, and a second hand slid the receptacle away from the edge. A head was the next thing to appear—the balding dome of the wardroom steward.

"We're bringing food to men at their stations," he said, without climbing up any further, his knuckles white with the fierceness of his grip, his face white for other reasons. "If you'll permit me Lieutenant, I should..."

"Of course, dismissed," she uttered after a moment. An expression of delight passed across the steward's face, and he began what was evidently a laborious climb back to the deck. How he had managed to get up with a tray in one hand she could explain only by the certainty of Malory's reaction had the steward refused or failed. An elderly fellow, he was occasionally required to pull on a rope but Colyer had never seen him anywhere near the rigging.

Daedalus and the Deep

She inspected the tray. It contained a cup of watered rum, half a biscuit, a dollop of pease pudding and a few pieces of meat. She continued systematically scanning the surrounding waters, allowing herself a sip of liquid and a mouthful of food only after completing a full 32 point review.

The sky continued to clear. That at least improved the light, but it extended the amount of visible sea and made the task slower. Instantaneously, Colyer realised her eyes were sore. She pressed herself to continue the lookout duty, changing direction after each third complete circle to introduce some variety, to try to stop her mind wandering.

As the layers of haze burned away, the sky above the corvette became a faint, weak blue and then a progressively hard, bright azure. Puffs of white cloud appeared distantly, and then closer. The puffs blossomed upwards over hours into uneven towers of hard, white coral. The towers loomed drunkenly, top-heavy, impossibly solid, their edges glowing with brilliance. They began to merge into one another, forming huge flat-based slabs.

Still Colyer searched. The sun wheeled higher. There seemed to be some kind of musket drill on deck. Four-bells rang, pointlessly. Six-bells, seven-bells. A flurry of activity on deck as topmen were mustered. They flooded up the ratlines and took sail in, before returning to their posts. She smiled. Someone was worried about the weather. Eight-bells, and the start of the forenoon watch.

The sickly rolling waves queued to the distant horizon. In the young lieutenant's mind, every peak threatened to become the edge of a fin breaking water, every shadowed trough a darkly slithering flank. And the light was beginning to make it hard to maintain the search.

The sun burned off the viscous water. It did not glitter or sparkle, as sunlight does from water that even the slightest zephyr plays upon. The swell rolled slackly, as the growing light turned a miles-wide quadrant of sea into an incandescent lake of molten copper.

Colyer tried to search the sunward stretch of ocean, which was aft of the starboard beam, through the cracks between her upheld fingers, but it was impossible to know what she might be missing. She could make out movement, but no form. Desperately, she tried to separate the rhythmic pulsing of the waves from any other motion.

It was no good. And she realised she was neglecting the rest of the vast disc of ocean on which the tiny corvette sat. But there was something mesmerising about the impenetrable glowing strip of water that resisted all efforts to learn what it might hide.

From out of the glare, came a whispering, that grew to a muttering, then a roar. She jumped to her feet.

"Mister Malory! MISTER MALORY!" scraped the hoarse but still-resonant voice of Captain MacQuarrie.

"Will one of you whore's bastards care to tell me what in God's name is going on with *my ship*?!"

In the silence that followed, Colyer could hear the individual droplets pattering back onto the sea's surface after each wave had passed along the hull.

Though the captain was clearly far from fit, his fury had given him strength. He had stood the ship down from its unorthodox action stations within moments of appearing on deck, and demanded a conference with the officers, leaving Gilpin with the deck. Colyer just had time to pass the word for the Starboard Watch's usual foretop lookout to take her place before hurrying after the rest of the commissioned officers. The officers assembled in MacQuarrie's cabin—which at that moment was still simply the end of the gun-deck. As the meeting began, the stern-chasers still gaped ashamedly out of the open ports, and seamen, their faces downcast, awkwardly re-erected the bulkheads.

MacQuarrie, though, had overreached himself. Though his head wound was all but healed, the days he had spent lying comatose in a cot had weakened him. He railed at Malory and the other officers by turn for letting the ship go to rack and ruin, but within a short time his fury had blown itself out. He had ignored Colyer in his rantings—perhaps he had tired himself before he got to her, she considered. More likely she was beneath his notice. The unpromising, low-class snotty who had become something between a pet and an experiment for Malory. Malory who the captain had come to rely on, and hated for it.

As the captain faded, Malory deftly took control of the situation again, flattering the captain's ego. They had attempted to follow his orders even while he was incapacitated. Had gone to every length to capture the beast—they owed it to their captain not to fail him. Until he had reawakened they had been standing at action stations—for hours in fact, determined not to let the beast get away again.

Colyer looked on astonished as MacQuarrie ordered Malory to resume their previous evolutions. No sooner had the men finished restoring the captain's cabin than they were instructed to begin taking it to pieces again.

"Oh, and Mister Malory?" asked the captain, just as he had seemed about to dismiss them to return to their assigned stations. "May I inquire what action you took following...I mean to say, after my...incapacitation?"

Colyer saw a flicker of despairing confusion pass across the captain's bewhiskered face, and for a moment he looked very old. She realised he had no idea what had happened. Malory, as usual, was ahead of her.

"Well of course you will recall, Sir, that a small group of the men had begun an organised disobedience?"

"Yes....yes of course...." muttered MacQuarrie. "And then?"

"I ordered two dozen lashes for each man who had shown insubordination. We have had no trouble since.

"Good...good...but what of...ahm..."

"We had ordered the protesters to stand down and quit their insolence, when that man Spencer evidently decided to take advantage of the situation to take his revenge on you, Sir. He had evidently blamed you for his undoing."

"The wretch!" MacQuarrie hissed.

"He struck you with a boarding pike."

A little of MacQuarrie's usual crimson rose to his face again for a moment, before pallor reasserted itself.

"What has been done with him?" asked the Captain quietly, carefully.

"Oh," said Malory conversationally, "Mister Colyer shot him through the throat."

MacQuarrie turned his eyes on her for the first time since they had been called to the cabin. He held the stare for several seconds, searching, evaluating, his eyebrows slightly arched. "Really?" he uttered: "Really? Well, capital. Well *done*, that, man. Well *done* indeed."

"Thank you, Sir," she responded, while the room spun and she longed to rush up on deck for fear that she might throw up on the chequer-painted deck covering.

She had half turned towards the companionway and freedom when a sudden, mighty thump resounded from the after end of the cabin and a simultaneous lurch of the deck sent the officers sprawling onto the canvas. A second thump was accompanied by a splintering of wood and glass—and a gigantic, slick snout shoving its way through the stern windows.

The officers scrabbled back, stunned, pressing themselves against the hull. Colyer glimpsed shock, defiance, outrage in their eyes. The beast gained another couple of feet, bowing a deck-beam —the cracking timber broke the spell and Malory yelled for weapons. Someone scrambled for a pistol, which misfired. The creature tried to open its mouth but the deckhead was too low. Still, its teeth were bared, just feet away from Colyer. Its breath was warm, damp, salty.

Feet were running, and dimly she became aware of men shouting. The creature's eyes were...

She stood, slowly, facing the beast. Its crescentic nostril flared. Its eyes gazed unfathomably. It tried to open its jaws again, and again could not. Figures ran past her, shoving long, pointed objects at the creature. It seemed to screech and started to pull its head back past the shattered windows. Something grabbed her from behind, dragging her back and she yelped, kicking in reflex.

"Ouch!" snapped Malory right in her ear. "You caught me in the shin you little fool! Get out of here, dammit, that thing could have had you!" His arms released her.

"Aye, Sir!" she squeaked in realisation, "Sorry, Sir," and ran for the spar deck, not looking back. Behind her, the stern chasers boomed, one after the other.

The glare of the sun off the clouds blinded her. She cowered in the companionway, shading her eyes, half expecting the serpent's huge form to loom out of the incandescence. Her sight adjusted—the creature was nowhere to be seen. Blinking, she stepped out onto the open space—*so open*—and moved to the quarterdeck.

Lambert and Douglas had reached the deck before her, joining Gilpin at the 'windward' rail (which could be identified only by the set of the yards—there was, still, not a breath of wind). The two lieutenants were both casting their eyes in every direction, in a completely disordered way. They would never see anything that way, she scoffed. At that point, the sea boiled furiously a hundred yards off the beam, the sun glinting off dark, wet flanks briefly visible. Not a man above decks could miss it.

Once again the ship was unready. After the captain had reawakened and stood the crew down the gunports had been closed and the powder drawn from the guns and muskets. The normal watch pattern had been reinstituted and the watch below had all retired to their hammocks, relieved to be able to sleep. Colyer wondered silently at the temperament of men who knew that the dangers had not diminished, but allowed a single order from a senior officer to absolve them of responsibility and act as if all was well.

The splashing subsided, only for the same thing to happen again on the opposite beam a minute or two later. Malory hurried on deck, visibly flustered, followed a moment later by Captain MacQuarrie, white as a sheet and leaning on his steward, and Owers the surgeon close behind. The sea serpent plunged out of the sea astern, and lanced back beneath the waves. The intake of breath from the watching crew was so simultaneous it was as if the ship itself had gasped. Colyer coughed artificially until Douglas and Lambert noticed, each staring quizzically at her before noticing the captain shuffling aft. They drifted down to the other rail letting MacQuarrie have the 'windward' side as was his right by custom.

"Beat to quarters," she heard the captain croak to Malory. The order was given and only a short while after the ship had been restored to stand-by, the crew were pulling it back to action stations. Some of those who had thought themselves free to sleep appeared bleary-eyed, irritable, but only for a moment. They knew what was at stake. And in any case, most of the men had at one time or another been pulled from their rest just to satisfy the whim of some sadistic officer trying to catch them off guard with pointless drills.

Despite the earlier disarray, *Daedalus* was ready in minutes. Colyer was about to scamper to the fore-top again, when she heard the doctor clear his throat and suggest that the captain's concussion might be reasserting itself. He fussed around a strangely compliant MacQuarrie, before nervously suggesting: "Sir, if I may examine you down in the Orlop, away from the noise and confusion, we may satisfy ourselves you are in no danger of a relapse into coma."

"Very well," said the Captain, "Malory, you have the deck until I return." He looked about to faint, but made it to the companionway without assistance.

As she ran over the gangway and swung onto the fore-rigging, it dawned on Colyer that this had been a piece of theatre, probably worked out before Malory and MacQuarrie had come on deck. MacQuarrie must have known he was barely fit to stand, let alone command a ship in combat—a strange combat at that. But he could not simply hand over the ship to Malory just because he felt unwell. Once again, the first lieutenant must have persuaded the captain without the latter realising he had been manoeuvred.

As Colyer clambered onto the fore-top, she felt a wash of relief that Malory was back in charge, then resumed her lookout procedure. The post was beneath her new role as acting lieutenant, but she no longer felt any resentment at that—she would far rather be up here than standing idle on that exposed quarterdeck.

With that thought, she caught sight of a sinuous form, slithering a few feet below the surface directly towards the bow with the rolling waves. "Deck there!" she yelled, "beast dead ahead! No, a point to port!"

"Bow chaser!" she heard Malory call, jogging forward, "Ready on my command!"

The big 56-pounder was fortunately offset to port of the bowsprit, facing the oncoming waves—to windward, or what would have been. Habits of the service were hard to break.

Malory looked to her expectantly. She spotted the serpent again, thirty feet from the bow, and pointed at it, keeping her outstretched arm aimed at the undulating shape. Ripples on the surface began to distort the view, and a moment later, its head broke the surface.

"It's coming up," Colyer shouted.

Malory waited for the briefest moment, before ordering "fire!" The big gun roared out, a load of grapeshot slicing across the water. It caught the serpent just as it had begun to launch itself at the beakhead. The creature took the full blast of the powder and half the load of one-pound balls on the underside of its head and neck, and the force flipped it end over end. Its limp body crashed into the water fifty feet away and it slipped gradually below the surface.

DAEDALUS AND THE DEEP

"You got it! You got it!" she screamed, and a cheer rang out from the deck.

"Silence!" snapped Malory. "It might not be done for. Keep looking," he added to the lookouts stationed around the ship, and Colyer herself.

Minutes passed. Surely the creature was dead. Though she continued to quarter the seas, the acting officer began to feel a mounting sense of relief. Her heart slowed gradually.

"Starboard beam!" howled the man in the maintop, an instant before the familiar long, dark entity speared into the air and latched onto the end of the mainyard with its jaws.

"Starboard battery, fire!" ordered Malory reflexively, and the guns pounded out a broadside—all missed. The serpent was too close and between gunports. The marines unleashed a volley of musket fire, which the beast just shrugged off, then another crashed out from the second file which had the same effect.

"Harpoons!" Malory yelled, at which point a handful of men with the whaling weapons ran to the starboard rail, but just then a mighty 'crack' emanated from the mainyard and it lurched under the serpent's weight. There was another 'crack' and the huge yard swung at a drunken angle. The serpent plunged back into the sea, and when the ripples subsided silence reigned once again.

Not for long. "Port beam, twenty fathoms!" shouted another of the lookouts. The serpent breached the surface and kicked its tail.

"Port battery, fire!" Malory commanded. The five heavy 32-pounders thumped out rapidly one by one. Grapeshot tore the surface to streaks of foam, but the creature had already gone. In a moment, it reappeared right below the mizzen chains, once again lancing high out of the water and grabbing the mizzen course-yard.

It means to wreck our rigging! Colyer thought, even as she jumped back away from the edge of the top in surprise. The creature thrashed from side to side and in a moment, the yard had ripped from its mountings, falling half way to the deck in a tearing cradle of cordage.

Her next thought was: *It's worked out that it takes us a minute or so to reload!* They must be hellishly careful about firing the main guns again. She was about to relay this information to the deck when she spotted Malory in conference with the gunner. Peddle moved away, gathering a few less occupied men and within moments she saw the small saluting-guns and quarterdeck carronades being loaded. The port guns were run in and reloaded, but not run out again. The port lids snapped shut.

The serpent breached again, this time several points aft of the port beam. On this occasion, only the small guns fired despite being well out of range. Nevertheless, a decent volume of smoke belched forth and the noise was not much quieter than the main guns had seemed—Colyer wondered if the decoy guns had been loaded with double charges to add to the effect. The barrels would not stand up to much of that, but with luck they would not need to.

As previously, the creature had plunged below the surface as the guns had fired, and the next obvious target was the foreyard. Her stomach turned, and she tried to guess where the serpent would emerge next. It seemed to learn quickly, so she chanced a quick scan to starboard in case it had ducked under the ship. Sure enough she sensed movement somewhere below the fore-chains on the opposite side.

"Starboard bow!" she yelped, stabbing furiously with her finger.

"Starboard battery ready!" Malory shouted, then just as the serpent launched itself at the fore-yard, the port-lids whipped open and Malory bawled "fire!". The cannonade crashed out, and a load of grapeshot from the foremost gun caught the serpent a glancing blow. It howled as it writhed in the air, changing course from a dart straight up at the yard to a backflip which took it down through the surface again, hardly a splash marking its position.

For a few minutes, peace returned to the scene. Not a ripple could be seen anywhere around the corvette. Then, "dead astern!" called Midshipman Gower in the mizzen top, and a moment later "gone again!"—at which moment the snout of the serpent shot up over the taffrail, grasping at the spanker boom. The crew of the stern chaser and the nearby carronades scattered, despite the roar of Malory demanding they stand their ground—as he was, even while the serpent hung overhead, worrying at the big spar.

After a few moments, some of the spare men brandishing harpoons collected themselves and ran aft. As they jabbed at the creature's neck, the topping lift gave way and the boom crashed to the deck with the serpent's jaws still clamped around it. This time the harpooneers fled—two were not fast enough and Colyer saw them knocked to the deck.

One seemed stunned, and crawled away slowly. The other's feet had been crushed beneath the falling spar, and he whimpered pitifully as he attempted to drag himself away from the serpent with his arms. The creature released its grip on the boom and drew its head back, regarding the crawling seamen with cold black eyes. Almost delicately, it poked its nose forward and picked up the second sailor by his wrecked feet. The man's whimper rose to a howl before the serpent casually flicked him back into its jaws, crunched down and swallowed him whole.

Everyone on the ship froze, horrorstruck. The serpent could slither aboard and take every man if it wanted. Then, there was a bang of gunpowder and a jet of smoke from somewhere near the starboard rail and the serpent recoiled, sliding hurriedly beneath the waves.

Colyer knew she had to keep up the lookout, but sneaked a glance for the gun that had gone off—Malory had swivelled one of the saluting guns onto the quarterdeck and managed to load and train it unseen. He had probably fired it with no shot just for effect, but it seemed to have done the trick.

There was a frantic splashing just off the starboard bow, the creature putting its head out for a moment as if to test the reaction. A brass carronade went off and the serpent's head dipped out of sight again even as Malory berated the gun's captain for firing without an order.

At that instant, something beyond her normal senses seemed to impel Colyer to look away from the battle below, to the West where the sky met the sea.

Across the horizon was a dark band, a strip of grey so dense it had a blueish tinge. She frowned. It had not been there earlier, had it? There was something odd about the strip, as if it were smearing the sea and the sky into each other.

The smear seemed somehow deeper than it had just a few moments ago. It formed a definite band now. The horizon looked much closer than it should be. Just a couple of miles—three or four at most. The guns boomed out again and she sensed rather than saw a violent splashing to port. A noise began to rise in the chests of the men below, the beginning of a cheer, that was choked off a moment later. With the battle against the serpent seemingly at its height, she still could not tear her gaze from that odd meteorological curiosity. A small part of her mind rebelled, screaming at her to look down at the creature below, at the guns and men desperate to kill it. She could not. Was it exhaustion finally coming to bear? Or had part of her finally broken under the strain?

Another salvo crashed out below and—was that...? Had she felt a breath against her face? A displacement of air from the cannon, perhaps? But not something she had ever experienced in all the practice shooting. Just a slight puff....

She stared at the grey streak, which had grown yet again, certain it was important, not knowing why.

Finally, the youthful lieutenant remembered her glass. She pulled it from her pocket, extended it and swung the lens toward the phenomenon.

The face of the streak was like a smooth, stone wall, completely featureless. Frustrated, she swung the glass upwards. The wall seemed to fade gently into the low cloud above. She trained the telescope downward instead.

It looked as though the sea was being torn up by its roots. The wall, seemingly so still, was churning up the face of the water and throwing ragged chunks of it into the air like blocks of pumice from an erupting volcano. Her hands fell, and the vision of the onrush without the glass seemed so much closer even in the space of seconds. A mile. Maybe two. Her heart jolted.

"SQUALL!" she screamed, not directed at anyone in particular. "A *squall,* big one, *five points on the port bow!*"

She already knew it was not just a squall—a gale, even a hurricane.

Malory gawped up at her, disbelief in his eyes, but he ran to the rail. In the eerie silence that had fallen over the ship she heard his muttered exclamation of "*Jesus!*" before he turned back to the afterguard.

"Leave the foretopsail! Get the main and mizzen tops'ls in, quick as your lives depended on it. Square the yards! And get the damned guns secured!" The men were already running, climbing, struggling, would be too late...

"Colyer!" Malory yelled up at her, his hands forming a trumpet, "Keep your eyes forrard, don't worry about anything else, if you see an obstruction, another ship or a whale, even a bigger than average wave, signal which way to steer to clear it. Like *this.*" He threw his arm out straight, first one, then the other. "Granby will stand at the mainmast and pass your instructions to the helmsman."

Colyer barely had time to squeak an acknowledgement, and wrap a couple of turns of a spare line around herself and the mast. Looking back to the squall she was just in time to see the water rising up like a curtain. The wind hit the corvette an instant before the sea did. A wall of air hammered into the rig, heaving the masts into a desperate heel. She whipped her head away from the wind, gasping. The onrushing sea burst against the bow, shattered, and spray like ground glass sliced at faces and hands. The rig shrieked, cables under tension howling in vibration, those loosened by the strain hammered against the spars.

The maintopsail blew into ribbons even while the men on deck wrestled with the buntlines. Those at the mizzen were quicker, luckier, and had their canvas secured before the gale could pluck at an unsecured fold. Beneath her she felt rather than heard the foretopsail straining, every stitch protesting. It held though, and through the mast Colyer sensed the ship raising itself up, bulling against the sea, and the head starting to fall off to leeward.

They were not finished yet, by God! There was still a chance. The bow shrugged off a weight of green water and carved to starboard. The masts, forced over by the drag of the wind, began to tremble upright again as the load transferred from the beam to the length of the hull. Through the bar-taught lines she caught a glimpse of four men at the wheel, fighting the spokes, Granby bound to the mainmast, staring up at her. As bidden, she turned her eyes forward, into the maelstrom while the screaming wind carried them on, to safety or destruction.

CHAPTER 32

CAPTAIN MacQuarrie stood on the quarterdeck of the corvette HMS *Daedalus*, a gale howling around him, staring down into a giant pit opening ahead of the bow. He resisted the temptation to recoil and stood his ground. The ship seemed to topple over the crest towards the abyss, but the sailing master directing the men at the wheel had already swung the ship's head a point to windward. Instead of plunging straight into the trough, the vessel skidded diagonally along the face of the wave. By the time the *Daedalus* had reached the foot of the giant swell, the steepness of the slope had smoothed out and the water was beginning to rise underneath the hull again.

For a blessed moment, the wind shadow of the great wave they had just surfed down masked the quarterdeck from the scream of the gale, and MacQuarrie had a chance to adjust his pose, stretch some of his aching muscles and push his hat back down hard onto his head. The corvette fought its way up the face of the next mountain of water, once again the sailing master keeping the course a point or two diagonal to the wind and the rushing waves, seeking out a longer, smoother course between crest and trough.

They had been doing this now for hours. The instinct of every man aboard was to hunker down and try to let the storm blow over them. To stay out of the wind which threatened to lift them off the deck and fling them into space, the water which jetted up and back off the bow slamming into raw skin and bruised flesh. It was an instinct that must be resisted at all costs.

The eyes of every man aboard blared with agony from the salt blasted into them every few moments. There was not a man aboard who did not long to close them for a while, or turn their face out of it for some relief.

They could not. If a single man failed to concentrate the ship could be lost. MacQuarrie recognised that the hardest task of anyone at that moment was the sailing master, and acknowledged Gilpin's skill with grudging respect. It was up to the old tarpaulin to decide, instant by instant, the corrections to course and rig that would keep the ship from disaster.

They had averted it so far, but the next moment could bring death, or if they survived that, the next or the one after that.

If they lost speed, there was a danger that the wave behind could break over the stern. If that happened, they were doomed—the water would tear through the ship, filling the bilges, smashing the steering...they would roll over or sink in moments. If they picked up too much speed they could pile into the back of the wave in front. If *that* happened, the ship would shudder to a halt but the rig would keep going under the force of the wind. They would be dismasted, and then pooped by the wave behind for good measure.

It was up to Gilpin to keep the ship on as even a keel as possible, stymie any sudden acceleration and prevent any loss of momentum. He could take not a moment's rest.

Through the bellow of the wind he heard the bosun yelling something to Gilpin, and the sailing master ordered another correction. The four men at the wheels heaved at the spokes and once again the ship seemed to skirt round the edge of a wave that had built itself up to abnormal height, clambering over the foothills of the mountain rather than attempting the peak.

He knew that the young temporary lieutenant, Colyer, was at the fore-top, signalling any obstructions. He hoped the man was up to the ordeal. Such a skinny fellow—still, MacQuarrie reasoned, for some reason it was the skinny ones who seemed to keep their energy up better than the hulking muscular types in these sort of conditions. As long as he kept pointing out the largest waves, the deepest troughs and anything dangerous lying in the water while they had a chance to take avoiding action, everything would be well. They could not see a thing from deck height.

The truth was that MacQuarrie felt horribly weak and old, and the storm seemed to be biting chunks out of him. For the first time in his naval career he felt that events were not in his control. There was no order, command, threat or insult he could yell that would make any difference at all. His entire sense of command seemed to have fallen away, but oddly it did not seem to matter. He watched Gilpin at work for a while, fancying that the man sensed the ship's very feel, analysing and responding to the slightest tremor starting to build in the rigging, or the signs of stress in the frames.

MacQuarrie then turned his gaze to Malory beside him. Malory looked like a half-tide rock, standing immobile while the gale seemed to swirl around him. There was a core of something tough to Malory, but his exterior was all theatre. He would make a good captain one day, perhaps, but an odd kind of captain. Looking at Malory now, he seemed to be built of disparate scraps. Like those newfangled steam sloops—there was something about Malory that made no sense to him.

He had evidently practised that look of implacable determination he was wearing, jaw set, arms clasped lightly behind his back, staring fixedly ahead. But MacQuarrie could see the uncertainty in his eyes. It was reassuring to see that his first lieutenant was human. He could not help but smile. Something told him that not very long ago that self-consciously calculated pose would have annoyed him, but now he was simply amused.

Perhaps the experience of the cruise had weakened him. He privately admitted that he would struggle in the hours ahead. MacQuarrie knew he was not in good health, having awoken from his stupor greatly weakened. He was of course not a young man. His skin was grey, and hung loose from his face. His body had wasted away and most surprising of all, he had not taken a drink since he had come around. In fact he could not bear to look at alcohol now, strange though it seemed. Since regaining consciousness he no longer seemed to want, or need, whatever it was that the many bottles and decanters in his cabin had offered.

There was a new, fearful clarity to the world since he awoke, but something visceral in the clarity. The time of chasing the serpent seemed like a dream. Absurd even. He wondered for a moment why it had seemed quite so important. This gale on the other hand was a real, solid ordeal—a seaman's challenge, and they would come through it by seamanship or not at all. There was nothing more important than how they faced this hour.

He wondered if the serpent was still chasing them, but could not make himself quite believe that the thing had ever been real. Had they fought only a phantom? It didn't matter. This tempest was challenge enough for any one man to deal with.

Daedalus and The Deep

He was tired and so cold he could no longer sense his hands and feet. He could feel a great lethargy trying to settle upon him, which he forced away. He would not succumb. Not this time. He had a duty to his men and his ship. There was a time when, youthful and vigorous, energised by the novelty of command, he had stayed on deck in storms for thirty-six hours or more. It was not that he needed to be there to give commands or make decisions. He could not do anything that would make the slightest difference—it was his very presence that was essential. He needed every man to see him there, standing firm. While he did, they could do the same.

There was every chance this storm would sink them. He would not cower in his cabin while that happened. If this was to be the end of his career—the end of his life—he wanted to face it like the man he knew he *should* be. And those bastards aft of the mainmast, and before it for that matter, would know that he was their Captain, who had done his utmost.

But they were not done for yet. And if he could stay here—stay conscious, stay alive—the men might not lose spirit. And if they did not lose spirit they would fight with every breath in their body to stay alive too.

As if managing the ship in a tempest was not enough the crew had to make good some of the damage caused during the last engagement. The damaged mizzen and main-yards with their wrecked sails had to be made fast lest they come loose and trail in the water like a vast, lethal sea-anchor. It had taken half the company four hours to repair enough of the rigging and haul the huge spars into a sufficiently secure position. They could not set sails on them until they had been properly repaired, but at this moment that was the least of their worries.

Nothing beyond the next wave, the next gust, concerned them now.

The ship climbed again, clawing its way up the face of a huge roller. The bowsprit dragged its dolphin-striker in the foam, and the bow followed it just as the hull reached the crest. A solid mass of water careened back along the spar deck, and MacQuarrie could barely grab at the mainmast pinrail before the living sea swamped him and every man on the quarterdeck up to the hips. A man swept by, borne along by the turbulence, and grabbed at MacQuarrie's ankles. The Captain hung onto the pinrail with both hands, fighting to stay on his feet. The sailor managed to stagger to his knees, coughing and choking, his face almost black. MacQuarrie risked taking a hand off the pinrail to grasp the man's collar, and helped him to his feet.

The seaman recovered something of his composure, coughing out gouts of water while staring at the Captain, and a look of mortification swept across his features.

"*Never mind that, back to your post now*," MacQuarrie shouted over the wind.

"Aye, Sir," answered the man, saluting and almost losing his balance again before staggering back toward the bow, a few feet at a time.

The green sea that had burst aboard a few moments before had stopped surging aft and was swilling about the deck at a depth of a foot or so, slowly streaming out of the scuppers. The *Daedalus* swayed dangerously to port, then starboard, top heavy for a moment, but the weight of the water was diminishing and gradually the corvette's rolling slowed. The Captain realised his heart was slowing too, though it was still thumping like an uncatted anchor swinging against his ribs.

MacQuarrie relaxed his grip on the pinrail but did not let go. In these circumstances it was very much a case of 'one hand for yourself and one for the ship.'

Over the constant blast of the wind he heard a muted cry from forward, which was taken up closer by. He saw a few men let go of whatever handholds they had found to struggle to the rail, despite the bucking of the deck, peering ahead into the tumult. The yell reached Gilpin, a few feet away. He still couldn't hear the words— *sounded something like 'Hye! Hye!'*—but Gilpin barked an order and the wheelmen heaved at the spokes. The head started to swing again, rapidly this time, and the corvette began another plunge down the face of a wave. Still the head came round, and instead of the skilful weave along the wave's face, the corvette kept turning to port, back where they had come from. The angle of heel increased and the single foresail they had set started to judder as its leading edge came too close to the wind, beginning to back a touch.

Gilpin was taking the ship beam-on to wind and sea! They could not survive it!

"Gilpin!" he howled, "Full and bye damn you!"

"*Hye, Sir, Hye!*" Gilpin shouted back, jabbing to leeward with a white finger.

Daedalus and the Deep

A jolt shivered through the planks beneath his feet, then another. MacQuarrie lurched to the lee rail to see a slab of grey stone the size of a dockyard lighter spinning lazily along the tumblehome. Not stone—ice. The floe bumped against the hull one more time, almost tenderly, before spiralling back into the storm.

Ice! Were they really so far south?

Gilpin was directing the helm up again, but the corvette had virtually come to a standstill. MacQuarrie looked to windward to see the wave they had just overtaken about to pile into their beam.

He screamed a warning, a meaningless noise that mingled with the whistle of wind through the rigging. A ridge of grey water broke over the deck, and this time nobody kept their footing. MacQuarrie hung onto the railing, his legs streaming horizontally while for a moment he was totally submerged. Just as suddenly, the water subsided and his feet found the deck again, but he was still up to his waist. A heap of bodies around his feet began to stir. *Daedalus* looked like it had been caught beneath a Biblical deluge. Here and there deck equipment and men poked out of the sea which washed over the whole vessel unbroken. The hull lurched and somewhere nearby he sensed a rope parting.

Gilpin had managed to hang onto the wheel, as had two of the four helmsmen, and began swinging the spokes to bring the ship onto a downwind course again. Momentum built, while the sailing master focussed on keeping the hull braced against the wind —too far downwind and there would be nothing to dampen the rolling. Once again the water slopped bit by bit off the deck, over the rail and out the scuppers. The ship began to feel less sluggish beneath his feet again.

MacQuarrie attempted to let go of the rail to make his way back to the mizzen, but as he tried to release his fingers they refused to moved and pain lanced through his hands. He could have cried out in agony, but stopped himself. His hands had locked rigid. He could not open them try as he might. The pain was joined by nausea, and for a few moments he was utterly insensible to the storm and the ship fighting for its life beneath his feet.

He recovered himself somewhat, and tried gripping harder to see if that would disengage something in the mechanisms of his hand. It did not. He tried leaning back, pulling against his grip with his arms and shoulders. The pain multiplied—his hands felt like they were made of driftwood and worn-out rope that would snap under the strain.

Slowly, his fingers scraped free of the rail. Another thrust of pain shot through the muscles and he gasped, trying to rub his twisted claws on his forearms. A little movement returned.... He staggered back to the mizzen, leaning against the pinrail with the heels of his palms, not daring to close his fingers around anything again. He felt a lump of sickness in the pit of his stomach, and dragged a breath into his chest. He wanted nothing so much as to vomit, or sit upon the deck.

"All right, Sir?" shouted Malory in his ear. The first lieutenant wore a concerned expression, with the usual wolfish glint in his eye missing for once.

"Fine, fine," MacQuarrie muttered. He glanced around for something neglected or left undone so that he could issue an order or two to restore his authority a little. The plunge through the wave had carried several of the braces away, sweeping them off their belaying pins. Some of the yards were in consequence swaying and banging on their parrels.

"There's a mess of rigging everywhere, Mister Malory!" he exclaimed. "Get it all squared away if you please."

Malory had placed his ear right beside MacQuarrie's face to pick out the order, and for a moment he looked confused, but then something clicked and he responded, "Aye aye, Sir, rigging, right away." Soon MacQuarrie could see Granby and his mates struggling about the deck, unravelling, replacing and securing the tangle of loose and broken gear trailing uncontrollably in the wind.

As the work reached a conclusion he saw the men fighting the elements on the deck and in the rigging as the ship bucked and started beneath them, and felt more old and worn out than he had ever in his life.

Chapter 33

COLYER felt as though she had grown into the mast and was now no more than part of its structure. She stood bound around the middle to the thick spar, feet braced to the foretop platform, the eyes of the corvette. For the first hour or so she had been sick with the worry, desperate that she should not lead them all to oblivion by missing a potential disaster in their path. There had been a few horrific moments early on when, unsure of how to direct the ship, she had unwittingly steered them into a particularly deep trough or an unusually steep crest.

After a time, however, she had acclimatised to the shape of this sea and could direct accordingly. For the most part, of course, Granby and Gilpin did not need her help. There had only been one moment of genuinely catastrophic consequences, when a large ice floe had loomed out of the sea and despite her warning it had bumped down the side of the hull. She prayed they had not been holed.

Since then there had been a few more pieces of ice, but smaller, and she had been able to direct the ship away from them. When you knew what you were looking for they were easy to spot, as the sea foamed white around their edges.

Nevertheless, it was a strain. She hoped desperately that the storm would begin to blow itself out, or they would pass out of it, or just that someone would be sent to relieve her. She missed the companionship of the quarterdeck—it was fearsomely alone up in the foretop.

Then, without realising quite when, Colyer was aware of another presence. She had heard or seen nothing, but it was as indisputable as the feeling of strong sunlight on the back of the neck. Her heart lurched. She whipped her head left and right, thinking there was someone else standing with her on the foretop. There was no one. Her gaze turned back ahead, and as the bow crested a steep hill of solid water, rising from the tearing mass with horrible grace, was the sea serpent, seemingly staring her in the eye.

The sun burned through the clouds just as the wave rose to its peak and the *Daedalus* slewed into the preceding trough. For an instant Colyer was struck with the impression of a mountain of refracting crystal looming overhead, a coiled serpentine form at its midst it as if set in amber. The clear light streamed through as she gazed *up* at the inverted tableau—ship below, sea above. In a moment the scene was gone, replaced with a shattering wall of steel grey and bilious foam, in which their enemy writhed. It came on relentlessly.

She waved furiously at the helmsmen, unheeded. *Starboard! Starboard!*

The *Daedalus* rushed on, unstoppable, the power of an ocean behind it. It climbed the face of the wave, rising up to meet the serpent as the creature slithered down toward the rushing corvette.

For a moment she felt an angry swell of euphoria—the ship must run the beast down. In her mind she saw it crushed, swept aside, smashed against the irresistible force. Then, like a sudden taste of bile under the tongue, the realisation dawned. The creature leapt from the foam like a salmon, whipped itself over the bowsprit and beak, and its head and front end plunged back into the water.

With a power that could not possibly belong to any living thing on this Earth, the serpent heaved the corvette's head round. The men at the wheel were flung away, one curving through the air to land on the opposite beam, as the rudder was wrenched from their control.

The hurtling ship balked, and yawed wildly. Diverted from its course directly downwind, the mighty forward motion arrested fatally, its stern slewed to starboard. As it did so, a wave broke over the deck, piling foam at the bulwarks and making of each man below nothing but a dark blob outlined by a streaming feather. The masts leaned and leaned, caught athwartships by the force of the gale. Still the serpent pulled.

The great weight of the ship fought against the struggling serpent's unnatural power. The triple reefed foresail strained to pull the corvette's head back downwind. For a moment the two forces opposed each other in perfect balance, while the wind screamed past the spars and howled helplessly through the rigging, and the sea thundered in frustration below.

It seemed that the foresail might win. The bowsprit made a slight lunge to leeward. The crew raised a cheer that Colyer heard the remnants of, even in the foretop.

Another wave, larger than the last, chose that moment to pile into the stern. It lifted the after end of the ship, hoisting it forward, pivoting around the dragging bow and the tenacious serpent.

A roaring gust joined the wave. Together they added their might to the forces straining to heave the hull over. Now catching the masts and the reefed foresail beam-on, the full strength of the gale punished the corvette.

Colyer thought madly of Hector, pursued three times around the walls of Troy by Achilles. Turning to fight. Being struck down in an instant.

She heard someone scream "She's going! She's going!" and thought it might have been her. The masts hovered at an unseen point of equilibrium, then toppled downward as the corvette began to capsize. The ends of the lower yards speared the surface of the furious sea.

She took a gulp of breath and shut her eyes tightly as she foretop plunged towards the water, while grasping feebly at the lashings. Knowing it was too late.

The final dive into the sea seemed to take an age. She opened her eyes and looked around. The foretop hovered above the waves, falling no further. The capsize had frozen before the masts hit the water. *Daedalus* had broached-to, but stopped short of turning turtle. The ballast had held secure and was, for now, holding the ship on its beam ends. The huge masts were tilted almost horizontal, but no longer presented such an inviting surface for the wind to push on. There was nothing to continue pulling the ship over. Colyer allowed herself the briefest sigh of relief. Now what to do?

The sea boomed and convulsed beneath her. She started pulling at the lashings holding her in place in case the ballast came loose—at the very least the corvette would invert, and most likely the mass of iron blocks would spear right through the deck planking. The vessel would go down in moments.

No one could survive in that sea for more than a few minutes, but her mind rebelled against the terror of being dragged below the surface with a sinking ship.

The mast seemed to start beneath her. She looked back down—across—to the deck. The hull was sound, and did not seem to be settling. With horror of realisation, she looked *up* the mast...

The serpent had slid from the bowsprit and was even now wriggling along the forestay, stretching its length onto the mast itself. Dully, she watched as it lost its footing and slipped back into the sea. The beast tried again, towering, unsupported from the water, undisturbed by the roaring turbulence. This time it hooked its fore-quarters over the cross-trees and began, with a disgusting rippling motion, to draw itself up onto the spar.

The whole ship seemed to shriek with the load.

The serpent wriggled, hauling another few feet of its length onto the topmast. Colyer felt her bladder let go. The creature seemed to look at her.

She felt, rather than heard, the shrouds creak with the strain, a trembling vibration buzzing into her through the lashings. She saw a few of the fibres unwind and break. The youth looked back to the serpent, seeing the mast bounce with the weight. In an instant of mad euphoria she wondered if the foot would be well and truly jerked out of the step this time. With a spike of hopelessness she feared the mast would come down, then with a little burst of defiance, hoped it collapsed under the beast. Why were the cables not breaking?

It was then that her eyes lit on the axe. She remembered she had considered it as something to defend herself with when mutiny seemed likely, if the worst came to the worst. Well, it had come to the worst and the last thing she wanted to do was attack the serpent with a hand tool.

...But perhaps she could attack the shrouds. A few good strokes and the strain might do the rest. It wouldn't be necessary to cut the shroud itself—just the thinner tensioning lines running through the deadeyes.

She fumbled with the axe's lashings, but could not reach far enough. She carried on untying the knots that held her in place. As the rope slackened, she felt for one horrible moment that the wind would lift her right into the air, but her weight held her, and she scrabbled at the thin line, after a moment remembering her pocket knife. A few hacking slices. Finally, the axe was free in her hands.

She clambered astride the mast and struck at the cable above her head with the blade of the axe—a few paltry strands parted. The rope could have been an iron strap for all the effect the axe seemed to be having. But the creature was looped over the fore topmast now, pitting its weight against the ballast, heaving the ship over, inch by inch. The entire ship seemed to be groaning. She thought she heard men roaring but couldn't be sure above the howl of the wind and the crash of the sea.

She struck the cable again, careful to mark the same place as before. A few more strands went. She began to thump the axe against the thick rope repeatedly, less seamanlike axe work, more like chopping firewood.

She dare not look at the creature. In her mind, it crawled sickeningly closer. Its jaws widened.... She kept chopping and chopping.

First, an ache started to bloom through her shoulders like warmth. She continued swinging the axe, and the ache spread to her chest, then her hips. She hacked and hacked, and through the ache, her joints became points of pain. She raised the axe and let it swing, giving the weight of the head whatever push she could. Her whole body was groaning with the effort now, her muscles felt like frayed rope running over splintered wood.

Stop, shouted her muscles. *No*, she replied through the tears, trying to quicken her pace instead.

Just rest for a while, said her joints.

I'll rest when I'm finished, she spat back.

Her arms felt as though they were full of acid, burning out from the inside. But still she chopped, dragging the axe up against the wind, heaving it at the rigging. The serpent heaved another few feet of its length onto the spar. The ship pitted its last reserves against its foe.

Colyer felt as though she had been chopping for hours, but that couldn't be right. Then it felt as if she had barely started. The shrouds swam before her eyes.

Just then, the fibres in the thick cable started to break of their own accord, strand by tiny strand. She kept up her chopping with a rush of hope, and with another two or three strikes, the cable parted, and the shroud recoiled like a whip, ripping the ratlines away for half its length and sending another mighty groan through the mast. But the other shrouds held. She dare not look for the serpent.

With her mind and body screeching at her to stop, or sleep, or die, Colyer started on the second shroud. She was barely able to do more than chew at the cable, and the axe was getting clogged with the Stockholm tar that the standing rigging was impregnated with.

She cleaned the blade's edge as best she could with her jacket sleeve, and started chopping again. It seemed to take fewer strokes this time, until the second cable started to part, the sound of the strands creaking and pinging even apparent over the howl of the wind. Finally, it broke with a sound like musket fire.

She had begun a feeble chopping at the third cable when, with a cannon-like boom, she felt the mast shift beneath her. The remaining shrouds broke in a ripple, and the topmast started to pivot around its doubling.

It was only relief that washed over her as she saw, as if through fog, the upper mast, with all its yards, and the sea-serpent, begin to fall away towards the maelstrom below. The ship began to swim upright again. In a burst of wild delight, she dropped the axe, which spun down and splashed noiselessly into the sea. She became dimly aware of a vast creaking, crashing, cracking that seemed to surround her. The doubled mast on which she had sat was no longer there. She shifted her weight towards the platform, but that was no longer there either. There was for a few moments, a rushing wind, but most oddly it seemed to be blowing past her straight *upwards*. Then she thumped into something cold, and slick, and very, very hard.

Something changed.

She was not aware of the change, but it must have been sudden, for one moment she was in space, the wind rushing past her, and the next she was suspended in a blue-green glow. It surrounded her and seemed to infuse her body with light. Slowly, her vision extended, radiating outward. First, she made out the bulk of the corvette's hull curving away beside her. Its thousands of copper plates twinkled in the gentle luminescence. The light was no longer all around her, but seemed to be coming from above, diffusing through the fluid in which she hovered. Below her, layers of the ether descended in progressively dark tones. It seemed to go on for ever, warm and comforting.

Her vision expanded again. A tangle of dark lines and curves hung in the glow ahead of her. After a moment the realisation pulsed through her mind that this was the topmast and its rigging. Dimly she remembered cutting the shrouds to cut the mast away so that…so that…

The tangle of rigging and spars seemed to be shaking. As her eyes adjusted, she saw something twisted around the thickness of the topmast.

The serpent.

It was caught in the jumble of cordage and spars. Colyer saw the heavy, tarred shrouds wrapped round the creature, as if they had torn away from their deadeyes and whipped back, coiling along the length of the mast. Binding the serpent as it did so. Again, she hazily remembered swinging the axe, strands parting…

The serpent stopped struggling, and turned its head toward her. She met its gaze once again.

She suddenly became aware of a crushing fear that, she realised, had gripped her every moment for months. She shrugged it off, and felt the weight of it slide off into the depths. The creature continued to regard her, unblinking. It was beautiful.

No moment of realisation came upon her, but she somehow already knew why it had pursued them across an ocean. Colyer understood its quest. That it would change the world, and the old order would be shattered, never to return. Euphorically, she resolved to go with it—with *her,* for the creature was of course female—back to the teeming black depths, overflowing as they were with mysterious and wonderful life.

The eyes called to her. Calmed her.

At that moment the blue-green glow ripped apart. A disturbance rammed through the ether, smashing the light and sucking the colour from the world. Something hard bumped against her. She tried to look round but found she could not move. The gentle luminosity of the atmosphere flicked into grey darkness, oppressive weight and choking pressure.

Acting Lieutenant Colyer began to drown.

Chapter 34

An age seemed to have passed, and yet nothing had happened.

The darkness had been replaced with light again. This was not the soft glow of the undersea though. It was a hard, white light. It swam, and resolved into a surface somewhere in front of Colyer's face. A smooth unbroken plane.

It was not unbroken though. There were lines across it. Thin but distinct, hard lines, then undulating groups of fainter lines swooping along roughly parallel to the harder lines.

Brushmarks. On wooden planks. White paint.

Idly she wondered why there was a white fence in front of her. It began to annoy her. It was blocking the way. There was somewhere she had to be. The fence was swaying slightly. She put her arm out towards it to steady the misbehaving panel.

Drunkenly, the world swung through a right-angle and instead of standing upright she realised with a jolt she was lying on her back.

The world seemed to telescope in and out at the same time, and Colyer found with a start that she was lying in a cot. Her *own* cot, in Spencer's old cabin. The events of the previous—day? week? lifetime?—rushed in like a Southern Ocean roller sweeping the deck. She grasped the sides of the cot, ludicrously afraid of falling.

More thoughts rushed into her head, competing for attention. Something old and worn hung in the background. Something important, that she must not let go of. Something that belonged to someone else but was hers just as much.

With a churn of horror she tugged back the blanket and found that she was dressed in clean cotton slops. Someone had dressed her. Someone else. On this ship of *men*.

She sat up. A sense of dread settled in her gut and she let out an involuntary croak of despair. Before the full notion of the discovery could take hold there was a knock at the thin board door. "Yes?" she rasped, sitting up. Her voice boomed in the tiny space.

It was Malory. He wore a grim expression and remained silent for a moment.

"Well, this is a pretty picture, isn't it?" he snarled finally, keeping his voice low so it could not be heard beyond the flimsy partition.

"You know then?" was all she could manage in reply. The universe switched again and it was as if she was looking at it through the wrong end of a telescope.

"Just me and the surgeon, thank God, and I've sworn him to secrecy. Do you know what would happen to you if the men found out?"

She could guess what he was thinking. She did not have the heart or the energy to mention poor Panna, who died an age ago, gladly keeping her secret.

"The ship?"

"Well, the ship is safe enough, thanks to your quick thinking," Malory allowed, not appearing happy about in the least. "The fore topmast went by the board after you took your axe to the shrouds, which righted us and the beast appeared to be tangled up in the raffle. We got away with it, and needless to say we have our best lookouts posted at the tops. Should it return..."

Malory paused, an intense expression on his face, his eyes like acid. He had not looked directly at Colyer in the minutes since he entered the cabin. Finally, he met her gaze and spat "I suppose you dreamt this whole ludicrous scheme up as some elaborate means of finding a husband?"

That yanked her out of herself. Colyer bristled, and drew herself up to as much of her five feet and five inches was possible while sitting in an Admiralty cot.

"I won't have that from you, *Mister* Malory any more than I would from a drunken landsman. I demand you take it back and apologise or, or I shall have to ask for...satisfaction." She had got through the outburst without her voice cracking, but her heart thundered in her chest.

The lieutenant did not move and for an instant his eyes shone with fury, then for a moment it looked as though he might laugh. Finally, he allowed the ghost of a smile to flicker on his face.

"Very well, very well, I withdraw the remark fully and humbly. God's teeth, Colyer, what are we to do with you? The only one of the whole damned gunroom of snotties who showed a bit of promise and it turns out you are..."

"So what do you intend to do, Sir?"

"That's the question, isn't it? Well, I shan't reveal you. And that means I can't disrate you." Relief welled in Colyer's heart but Malory went on. "You shall remain *Mister Acting Lieutenant* Colyer for a spell, but I cannot allow you to continue to serve after we return home. I shall secure you an honourable discharge from the service—perhaps you might be good enough to consider some family crisis that you will find compels you to return home..."

She did not have to think to hard on that account, she reflected bitterly—her family had suffered a son killed and a daughter run away to sea.

"And, if I ever see another Colyer on the Navy List," Malory went on, "I shall seek them out, in person, just to make sure they aren't you."

He paused and tried to pace again but ran out of space after a step and a half. "You can't help it—I understand," he said with hauteur. "Women are naturally deceptive in everything. But this must be the end, do you understand?"

Colyer nodded, mutely. So that was that. Back home to a life of service, or a post as teacher or governess if she were lucky.

"Well, then I'll leave you." He bowed to exit the tiny cabin before turning back. "By the bye, would you really have dueled me over that comment?"

Colyer smiled bleakly. "If I shot you, Sir, surely that would have solved all my problems." With a strangely hollow voice, she added, "Perhaps if you shot me, the same would apply."

This time Malory did laugh. "It's a damned shame," he chuckled, "a damned shame. But there's nothing to be done. Go home. Get married and have a son, then when he's eight or nine, for I should be made Admiral by then, send him to me." He withdrew and closed the door.

Colyer allowed the feelings of desolation, loss, outrage, despair and insult to swirl around her head before she lay down in the cot and hoped, vainly for sleep to come. Instead, there was another knock, and Malory's head reappeared in the doorway. He appeared somehow as a different man, or one who had just removed a mask.

"I meant to ask you...what is your name? Your real name?" Colyer looked at him askance. She rolled the word around in her mind but it sounded oddly alien in her head. The person with that name did not exist. Just as she was about to respond, he held up his hand.

"No...best I don't know. Best I think of you as little snotty Tom Colyer 'til we reach Portsmouth. Well, good-night." And he was gone again.

The following morning she felt a little better, so rose, dressed and found the surgeon. He looked at her strangely, but cleared her fit for work. She didn't wait around for him to ask any awkward questions or change his mind, and went immediately on deck.

The ship resembled a scene from a dockyard and cordage store combined. The course-yards had been lowered to the hammock netting to reduce strain on the masts while repairs were conducted. Spare yards littered the deck in various states of preparation, and a sort of crane had been built around the foremast. A jury-topmast intersected the mast at a drunken angle, the operation to sway it up abandoned temporarily.

The storm had largely blown itself out, leaving a fresh, cold breeze that whipped the waves into a short, thumping chop. The sky was now mainly clear apart from the remnants of the storm clouds, ragged chunks of dark fluff, tumbling and racing along on the wind. She noticed the lookouts posted at each of the tops and crosstrees, and around the deck.

Looking out for the serpent. She alone seemed to know it would not be back.

"Colyer!" came a shout from aft. It was Lambert. She approached him with trepidation, but he strode towards her, grasped her by the hand and pumped it furiously. "Capital to have you back, capital! It's a wonder to see you up and about so soon. We thought the monster had you for certain until Gilpin fished you out."

She smiled weakly. Her muscles were already beginning to hurt. "Now," he went on, "do help me with the jury rigging of the fore-topmast won't you? After all, it's your fault the proper one came down. I can't judge the angles from both sides, you see..."

She clasped her hands behind her back listening to his plans. At least there was plenty to keep her busy for the time being. A tiny glow of something reassuring flickered in her breast. It was almost pitiful, but she held on to it tight, and managed another sad smile.

Chapter 35

THE ship reached Gibraltar one evening, early in the first watch, and put in for stores. Douglas took a boat ashore and brought back a bag of mail, and Colyer found a letter which had been waiting for her—for *Tom*, she corrected herself—for several weeks. Her stomach roiled—there was in all probability only one thing the letter could mean. She opened it.

As expected, the letter was from her father. And although the envelope was marked for Tom, the letter within was addressed, more in hope than expectation, to her. Her father recounted how he and her mother had returned to the house after they had seen Tom's body to the undertaker and dealt with the constable, only to find her missing. When she had not returned, they had searched the area, putting up notices and knocking on every door.

After a while they had noticed Tom's sea chest was missing as well, but thought nothing of it—they had known it had been left in the porch waiting for the coach to take both Tom and his luggage to Portsmouth, and assumed that the coachman had picked up the chest because of its label. Not that they cared about this at the time.

The family continued to search for her, fearing that in her grief for her brother she had thrown herself in the sea or run off to end her life—that was the only explanation they could find as no trace of her had ever been found.

It was only when Tom's pay began to arrive that her parents had realised something unusual was taking place. Her father had written to the Admiralty asking why the pay was being sent to them, but not mentioning Tom's death—the pain was evidently too acute for him to write the words, or perhaps he already sensed something of the truth. After some time, a response was received indicating that Midshipman Colyer had made those arrangements when he had arrived at Portsmouth on such-and-such a date, before taking ship to Gibraltar where he had joined the corvette HMS *Daedalus*.

With that, everything fell into place. Her father evidently knew his daughter well enough to sense that she might have the nerve to start a career at sea, and had written her this letter. By now, the message was months old. It had contrived to follow her to the East and back via the Cape, only overtaking the ship thanks to the corvette's extended cruise in the Atlantic.

The writing expressed the fervent hope that she—if indeed, it was her and there had not been some dreadful mix-up at the Admiralty—was well, and wished her to know that her whole family only wished to see her home safe once again. He desired her to know that she was in no trouble whatsoever—and even that they had been keeping aside as much of her pay as they could spare!

By the time she had finished the letter she was sobbing, silently, with guilt.

She sealed it up again and buried it at the bottom of her seachest for the short voyage home. In a while she would present the news to Malory—that her brother was dead and her family required her to quit the Navy. But not yet. It was almost eight bells in the first watch, and the middle watch, her duty watch, was about to start. She went up, took over the quarterdeck from Lambert, and went over all the myriad of details to be checked even on a ship at anchor. She allowed herself a moment of thinking about nothing at all, simply listening to the ageless throb of the waves.

The watch passed as uneventfully as any since they had left Borneo. It was a blessed relief in some ways, but Colyer still wished passionately that she had something to occupy her mind. She ordered an observation of the level of water in the well, the running rigging checked over for wear, and the temporary repairs on the rig examined. Everything was in order of course.

The watch seemed to take an age, and at the end of it the end of her time in the Navy seemed noticeably closer. As Gilpin took over, she resolved to seek out Malory, but at that moment the first lieutenant appeared on deck.

"If I might have a word, Sir," she almost sobbed. He nodded and they moved to the opposite side of the quarterdeck where a little more privacy could be had. She blurted out that she had received a letter, relayed the story of her brother's death and the family's struggle, and that they needed her to come home. Malory raised an eyebrow, evidently wondering if she was making it up, but the faintly amused expression he had worn slipped away as he realised there was something behind her story.

He agreed that she could be released from her duties when the ship put in at Devonport, raising his voice slightly to make sure Gilpin and some of the afterguard could hear.

She fled below decks again, grateful for the relative solitude of the hutch-like cabin. When she rose in the morning she received an invitation for dinner with the captain and the officers in the evening, after the *Daedalus* had got underway once more. She was mortified and delighted in equal measure to discover that the occasion was in her honour, a farewell of sorts. A toast was drunk to her, and Douglas, Lambert and Gilpin seemed genuine in their sadness that she would be leaving the service.

Even the captain seemed to have accepted her, with a few words of praise about her conduct in the recent gale. Malory was gracious but distant. There was no mention of the serpent, an omission which made the event seem a little surreal, and even more awkward.

Even so, she drank at least a glass more wine than she would normally allow herself, and when the gathering broke up she felt pleasantly numb. She made her way above decks in the hope of clearing her head, finding a clear space at the break of the quarterdeck.

After a while, Malory joined her there. He said nothing for what seemed like hours, simply looking out into the black night, before eventually breaking into the silence in a low murmur.

"I presume you are unlikely to speak extensively of your...adventures when you return to your normal life," he said levelly. "But I must ask you to refrain from revealing anything of our...diversion," he added. She said nothing, and he went on.

"We intend to indicate sighting the creature, but no more than that. We cannot afford to have departed from our orders so extensively without success. Had we beaten the beast it would be a different story, but as it is we have too many questions to answer about our collective...behaviour. Something may appear in the news sheets, or it may not. We may be a minor sensation or a laughing stock. In any event I would be grateful for your...discretion."

He paused again. He had clearly thought this through, and she imagined he had persuaded the captain of his views as usual. She realised his primary concern was his career—a fantastic tale like the one they had lived through could be a blot on the progression of an ambitious officer. Nevertheless, there seemed to be a struggle within himself.

"The damage and casualties—those we sustained in the storm, of course," he continued. "In fact, I understand several ships were lost, so it might have happened just so. I believe the men are to be transferred to other ships on our return. They won't be permitted back home until any controversy has blown over. It will cause a fuss no doubt but we will have to manage it." After another pause, he concluded. "Very well, I know I can rely on your good sense in this matter."

He made to withdraw, but she stopped him. "Sir, I..." It was important. He looked at her again, eyes questioning. "Everything I did on this ship, Sir, I...It was all in good faith. I wanted to do my best for...Well, that's all."

He gazed at her, lips curling, eyes staring into hers as the serpent's had done. Then he nodded, ever so slightly, and walked away.

Gilpin acknowledged her and she crossed over to him, blessedly grateful for sympathetic company. She would miss the old sailing master.

Six days later, Her Majesty's Ship *Daedalus* dropped anchor in the roads outside Plymouth. Shortly afterwards, her launch pulled away from the entry port, bulling easily through the short chop in the roads. After the rowers had found their rhythm, and Acting Lieutenant Colyer had found the best angle for the tiller to steer them across the tide, she turned for one last look at *Daedalus* as one of its officers. In a few minutes, she would be leaving this life for ever.

Even with its scars and jury-rigged fore-topmast, the ship was utterly beautiful. The lines of the vessel were in perfect proportion, after everything it had been through. Especially so. The lumps out of her rail, the worn paint and the mismatched spars just added to the effect. *Daedalus* might be outmoded, but she was pure. Some of her men might have been flawed and unworthy, but the ship had never let any of them down. Colyer thought if only she could take the old corvette, find a crew of volunteers and sail back into the broad oceans again, it would be all right.... Home.

As it was, she would never return. In her pocket she carried a letter from Malory, countersigned by the captain, authorising her discharge from Her Majesty's Navy.

She wondered if she would look outwardly the same, or changed utterly. She had worn a different person's life for a year and more. She had been through fire and water and stepped into a new world, only to be ripped back into the old one. The damage she had suffered had been jury-rigged too, and she could not see how it could ever be put entirely right. Or if it should be.

"Ow about a song while we pull, eh lads?" puffed Carson, "with yer permission o' course, Le'tenant Colyer." He nodded in her direction as an afterthought.

"Go on, then," she agreed. And before the men could lift their voices, she began to sing, high and clear, the notes carrying out over the waters and the anchored ships.

"*Our anchor's aweigh and our sails are set,*
Bold Riley, oh, haul away,"

The men at the oars glanced at each other in surprise, but she carried on.

"*The folks we are leaving, oh, we'll not forget,*
Bold Riley, oh, has gone away.
Goodbye, my darling. Goodbye, my dear-o,
Bold Riley, oh, has gone away,"

The men were smiling now, and joining in. Her face felt oddly cold and she realised the gentle breeze was cooling the tears that were flowing freely down her cheeks.

"*The rain it rains now, all the day long,*
Bold Riley, oh, haul away,
And the northerly wind, it blows so strong,
Bold Riley, oh, has gone away."

The rich tenors of the men mingled with her high alto creating a sound that had the men on the anchored ships in the roadstead pricking up their ears in wonder. It was more than one who might have confessed to a tear in one eye or two, as the normally boisterous shanty seemed to encapsulate something inexpressibly sad.

Daedalus and The Deep

Colyer carried on, singing and crying, for poor dead Tom, for poor wrecked Seaman Panna, for poor mad Spencer, and for her own life on the wide, deep, beautiful ocean that would last only a few more precious moments.

"We're outward bound for the Bengal bay,
Bold Riley, oh, haul away,
Get hauling, me boys, it's a hell of a way.
Bold Riley, oh, has gone away,
"Goodbye, my darling. Goodbye, my dear-o,
Bold Riley, oh, has gone away."

And back on the quarterdeck of HMS *Daedalus*, Second Lieutenant George Douglas turned to Third Lieutenant Simon Lambert, and said, "Well there's a thing indeed. I had no idea Colyer had such a damnably fine voice."

"Yes, it's a surprise all right. Very fine." replied Lambert. "It sounds a touch...feminine though, don't you think?"

"Hmmm," replied Lambert. "'Twas a little funny that his voice never did break." And after a moment the two men's eyes widened and they looked at each other in surprise.

Epilogue

WHEN she finally disentangled herself from the mass of spine and musculature shed by the giant creature, the beast itself had long since disappeared. She reluctantly accepted that she had failed in her task to fight and kill one of the giants of the upper space.

The turbulence in the thin substance of that space raged around her. She was not ready to crawl back to her own society yet, with nothing to show for her odyssey, so she swam on, pushing through the foaming surface waves. Eventually, she dipped through the surface into the calm, and swam on in the opposite direction from that the creature had taken.

She continued just below the rippling edge of space for some hours, and began to prepare herself for the inevitable return to her home world.

It was then that she found the first of the discarded symbiotes. The tiny creature swirled in the vortices, its limbs drifting with the currents. She approached it tentatively as it fell slowly, and sniffed at it. It was dead. Oddly, a length of the hard, heavy fibre that had been flung at her on more than one occasion—once nearly choking her—was hanging from one of the symbiote's limbs.

This was no surprise. If the massive animals could shed large parts of their own bodies when threatened, discarding the symbiotes did not seem very significant. She did not think it could be from the creature she had been chasing, though. Its surface covering looked different to those she had struggled with before, and there was that odd fibre dangling from it, pulling it down into the depths. And the other creature had been heading in the opposite direction—it must be far away by now.

Then, in the distance, she saw a second discarded symbiote. She swum towards it, through waters stirred up by the thundering winds above. It was somewhat similar to the last, down to that heavy strand attached to it. As the great creature must be miles away by this time she decided to risk a pulse or two of echo-location. She had rarely dared previously for fear of giving herself away. The sound waves revealed more of the symbiotes, many more, slowly sinking as they receded into the distance in a ragged line. She kicked her tail and flicked her long body in that direction.

There was a trail of them. Surely for a creature to lose so many of its symbiotes was not normal.

And there, on the surface, was another of the giant creatures. She followed it for a while. It had only two long spines, instead of the three that the last beast, her nemesis, had boasted. There were but a few thin scraps of membrane stretched between the great dorsal quills. Like the previous creature, it was piling along in the direction the turbulent gases were blowing, at some speed. She surmised that the chaotic atmosphere excited the creatures and spurred them to run along with it as fast as they could.

The symbiotes were splashing into the raging sea every few minutes. The creature was rolling heavily from side to side. It did not look so fearsome as the first, larger beast, she thought. An idea occurred to her, and then a plan took root. Could she grab this creature unawares and drag it under before it even knew she was there?

It seemed to be struggling, bouncing around on the raging waves. She crept closer, carefully moving as near as possible. The creature did not seem to detect her. The symbiotes seethed on its upper levels. More of them dropped into the sea, creating a creamy swirl on the surface which was quickly swept away.

As she drew closer, the differences with the first creature grew more apparent. Apart from the lack of a third spine, its body was much slimmer. Slim enough for her to coil around, perhaps?

She rippled her fins more rapidly and drew alongside the beast, just below the surface, not disturbing the upper edges of the waves. Her quarry did not change its course. As it fell into a trough, she pounced, darting her long head over the middle of its *body and back into the sea. She pulled the loop her body had made tight, and felt the carapace beneath her give with a reassuring crack. She expected the beast to bellow like her previous prey had, in that unearthly 'boom, boom, boom' that it made when it spat out its defensive projectiles. But it did not. She thought she heard, through the hurricane, tiny, thin noises from the symbiotes, but the creature itself just gave in to her embrace, creaking and snapping.*

With a ripping crunch, the creature seemed to flop, its integrity gone, its back broken. Its air-sacs must also have punctured, as she felt the beast start to settle into the water. It was working—she did not even have to drag the mighty animal below.

She relaxed her grip a little, and slipped back into the water. She oriented herself according to the energies running through the ocean that told her which way she needed to travel. She looped her tail around the creatures beak and its single tusk, and began to swim towards home.

The beast was sluggish, acquiescent. Even while still on the surface, it allowed itself to be dragged without resisting much. It was clearly already more dead than alive. Even so, the mighty rippling of the upper surface of the atmosphere dragged at the body and the thin, roaring gases tugged the dorsal spines. She was pleased when, after many miles, it finally gave up its grip on the upper space and slid slowly into the liquid atmosphere.

She transferred her grip to one of the spines and concentrated on preventing it from sinking too fast. If the corpse reached the floor of the ocean before she had reached her goal, it might be impossible to lug the inanimate beast to the convocation. Still, it was no heavier than a Sperm whale, examples of which she had killed and brought home in the past, and about as buoyant. It was rather more awkward though, and every current seemed to yank at her prize so she was constantly needing to heave it back onto the right course.

It was tough, tough going. She had travelled further than she had intended from the homedepth, and further she strayed, the further her prey had to be lugged back. She was exhausted from her struggles with the larger creature but her muscles and wounds had stopped hurting so much. The pain would come, she had no doubt of that, but for weeks she had endured the thin upper atmosphere and the vicious attacks of the alien creature.

Daedalus and the Deep

She had not submitted to pain in all that time, nor would she. Her nervous system had recognised her tenacity and respected it. Pain served no purpose—it would be bypassed.

Every so often she had to abandon the track she was swimming to drag the dead beast back closer to the surface again. The gradual thickening of the ocean told her how far she had sunk back towards the homedepth, and however much she wanted to let the creature fall, and sink to the bottom after it, she must not. If she succumbed to the desire, all would be for nothing.

She felt its shattered body creak and strain with the load she was putting on it, and wondered if it was decomposing already. She imagined her hard-won prey crumbling away before she reached the convocation. If that happened she deserved nothing. She would crawl away and give her own wrecked body to the ocean.

But not yet. There was still a chance, and so still she must fight.

Finally, she reached the place. She sensed the string of huge mountains many miles ahead of her, where they thrust up from the ocean floor so far they penetrated the entire atmosphere and up into space. It was by one of these mountains that the first great creature, the one that had bested her, had stayed to rest after she had lured it across the ocean. Skirting those vast peaks was the homedepth—the great, black, trench that was home to her people. Her complacent, vainglorious people.

At this moment they would be gathered at convocation. For the first few weeks, little of substance would have been done—the stories of great serpents of the past recreated in dramatic form, the distribution of meaningless ceremonial roles for those of merit that had no real power and were designed to keep the lower orders content.

After that would of course come the challenges—by now more ceremonial than real. It would start with days of posturing, then the hunting would begin. The champions would strike out and do battle with the biggest, fiercest creatures of the atmosphere according to the ancient lore. The serpent that achieved the greatest feat by common assent would rule until the next convocation. This would go on for weeks, with increasingly larger and more powerful creatures being brought back to the convocation over time until two of roughly equal proportions and viciousness would be produced. Some theatrical arguing would follow, after which the winner would be decided.

In the past there could even be challenges to single combat and a fight to the death between serpents. But no longer—not for aeons as far as she knew. Not since the serpents had become civilised, as they saw it. The whole of convocation was a throwback to an earlier era, and nowhere was this more true than in the ritual of the hunting.

She had even considered the path of single combat, but ruled it out as she knew that in a straight serpent-to-serpent fight she could not guarantee victory, or even that her challenge would be accepted. She knew she needed the boldest of strokes—something that meant no one could deny her what she meant to take. No flexible interpretations of the law, no ancient precedents ruling her out. It had to be the oldest and clearest of ideas.

The biggest, fiercest creature of the atmosphere. She knew no sperm whale or colossal squid would be nearly good enough—these days the old families had carved up the rulership between them, and the 'challengers' put forward had their clans to help them fight and subdue another sea creature. The way it was going to go would have been decided months if not years ago, in discussions between the representatives of the favoured few, hiding behind rocks and black smokers as they divided up and parcelled out her people's future.

Strangely, she could not remember when she first had the idea to find, kill and bring back one of the giant space creatures of legend. It seemed to have been with her always. She had never told any of her family or companions—they would have thought her insane. Perhaps she was. After all, not all the serpents even believed that the space creatures existed. There were plenty of stories of course, but only a few sightings in living memory and these had been hotly disputed.

They would not be able to deny it for much longer.

Subtly echo-sounding, she fixed her position, and heaved the dead creature's bulk over the lip of the sea-floor canyon that her people called the homedepth. Taking quick sightings and occasionally pinging a tightly-focussed sound beam against the rock, she adjusted her descent. After a while, sounds reminiscent of a large gathering of sea serpents began to penetrate the cold, viscous water. at first a homogeneous mush of noise, as she approached the sounds separated into the swishing of tails and *fins, the bark of long-wavelength echo pulses uttered in agreement or dissent, the rhythmic snap of jaws to gain attention...*

She intended to gain attention—their undivided attention...

At the moment she judged she was directly above the largest concentration of noise, she let go of the creature. Relief welled briefly as she finally allowed it to sink, but even then she knew that the greatest challenge was still to come. She fluttered her fins and dived after the giant corpse.

It settled slowly, by now being totally filled with water. She caught up with it and spiralled around it as it sank.

Just before the giant was about to fall on them, the crowd sensed something massive approaching them out of the gloom, and scattered. The great, dead monster impacted softly onto the floor of the homedepth, creating a puff of silt followed by an eerie shriek, as of old bones grinding together. As the pulse of sound emitted from the landing reverberated around, she opened her jaws and bellowed:

—I AM HERE I AM HERE

She sensed the shock of the other creatures. It would have seemed as if some great, silent whale was about to attack, and then the giant space creature had appeared, conquered.

Sending out a few echo-pulses she noted a large sperm whale lying dead in the gathering space, with some smaller whales. There was something tangled up there too—a colossal squid. She raised her voice again:

—I HAVE KILLED THIS CREATURE AND BROUGHT IT BACK I CLAIM MY RIGHT

A murmuring darted around the gathering. Creatures drew back into a defined group from the positions they had fled to. They held back from the creature, inspecting it at a distance. Then, two or three approached it more closely, skirting round its shattered bones, inspecting the giant spines on its back. One of them turned back to her.

—I HAVE RIGHT I HAVE CLAIMED IT

A young male, scion of one of the leading families. Malleable, unchallenging. He would maintain the interests of the powerful few for another generation, until his successor was chosen to do the same.

—NO I SAY NO I HAVE TRAVELLED TO SPACE AND BATTLED THIS CREATURE I BESTED IT AND BY ANCIENT LAW RIGHT IS MINE

The murmuring broke out again. The note of shock was still there, and fear, but there was something else. Admiration. Hope. She pressed her point.

—DO YOU DENY MY RIGHT WHO HERE DENIES BY ANCIENT LAW THE GREATEST CONQUEST WINS RIGHT

The male put out his frill, anger in his black eyes.

—YOU ARE NOBODY YOU PRESUME TO CLAIM RIGHT NEVER NEVER

She bristled, and assumed a threatening pose. The young male looked surprised, worried even, and blurted:

—YOU DIDN'T KILL YOU FOUND IT DEAD

The gathering fell into silence. This was a powerful slur. Her hackles rose.

—THIS CREATURE BREATHES FIRE LIKE BLACK SMOKER AND HURLED GREAT ROUND ROCKS AND SHARP STONES LIKE TEETH IT HIT AND STRANGLED YET I KILLED IT I WILL SHOW YOU HOW I KILLED IT IF YOU SUBMIT TO COMBAT

The representatives of the ruling families slide forward alongside their chosen. They did not confer but one spoke up:

—WE DENY YOUR RIGHT AND ACCEPT YOUR CHALLENGE TO COMBAT

That was it. She was finished. With everything she had been through. To be beaten by their rules once again. She would fight for all she was worth but her body was worn out and broken. She would not win against a halfway skilful serpent in his prime. She rallied her anger into defiance:

—YOU INSULT I KILL THIS CREATURE WHICH NO ONE HAS BEFORE I WON YOUR BARBARIC CHALLENGE AND YOU CHANGE THE RULES I WILL BEAT YOUR CHOSEN AND RIGHT IS MINE

The representatives slid back into the anonymity of the crowd. The chosen one looked at her, his frill still standing out. Then he looked at the creature. The sheer size of it. The otherness of its appearance. Something settled within the decaying body and it emitted a rumbling crash. The chosen one started.

Daedalus and the Deep

She extended her fins and rippled her tail, letting everyone see the wounds she had sustained. Her fins were ragged-edged, her body scarred in a hundred places.

The chosen one assumed the posture for a challenge, drawing his head up and back, poised to strike. She did the same, angrily, thinking LET'S GET THIS OVER WITH.

The chosen one straightened his neck. He looked back at the giant creature, its mighty spines looming over all of them. And he put his head down.

—I SUBMIT RIGHT IS YOURS FORGIVE INSULT

A howl rang out from the cabal of the top families. Several of them darted forward, shouting at the chosen one to resume, but he had already begun to slink from the field. Two of the ceremonial elders swam towards her. She felt something radiating from them. Uncertainty but optimism. It had come out of the blue sky, but in those few moments she had broken the deadlock of centuries. They spoke:

—YOURS IS RIGHT TO RULE UNTIL NEXT CYCLE BY LAW

—GOVERN WISELY THE HOMEDEPTH FOR THE SAKE OF THE PEOPLE

—ACCEPT THE LAWS AND RESPECT THE RITES

These were ceremonial words, but they smacked of inertia, of unwillingness to change. Well, they would have to get used to doing things differently now. She responded:

—I WILL GOVERN WISELY WITH COUNSEL OF ELDERS

And she added,

—AND HOPE OF YOUTH

The people looked on expectantly. She read their expressions. Was this a coup in their eyes? A mere power grab? Would the names at the top be the only thing to change?

—I INTEND TO CHANGE LAW IN MANY WAYS TO BEGIN WITH THIS WILL BE THE LAST RULERSHIP DECIDED BY CHALLENGE FROM THIS DAY FORWARD ALL RULERS WILL BE CHOSEN BY PEOPLE

A ripple went round the convocation, that became a chatter, and then something like a roar. There was much to decide. She would need to gather a group of the wisest to work out how things would be. She might fail, and the powerful might seize the right once again. But after her struggles with the giant creatures of space, her impossible dream did not seem so impossible any more.

The ritual was at an end, and those she had known and others she did not swarmed forward full of questions about space, the creatures, and her battle.

She could not help feeling that after everything, her battle was still closer to its beginning than its end. But she had time. There would be those who wanted to see her fail, but glancing around the faces of her people, she knew that they would seize onto this and not let the opportunity go. The looming form of the conquered giant would serve as a reminder of what could be achieved by just one serpent and the power of will.

She felt the future opening out like the mouth of the homedepth, and brightening like the sky did as she had approached, with hope and determination, the edge of space.

HISTORICAL NOTE

THIS account is fictional. The characters and much of the action are unequivocally the product of imagination. However, the story has its roots in real events.

HMS *Daedalus* was a real ship, a *Leda*-class frigate built in 1820 and later re-rated to corvette. In 1845 boats and men from HMS *Daedalus* took part in a raid on pirate strongholds and the action described in chapters 1 and 2 is based on contemporary accounts.

HMS *Daedalus* was best known in Victorian Britain, however, for the sighting of a giant sea-serpent between the Cape of Good Hope and St Helena in 1848. The description of the serpent in this narrative is based on those in contemporary reports from the officers of the frigate. Exactly what those men saw in the Atlantic on that August day remains a mystery. The other accounts of sea serpents which Colyer discovers during her research are equally based on factual reports—and equally mysterious.

The chase of and battle with the serpent is entirely my own creation, with the slight qualification that the island *Daedalus* touches in the south Atlantic is very real—Zavodovski Island is part of the South Sandwich Island chain, and is indeed home to the largest colony of chinstrap penguins in the world.

The narrative following the sighting of the serpent was inspired by my scepticism that the scientific and curious officers of the 19th century Royal Navy would be content to sight an entirely unknown creature and not pursue it. What follows is an exploration of the question 'what if...?' The officers and crew of the *Daedalus* are similarly fictitious. It did not seem right to attribute my own motives and actions to real people. There were, to the best of my knowledge, no women serving on the ship in this period although a great many women, some disguised as men, went to sea on Royal Navy ships throughout the 18th and 19th centuries.

HMS *Daedalus* is no longer with us. She was laid up in 1853 and eventually broken up in 1911 after having spent more than half a century training cadets. Two of her close sisters, however, survive and a visit to both is thoroughly recommended. HMS *Trincomalee*, now beautifully restored at Hartlepool, was a slightly earlier incarnation of the Leda-class but was rebuilt in 1845 as a corvette with more modern features and armament in a very similar way to *Daedalus*. *Trincomalee*'s first commission was underway at the same time that *Daedalus* was recording its sighting of the sea-serpent. For readers desiring an impression of *Daedalus*' upper decks and rig, HMS *Trincomalee* demonstrates these features perfectly.

HMS *Unicorn* was almost identical to *Daedalus*, being part of the same batch sometimes referred to as the 'modified Leda-class' with a round stern and Sir Robert Seppings' 'small timber' construction. *Unicorn* was never commissioned and remained 'in ordinary' from the day she was launched to the present. This fascinating ship is preserved at Dundee. Readers looking for a clearer sense of the interior of HMS *Daedalus,* and the look of her stern and Captain MacQuarrie's cabin could do no better than to visit *Unicorn*. It seems entirely appropriate that HMS *Daedalus*' surviving sister bears the name of an elusive mythical creature.

Any similarity between any sea-serpent in this novel and any other sea-serpents, living or dead, is almost entirely coincidental.

About the Author

Matthew Willis was born in the historic naval town of Harwich, Essex in 1976. He grew up nearby, never far from the sea, becoming a keen racing dinghy sailor in his teens.

Willis studied Literature and History of Science at the University of Kent, where he wrote an MA thesis on Joseph Conrad and sailed for the University in national competitions. He subsequently worked as a journalist for Autosport and F1 Racing magazines, before switching to a career in media relations for the National Health Service. His first non-fiction book, a history of the Blackburn Skua WW2 naval dive bomber, was published in 2007. Willis currently lives in Southampton with his University lecturer wife Rosalind, and writes both fiction and non-fiction for a living.

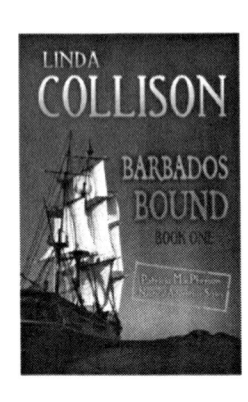

BARBADOS BOUND

BY

LINDA COLLISON

Portsmouth, England, 1760. Patricia Kelley, the illegitimate daughter of a wealthy Barbadian sugarcane planter, falls from her imagined place in the world when her absent father unexpectedly dies. Raised in a Wiltshire boarding school sixteen-year-old Patricia embarks on a desperate crossing on a ship bound for Barbados, where she was born, in a brash attempt to claim an unlikely inheritance. Aboard a merchantman under contract with the British Navy to deliver gunpowder to the West Indian forts, young Patricia finds herself pulled between two worlds -- and two identities -- as she charts her own course for survival in the war-torn 18th century.

Fireship Press
www.FireshipPress.com

WWW.FIRESHIPPRESS.COM
HISTORICAL FICTION AND NONFICTION
PAPERBACK AVAILABLE FOR ORDER ON LINE

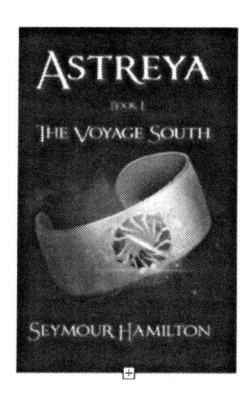

ASTREYA

BY
SEYMOUR HAMILTON

Astreya isn't like the other boys in his remote fishing village.

When Astreya leaves home, his widowed mother gives him his father's knife, a riddling notebook, and a bracelet with a mysterious and powerful green stone. He sails south with an adventurous fishing boat skipper, hoping that in the world beyond, he can find out who his father was, what the three enigmatic gifts mean, and whether there is any value to the looks, skills and talents that have set him apart from everyone he has ever known.

They voyage to a village where all the inhabitants have met a grisly end, and fearing this may be the work of the legendary sailors cursed to sail forever, they dare the open ocean. A storm blows them to a land unlike their own, where Astreya is betrayed by his shipmate and abandoned by his skipper. Escaping slavery, he makes his way to The Castle, where he believes he can learn more about his father's gifts.

Along the way, he meets Gar, an itinerant painter, and his striking assistant, Lindey, who can take care of herself with the forces of truth, logic, reason, and the occasional shrewd blow from her quarterstaff. They learn to trust each other, even though all three guard secrets. Accomplished painter, able seaman, and now a proven knife fighter, Astreya is just imagining a new destiny with Lindey when a man from the past he never knew alters the course of his life toward the adventures that continue in Book II, *The Men of the Sea*.

Fireship Press
www.FireshipPress.com

HISTORICAL FICTION AND NONFICTION
PAPERBACK AVAILABLE FOR ORDER ONLINE
AND AS EBOOK WITH ALL MAJOR DISTRIBUTERS

CONFESSIONS OF THE CREATURE

**BY
GARY INBINDER**

The story of Frankenstein's monster continues

In the Arctic waters of the Barents Sea, the creature has taken the ultimate revenge on his creator, Frankenstein. He travels south, where a chance meeting with a witch gives him the opportunity to overcome what he is, and perhaps become who he was meant to be.

Transformed into a normal-looking man, but retaining his superhuman strength, the creature journeys to Moscow, where he becomes the protege of a wealthy natural philosopher and the lover of his daughter, Sabrina. Taking the name Viktor Suvorin, the creature wins acclaim as a military hero while Napoleon rages across Europe. Following the wars, Viktor and Sabrina travel to Switzerland, where they meet Byron, Percy Shelley, and Mary Wollstonecraft Shelley, who bases her novel on Viktor‚Äôs memoirs.

Viktor faces a final challenge to his hard-won humanity when tragedy strikes his family and he returns to the Arctic. There, on a frozen sea under the shimmering Northern Lights, the creature must confront the meaning of his creation and his life.

Fireship Press
www.FireshipPress.com
HISTORICAL FICTION AND NONFICTION
PAPERBACK AVAILABLE FOR ORDER ONLINE
AND AS EBOOK WITH ALL MAJOR DISTRIBUTERS

Lonestar Rising

The Voyage of the Wasp

by

Jason Vale

Fans of Alternative History celebrate! Jason Vail's compelling novel, Lonestar Rising: The Voyage of the Wasp, is must-read literature.

The American rebellion has failed. George Washington is dead. The surviving revolutionaries have retreated to Tennessee, only to be routed again. In 1819, John Paul Jones, Jr., a smuggler, plies the waters off the coast of New Spain, while a new generation of rebels have settled in Spanish territories and the wasteland called Texas. But Andrew Jackson is not content to be a Spanish subject. He dreams large. Texas must be free and independent from the corrupt old empires of Europe. But with no army other than the Texas Rangers, and no navy, Texas has no hope of opposing the mighty forces of Spain. No hope, that is, until David Crockett recruits the sardonic John Paul Jones. Together they buy and refit a broken down warship to become the first ship of the Texas Navy. With a handful of Crockett's men, the blessing of a voodoo queen, and a dubious crew of French pirates, they set sail to seize Spanish treasure and remake history in a ship called the Wasp.

Fireship Press
www.FireshipPress.com

WWW.FIRESHIPPRESS.COM
HISTORICAL FICTION AND NONFICTION
PAPERBACK AVAILABLE FOR ORDER ON LINE

**For the Finest in
Nautical and Historical
Fiction and Nonfiction**

WWW.FIRESHIPPRESS.COM

Interesting • Informative • Authoritative

All Fireship Press books are now available
directly through www.FireshipPress.com, Amazon.com
and as electronic downloads.